QU ···PIES

Also by Brian Landers

Empires Apart: The Story of the American and Russian Empires

The Dylan Series:

Awakening of Spies
Families of Spies
Coincidence of Spies
Exodus of Spies

QUIVER
OF SPIES

BRIAN
LANDERS

Red Door

A RedDoor book
Published by Ember Press 2023
www.emberpress.co.uk

ISBN 978-1-9997701-5-0

A CIP catalogue record for this book is available from the British
Library

Cover design: Rawshock Design

Typesetting: Jen Parker, Fuzzy Flamingo
www.fuzzyflamingo.co.uk

Printed in the UK by Severn

For Jocelyn and Louis

I

Half a century and 2,500 miles separate the deaths that led to Roger Montacute's disappearance. There is a temptation to find spurious similarities between those deaths, to look for patterns where none exist.

The victims were all male. The seven Spaniards in the hills outside the village of San Blas de la Ciduela had been coldly executed, as had the two Russians in the inhospitable mountains between Georgia and Turkey. The dead men were all soldiers of one sort or another, like their killers, but then again not like their killers. Those who had pulled the triggers had the sense of invincibility that comes from belonging to self-professed military elites: the Tiradores de Ifni in Spain in 1938, the Spetsnaz in Georgia in 1989. They had been hardened by war and killing had long since ceased to arouse any emotion at all. The Spanish bodies remained undiscovered for nearly forty years; the Russians' bodies have never been found. Spain in the 1930s had collapsed into civil war; some expected the Soviet Union at the end of the 1980s to do the same. But these are merely coincidences.

Before Dr Montacute's disappearance nobody could possibly have connected the events in Spain with those in Georgia, for the truth is there was no other connection. The missing Cambridge academic was the only link between the two events and that only became obvious much later.

The killings in Spain were just an unremarkable footnote in the history of the Spanish Civil War, one more example of bloodshed in a conflict drowning in blood. Even at the time the deaths were of no interest to my Service. In the Broadway building behind St James's Park Tube station, where the Secret Intelligence Service was then housed, no incident reports were ever requested, no case file was ever opened. And nearly forty years later, in 1976, when the remains of the seven dead men were accidentally uncovered, there was even less reason for the Service to take any notice.

Thirteen years after that, the deaths in the Soviet Union were different. They mattered. They could have consequences. Cables hummed across the world, meetings were hurriedly called and files opened on both sides of the Atlantic.

'We have an unexpected eventuality,' announced a senior CIA official who happened to be on a courtesy visit to London. My new Desk Officer, Neil White, nodded politely as if that was news to us. According to our American colleague the two principal Russian intelligence agencies, the KGB and GRU, were falling over each other to piece the story together. The fact that the Russians themselves didn't know what had happened to two of their own soldiers had already made finding out a priority for us.

At the time I was based in Century House on Westminster Bridge Road. The Service had long outgrown the Broadway Buildings but had not yet acted on the National Audit Office report which had pointed out how totally inappropriate it was for the headquarters of MI6, the Secret Intelligence Service, to be in a glass-windowed tower block and, even worse, almost on top of a petrol station.

By then I had been in British Intelligence for fifteen years.

Not much had changed in the Service in that time. Those of us who had been at university in the sixties and seventies had started to work our way up through the organisation, but the men at the top, and they were nearly all men, were still wedded to the values that had protected the British Empire from foreign contagion. Tradition was everything. Anyone describing Neil White would invariably start not with Neil's own achievements but with the legendary role played by his father, Archibald, during and after the war.

'Neil's a chip off the old block,' was the highest compliment he could receive.

***

The Swinging Sixties may have marked a cultural watershed for Britain but life in the corridors of power continued much as before. Change was more dramatic elsewhere.

In 1975 the Spanish dictator Francisco Franco finally died. The following summer I remember was exceptionally hot. The blistering sun caused long-buried shells on the battlefields of Ebro to explode in a final ironic salute to the memory of the man who had kept a stranglehold on life in Spain for nearly forty years. That summer the people of Spain were given cause to remember the Civil War that had brought him to power. The old tensions, like the shells not far below the surface, bubbled up and exploded into riots, kidnappings and assassinations. In Spain, as in Portugal not long before, a dormant nation started to awaken as left and right clambered over each other in their rush for power.

I'm sure that the school children scrambling over the hills above San Blas de la Ciduela gave no thought to politics.

For them the civil war was something in the history books, something old men talked about only when the red wine flowed freely and old women talked about not at all. The national figures of an earlier age, Negrín, Mola, Líster, even Franco, meant nothing. The local heroes and villains, Pablo Bustamante, the Casares brothers, were just names muttered in benediction or curse. Then they found the body of Juan Manuel Casares.

Little Rafael Agüero, son of the village butcher, found him. At least he found the first bones. Rafael was digging a pit for a campfire when the shovel struck something unexpected. He was on his own and carefully dug around until he could announce in a small piping voice that he'd found a hand.

He kept digging as the others crowded in until an adult came to see what the shouting was about. Rafael was pulled away before being sent off to fetch Pejérez, who formed the entire local police force. This despite the boy pleading to be allowed to keep digging to find the other hand.

Had he stayed, young Rafael Agüero would not have found the other hand. Juan Manuel Casares had lost it when the communists turned on the anarchists and stormed the telephone exchange in Barcelona.

But he might have found the gold Australian dollar that had been stuffed into Casares' mouth. It was the looted coin that reignited stories of buried treasure and eventually led Dr Roger Montacute to my wife Julia's door.

The missing hand helped identify Casares' remains. The identity of the other six skeletons was more difficult to establish.

The question of identifying the bodies did not arise when

4

two Russian conscripts disappeared in 1989, however. Their names were known but their burial place was lost for ever. They had left Khelvachauri and simply vanished.

Khelvachauri, close to the border between the old Georgian Soviet Socialist Republic and Turkey, used to be one of the largest army bases in the Soviet Union, home to over 2,000 infantry, tank and special forces troops. That was before the Union of Soviet Socialist Republics ceased to be a union and the Georgians, among others, decided they were better off on their own. Twenty years later, when newly independent Georgia tried to shake its puny fist in the face of its old Kremlin masters, the Russians would decide that if they couldn't have the base nobody should: it was flattened by Russian bombers.

But back in 1989 the barracks were still occupied by Soviet forces, and the only unusual thing about the drab ZiL truck bearing the insignia of the 87th Motorised Rifle Division when it drove out of the base was the time at which it left.

'One o'clock in the morning,' I imagine the driver grumbling. 'What needs driving to the docks at one o'clock in the morning?'

His companion probably didn't answer. In the Red Army orders were orders. 'At least there's no traffic,' would have been his only comment.

The truck turned towards the port city of Batumi but it didn't get far. One of the new BTR-80 troop carriers was parked by the side of the road and as the truck approached, it pulled out, blocking the way forward. Four men in army fatigues jumped out, three carrying the AS Val rifles favoured by Russian special forces because of their built-in silencers.

The two occupants of the truck were bundled into the back of the armoured personnel carrier which then set off in the opposite direction, towards the Turkish frontier, with the truck following on.

The border between Turkey and the USSR had been closed for many years. Now, with Gorbachev in the Kremlin, plans were being made to establish a border crossing at Sarpi where a road could be reopened between the steep cliffs and the pebbled beach. But that was not the destination that night.

Stalin had asserted that the land on the Turkish side of the border rightfully belonged to his native Georgia and generations of Red Army strategists had developed plans for regaining the 'lost' territory. Special forces troops regularly rehearsed infiltrations across the border and they knew a far less conspicuous crossing point further east that would still avoid the heavily militarised area around Borçka.

Soon after five o'clock in the morning the whole operation was over. The armoured personnel carrier was back at its base in Khelvachauri and the truck had been dumped in a back street in Batumi. The truck's original driver and his companion lay in a shallow grave in the mountains north of Güreşen, each with a single bullet in the back of the head. The truck's cargo, now in another nondescript truck, this one with Turkish plates, was rattling along the road that followed the Black Sea to the Turkish port of Trabzon 150 kilometres away.

We would only discover that later. By then I too would be setting off along Turkey's Black Sea coast, coming from the opposite direction, from Istanbul.

Turkey was not really my patch; indeed I had never been

there. I was attached to what was then called the Soviet Operations Desk, a term that was soon to become obsolete. As a Deputy Desk Officer I was responsible for analysis and policy but only occasionally for actual operations. For me the trip to Istanbul was a welcome break from the routine of Century House, an opportunity to get out into the field, even if only briefly.

I might even be able to find a moment to buy a memento for my wife. When we were stationed in Moscow Julia had flown to Ankara to attend a funeral and returned with a jar of rose petal jam that she had taken a fancy to. There would be no time for me to explore Istanbul's Grand Bazaar but I was confident I would at least be able to find somewhere to buy jam.

In fact what I found when I reached the Black Sea was something quite different: men with guns in their hands taking careful aim directly at me.

II

At some point in the late 1980s everything changed. The certainties the intelligence world had known for forty years disappeared. Perhaps it was the moment on 26 February 1986 when Mikhail Gorbachev addressed the 27th Congress of the Communist Party of the Soviet Union and told them their world could not continue as it was. Intentionally or not, he had ripped up the rule book. We didn't know it then but the Soviet Union was about to disappear.

Suddenly *glasnost* and *perestroika* were being bandied around by politicians and commentators in the West whose previous knowledge of Russian had been limited to *balalaika*, *sputnik* and *samovar*. They might have added vodka to the list, although Poles would insist that word was theirs.

My wife, Julia, who had learned some Russian in our time at the Embassy in Moscow, gave up correcting people who pronounced the first vowel of *perestroika* as if it was the first vowel of peasant. It still grated with me.

'It's pea,' I would tell my acquaintances, 'like the vegetable.' Or as I told my closer friends, 'Just think of pee.' Actually, even that was not really exact.

My own Russian was almost fluent. The Service had sent me for intensive language training when I transferred over from the Defence Intelligence Staff; the Portuguese and

8

Italian I had studied so assiduously at university were of no value to MI6.

The Service had to adapt rapidly to the world created by Gorbachev. Our political masters had become comfortable with the predictability of the Cold War. They were more interested in the intentions of the Irish Republican Army than the Red Army. That suddenly changed and we were expected at a moment's notice to produce emergency briefings on subjects that had previously been of no interest to ministers: unexpected Soviet troop movements in Armenia, for example, or the psychology of General Snetkov, the Russian commander in Berlin.

For security reasons all our papers had to be locked away each night and Neil White prided himself on carefully returning every file to its proper place before going home. I tried to do the same but as the pressure of events increased, I often found myself suddenly noticing the time and shoving any papers on my desk into the safe in my office to retrieve in the morning. Unlike White I had a wife and child to go home to.

As the demonstrations across Eastern Europe grew more widespread, politicians debated whether the West should intervene in the name of freedom or make sure that we avoided being sucked into a new world war. Self-declared experts insisted that the long-awaited birth pangs of democracy had arrived behind the Iron Curtain while others, with equal certainty, were sure it was only a matter of time before it all ended in bloodshed: the Red Army would never stand aside and let everything it had achieved at such sacrifice in the Second World War be destroyed.

Not only were the nations of Eastern Europe about to

shake off their shackles but, to the astonishment of nearly everyone, nations many people had never heard of suddenly sprang up within the USSR. Newspapers condescendingly explained that Lithuania and Latvia were neighbouring countries on the Baltic, but then struggled to say why the political conditions in one were so very different from the other. In the US academics tried to teach geography to bemused TV anchors who had just discovered that Russia also seemed to have a state called Georgia.

Of course at that time very few of us knew about the two Red Army conscripts missing in Soviet Georgia.

Behind what was still an iron curtain, albeit one corroding by the day, the world was in ferment but there were also smaller developments on the other side of the Atlantic. The Iran-Contra affair had made clear what everyone in the business already knew: that the Intelligence establishment in the US was fractured into competing fiefdoms, not all of whom paid any attention to the letter of the law let alone the spirit. Congressional enquiries were trying to find out how staff at the National Security Council, which was supposed to be concerned with policy not operations, could secretly arrange for the Israelis to sell American arms to Iran and then use the profits to buy more arms for the CIA to deliver to the Contra guerrillas in Nicaragua. All this at a time when US policy, expressed in laws passed by Congress and signed by the President, was absolutely clear: no arms sales to Iran and no arms deliveries to either side in Nicaragua.

The reputation of the Intelligence community in the US had been dented by the Iran-Contra scandal but its work on our side of the Atlantic was largely unaffected. In some ways, as the situation in Eastern Europe became more unstable the work of the CIA became easier. New informants made themselves known and the challenge became not to recruit new sources but to decide which ones to believe.

I suspect it was from one of these new sources that the Americans had first learned about the events near the Khelvachauri barracks, although as usual our friends across the pond would not say anything that might reveal their source to us.

The Russians, it was reported, had launched some sort of major search operation around the Georgian city of Batumi following the discovery of a stolen army supply truck. Two conscripts from one of the Motorised Rifle Divisions based nearby were reportedly missing. Shortly after came the news that when it had left the barracks the abandoned truck had contained fifteen surface-to-air missile launchers along with thirty missiles. They were also now missing.

We learned all that from the CIA's London station. Despite occasional rivalry our relations with the 'Company', as we usually referred to the CIA, were close. I had met their London station chief and his number two and been alarmingly impressed. Not only were they thoroughly briefed on Soviet operations, the subject of our meetings, but their knowledge of political developments in the UK was startling: it had certainly not been acquired by simply reading the British press and chatting to official contacts.

Neil White returned from one of his regular meetings at the US Embassy in Grosvenor Square with a blue-covered file bearing the CIA logo with its sixteen-point red star. Emblazoned on it in enormous letters were the words 'Top Secret', as if the file was specially designed to draw attention to itself.

'Our friends gave me this,' White explained. 'They want us to keep our eyes open. I tell you something, normally they would only pass over a report with this sort of security classification if they thought we already knew what was in it. As we didn't know anything at all about this Khelvachauri business I think they really want our input. I'm going to send out an all-stations bulletin.'

The thought that fifteen surface-to-air missile launchers with missiles could now be on the open market was alarming to both us and the Company. 'This could be a sign of things to come,' said White. 'In the past the KGB could terrify everyone into obedience, but now who knows? There are a lot of people out there who would pay good money for surplus Soviet hardware.'

The alarm deepened when the Company's source discovered that the missiles were the latest version of the new SAM-18s rather than the usual SAM-7s which had been around for a long time. Hundreds of thousands of SAM-7s had been made and NATO forces knew how to deal with them. But the Red Army had been phasing out the SAM-7s in favour of the SAM-18s which were far more effective in dealing with the counter-measures developed by the West. I knew that someone armed with an SAM-18 could bring down a jet flying directly at them, a dangerous advance on the SAM-7 which locked on to the heat of a jet's engine only when it had gone past. The missing missiles were a new and radically updated version of the SAM-18, what the Russians called *igly*, or needles.

The Russians apparently believed that the missiles had been smuggled into Turkey. They were therefore potentially available to all sorts of unsavoury Middle Eastern customers.

Finding them became a major priority at a time when, to be honest, we had a lot of major priorities.

In Lebanon the bloody civil war was approaching its endgame but few would have guessed that at the time. Shellfire continued to devastate Beirut and the only people for whom business could continue as normal were the arms dealers, although most of the big dealers had long since decamped to Cyprus.

Our Station in the Lebanese capital was once one of the most important postings in the whole Service. Beirut had been a civilised, for which read Europeanised, outpost from which a critical region could be monitored without having to experience the poverty, heat and corruption at first hand. At least that was the theory; in practice it was a city where the poverty could be ignored, the heat was bearable and the corruption made our job easier.

With the advent of the civil war, the Station had been significantly downgraded but our Head of Station remained impressively well plugged into the feuding factions in the country, and to the men who supplied their weapons. His was the only reaction to the all-stations bulletin. He responded with a cable which simply quoted the number of the bulletin and suggested a secure call today 'AM'.

'Well a.m. is not going to be possible,' Neil White said, glancing at his watch. 'It's nearly noon here now, and way past that in Beirut.'

'I don't think that's what he means by AM.'

White looked at me quizzically. In my time on one of the Africa desks I had come across AM. Andranik Mkrtchyan, known to everyone as AM, had supplied guns to one side or the other, and often to both, in half the wars in Africa. His base was in Lebanon, although I heard he had gone out of business.

Half an hour later we were settled in one of the soundproof cubicles in the centre of the building to receive the call.

'Bring your coffee,' White had warned me. 'This may take some time.'

The Beirut Head of Station was known for his long-winded ramblings, which were only tolerated because he knew the Middle East like nobody else in the Service. When we got through it was clear we were in for a lecture.

'Andranik Mkrtchyan,' he announced. 'Armenian. Born in 1924 in a place you won't have heard of, the Sanjak of Alexandretta, an odd little statelet carved out of the collapsed Ottoman Empire by the French after the First World War. Cosmopolitan sort of place, primarily Arab, but for centuries home to people from all over the Eastern Mediterranean and beyond. But times were changing. The Turkish minority turned on everyone else, very bloody. In 1938 cosmopolitan Alexandretta became Turkish Iskenderun. The Armenian community vanished, the Mkrtchyan family fleeing down the coast to Beirut.

'What happened to AM when WWII reached Beirut is not altogether clear. He was only seventeen when the Vichy French forces surrendered to the Australian 7th Division. Five years later when Lebanon and Syria achieved their independence, the young man was already in business selling military equipment abandoned during the war or left behind by the departing French and British troops.

'It was a small step from that to buying US Army surplus rifles on the open market to supply the Lebanese army and

14

then to acquiring Soviet bloc weapons to supply to anyone willing to buy them, first in the Middle East and then in North Africa and afterwards throughout Africa. After arming those fighting the French in North Africa, he sold guns to the Algerians to give to the Polisario guerrillas in Morocco and just moved on south. It's alleged that a lot of the explosives used by the ANC terrorists in South Africa came from AM.

'When the civil war started and the Israelis invaded, he considered moving his business elsewhere but his Lebanese wife persuaded him to stay. Her brother arranged a permanent guard of Phalangist militia.

'Then he suffered a heart attack that nearly killed him. He was just sixty-three.

'It was time for a new generation to take over. His son Miqayel was soon supplying weapons to the regime in Iraq and it seemed the Mkrtchyan business would continue as usual. A bomb under Miqayel's car ended that. AM's younger son, Poghos, returned from the US, where he'd been studying at the University of Nevada. Inevitably he's known as PM. He's the key figure for us and he's an unknown quantity. My source in AM's circle is very dismissive of young PM, bit of a playboy apparently, a gambler.

'What I do know is that AM has been approached and offered the very latest Russian surface-to-air missiles—'

'Who by?' White interrupted.

'That I don't know. AM is well known but anyone active in the business would know that he's no longer a player, and they would know that Miqayel is dead. If they really knew the market they would have gone somewhere else. AM turned them down, but here's the twist. PM heard about it and insisted he would go ahead. There was a big row between father and son. But PM is going to meet these guys, in Turkey. He leaves for Istanbul the day after tomorrow. I'll send you the flight details and a mugshot.'

'What's he going to do with the missiles if he gets them?'

'I've no idea. I'm not sure he's thought that far ahead. He just wants to show his old man that he's got what it takes. The problem for us is that his father knows the rules of the game. AM's worked with the Americans, he knows what they will and will not accept. His son is different. If he gets hold of those missiles, he could sell them to anyone. Sorry about the pun but PM is quite literally a loose cannon.'

When the call was over we returned to White's office. 'What do you make of that?' I asked.

'We will have to wait and see, but one thing is certain. I want our Desk involved. Our Station in Istanbul is going to need a fluent Russian speaker. You better pack your bags.'

III

Neil White reminded me before I left London that I would be in Turkey purely for 'some discreet surveillance'. White was a keen photographer and had managed to requisition one of the new Canon EOS-1 SLR cameras. 'A professional's camera,' he told me. 'Look after it. Try to get some close-ups of anyone PM meets and then we'll let the analysts get to work on them.'

At this stage our aim was just to find out who had the stolen missiles; we didn't yet want to do anything about it.

And we didn't want to step on anyone's toes. We hadn't told the Millî İstihbarat Teşkilatı, the Turkish National Intelligence Organisation, what we were doing in their backyard. They wouldn't be happy if they thought we were mounting any sort of operation on their turf. And in any case, in those days Turkey was usually considered American territory so we should probably have just passed the mission over to the CIA. They had a far bigger operation in Istanbul than we had. But the Americans had other things to worry about. The Panamanian dictator, Manuel Noriega, had just suppressed an attempted coup which much of the media believed had been organised by the CIA. If the CIA had been involved they had made a mess of it; the coup attempt was a fiasco and the coup leader, Moisés Giroldi, ended up dead.

Neil White was determined that the Service would grab any glory going. The lead from Beirut was ours and we were determined to follow it. As he later observed, the CIA's London Station Chief sits on Whitehall's Joint Intelligence Committee, so he could have objected if the Company had wanted to take over the operation itself.

I was even more determined than White. The more I could uncover the better for the Service, and for my career.

'I think it's you not Neil who's after the glory,' my wife commented with a smile.

She was right. Julia's own career had seemed to be over when she was compelled to leave the Defence Intelligence Staff on the birth of our daughter. Being both an RAF officer and a mother was simply not allowed in those days. However, she had joined some of her former DIS colleagues to establish a strategy consultancy they called Exodis. Somewhat to her surprise the firm was doing well and she was now a full partner. Since joining Exodis Julia had found a renewed sense of purpose. As Exodis grew, every week seemed to bring fresh challenges. The same was not always true for me.

The changes in the Kremlin created interesting times for the Soviet Operations Desk, but my own life seemed to be settling into a fixed routine and routine was not one of my strengths. Nor was writing reports that disappeared into the Whitehall ether. I had joined MI6 to help change the world, not to describe it. The point of collecting information is to then use it: intelligence is there to be pursued, not merely perused.

In Istanbul I hoped to get more than a few photographs. I wanted background, plans, names. Who was PM planning to buy the missiles from? More importantly, who did he think he could sell them to? I wanted something that would enable me to escape from the paper that festooned my desk each day. I had spent long enough in Century House; it was time to get back into the field.

Julia didn't altogether agree. When we were stationed in Moscow she often commented that in our business people don't get promoted in the field. You need to be right under the noses of the decision-makers to get noticed. When it comes to career advancement all bosses find it easier to deliver good news to those close by and bad news to people they don't have to see every day.

On top of that there was always a list of things to do around the house that Julia hoped I would find time for; perhaps that was another reason I looked forward to hopping on a plane.

I arrived at the recently renamed Atatürk International Airport twenty-four hours before our target was due. We had discovered that PM would be collecting a hire car when he arrived. I did the same and then drove to meet our local Head of Station.

I only got lost once on the way from the airport.

'That's not bad,' Vernon Forbes told me. 'It's much quicker, and safer, to use taxis in this city. I've no idea why our man is hiring a car. Driving here is like doing the Steilste ski run with your legs tied together.'

Vernon Forbes was one of the Service's younger Head of Stations but out of the standard Service mould: public school (in his case St Paul's), Oxbridge (Clare College, Cambridge) and a year out in the 'real world' before joining the Service. His year in the real world I discovered was spent at a private

Swiss bank owned by a friend of his father. I suspect he hadn't done that out of a passion for banking. When it had come to choosing his Service cryptonym he had opted for 'Kandahar', not out of any connection with Afghanistan but because that was the name of his prestigious ski club in Mürren.

Forbes' allusion to the Steilste run was one of those in-group references intended to mark out who was 'one of us'. I could have replied that my wife had belonged to the Downhill Only Club in Wengen and knew Mürren and the Steilste well but I didn't feel the need to play silly games. In any case, Julia had then been attached to a ghastly man named Rupert and I had no desire to bring him into the conversation.

'My only skiing is on water,' I responded. 'Not so far to fall.'

Forbes let that go.

We were in the mock renaissance style palace that Sir Charles Barry, the architect of the Palace of Westminster, had designed as Imperial Britain's embassy to the Ottoman Empire. Now that the Embassy had moved to Ankara the building housed our Consulate General.

'I gather PM has told the car rental people that he must have a Mercedes,' Forbes continued. 'He'll have a hell of a job trying to park that safely. I hope you haven't done that.'

'No, I picked up a Renault 12.'

'That's good, suitably anonymous. They're built here. No good for speed of course, but there won't be any car chases in Istanbul.' He sounded disappointed. 'My wife has one. I'll use her car tomorrow, my own Rover's far too conspicuous.

'There will be just three of us at the airport when PM

arrives,' he continued. 'You, me and Turgut but we'll manage. Turgut's a local, we've used him for surveillance and suchlike for years, very reliable. Drives a taxi, which makes him almost invisible.'

'That's still a small team for surveillance in a city like this,' I commented.

'We're pretty stretched at the moment,' Forbes responded. 'As I say we'll manage. Our job is just to identify anyone PM is meeting. My deputy has to be in Ankara tomorrow, so he won't be able to get here until evening. That should give us a reasonable team on the spot. If PM leads us to the chaps with the missiles we forget about him and concentrate on them. Even if we can't find their names, if we could get some clear photos London can go to work.'

Forbes had a way of talking that made it clear that whatever our theoretical ranks in the Service, in his town he was the one in charge. He spent half an hour filling me in on the practicalities of life in Istanbul before arranging to meet the next day at what he still referred to as Yeşilköy Airport. Before I left he passed me a clunky Philips two-way radio.

'Leave that in the car. They're getting very touchy about security inside the terminal building.'

I spent the rest of the day trying to familiarise myself with the city. I drove from the Consulate through the area around Taksim Square and located the big modern hotels, like the Hilton, Sheraton and Divan. It was likely that PM would be meeting his contacts in that area, but the real glory of Istanbul was elsewhere. My hotel was in Sultanahmet, in the heart of the old city, prime tourist territory. The Topkapi Palace, Blue Mosque, and the magnificent Hagia Sophia were all an easy walk away and in the evening I explored the

21

Old City on foot. It struck me that the Obelisk erected in the Byzantine Hippodrome by Theodosius the Great 1,700 years ago, and already 1,700 years old when he brought it from Egypt, looked eerily modern, like a giant version of one of the missiles I was here to chase.

I had been assured that the weather in Istanbul would be dry, but as I returned to the hotel a soft rain began to fall.

The rain seemed to clear away overnight. After a breakfast of crumbly white sheep's milk cheese, black olives and sumac-sprinkled eggs I was back at the airport well before PM's plane was due to land. I needn't have bothered; the flight was running more than an hour late. Vernon Forbes turned up just as it landed.

Poghos Mkrtchyan, PM, was taller than I expected, tall and slim. He looked fit but it was the fitness of the gym not the sports field. As he emerged from the arrivals gate, he stopped to put on dark glasses. His face was tanned and unlined, his straight black hair cut just too short to be fashionable. I knew that he was thirty-one years old but he looked younger. 'Perpetual student,' Neil White had muttered disparagingly when we saw the background briefing from Beirut. He was wearing high-waisted, tapered denim jeans and a plain white shirt with a Tommy Hilfiger sweater thrown casually around his shoulders. He carried a matching denim jacket and a leather overnight bag. PM was clearly not planning to stay for long.

Turgut was outside the terminal, where he could keep an eye on the Avis cars waiting for collection. He had a copy of the grainy photo of our target we had been sent from Beirut. Nevertheless, Forbes hurried off to let Turgut know what PM was wearing and to collect his own car from the car park.

I stuck with PM. He went straight to the Avis desk. I held back but he didn't look around. He seemed to be having difficulty making himself understood but a wiry American stopped to help. That should have struck me as odd as I knew from my own experience that the Avis rep spoke perfect English, but that thought only occurred to me later. He was soon scribbling his signature on a multitude of forms. I followed him to the parking area where Turgut took over. The rain clouds were starting to gather again.

I rushed off to the car park. Forbes was still there. As I arrived I could see that he was changing a tyre on what I assumed was his wife's car. Both his front tyres were flat.

'Come on,' I shouted. 'We'll go in my car.'

He pointed at a row of cars some yards away. 'Is yours the blue Renault 12?'

'Yes,' I replied.

'Better take a look at it. Then bring me your spare tyre. And bring your fancy camera.'

I ran over and saw that the front tyres were also flat; somebody had put a knife in the sidewalls of both of them. There was only one thing to do. I pulled open the boot, removed the spare tyre and rushed back to Forbes. He had finished replacing one tyre and was trying to loosen the nuts on the second which had clearly received the same treatment as mine. By the time we had replaced that tyre PM would be well away.

'Try the radio,' instructed Forbes.

I did as he suggested and Turgut's voice boomed into the car. 'I'm on his tail. Where are you?'

'We got delayed. Which way's he going?'

'I don't know. He's not heading the way we expected. He

23

could be going to cross the Haliç Bridge.'

So he's crossing the Golden Horn, I thought to myself. 'He must be heading for Beyoğlu,' I said, keen to show that I had familiarised myself with the local geography.

'Perhaps,' responded Forbes doubtfully. He was right. By the time we had finished changing the tyres and crossed the Golden Horn ourselves it was clear that PM had no intention of stopping anywhere in Istanbul. Fifteen minutes later, after an exchange with Turgut in Turkish, Forbes announced what I had been beginning to suspect. 'Our man is leaving Europe.'

When it was constructed the Bosphorus Bridge linking Europe and Asia had been the longest suspension bridge in Europe and in Asia. The Humber Bridge had usurped its European title and just a year ago it had stopped being even the longest bridge over the Bosphorus.

'I still love this bridge every time I drive across,' commented Forbes. 'Wonderful engineering but thank God they've built another one further north. I swear this city has more lorries and cars than people.'

It was only when we crossed over the bridge that Forbes voiced the questions that had been plaguing me since we left the airport.

'What happened back there?' he asked. 'How the hell did anybody know we were at the airport waiting for PM? How could they identify both of us? I could've been under observation but you only arrived yesterday. How did they know what car you would be driving?'

'And who are they?' I asked.

'Well, it must be whoever PM is planning to meet. London seem to think they're renegade Russians. Somebody inside the Russian military. I tend to favour Georgian gangsters of some sort. There are still people in Turkey with family connections in Georgia. And Georgia's always been a pretty dangerous place. That's where Stalin came from,' Forbes added irrelevantly.

'Even if it was the local mafia who stole those missiles they must have had help from inside the Khelvachauri base,' I replied. 'My money's still on renegade Russians.'

There was no point saying anything more. What was important was that we caught up with Turgut and PM.

'Where are you now? Where's our man going?' Forbes asked Turgut.

'He's still heading east. He could be going anywhere.'

'Ankara?' I suggested.

'No way,' responded Forbes. 'You forget how big this country is. He would have flown there. Ditto if he wanted to go to somewhere like Trabzon closer to Georgia. He will stop soon. I thought he might have been heading for Karacaahmet. He's not though, we've just passed that.'

'What's special about Karacaahmet?'

'Largest Moslem graveyard in the world. Pretty secure place to meet.'

I wondered if Forbes was joking but a quick glance showed me that he wasn't.

We left the overflow from Istanbul behind and the countryside became more rural, the road lined by fields and forests. The car bounced around on the uneven road as Forbes tried to close in on our target, overtaking with the same reckless abandon as the locals. We caught up with a crowded minibus that, Forbes explained, was known as a dolmus, which means 'stuffed'. I could see why. When the dolmus stopped on a bend I was amazed to see yet more passengers pushing their way aboard, one carrying what looked like two bicycle wheels. Forbes took the opportunity to overtake, his hand on the horn, oblivious to anything coming towards us through the rain.

I had always thought of Turkey away from Istanbul as a fringe of gloriously sunny beaches on the Aegean and Mediterranean with a dry, barren hinterland behind them. I was wrong, as Forbes was keen to tell me.

'A quarter of Turkey is forest. The Black Sea coast is pretty lush, cool in summer, cold, even snowy, in winter. And lots of rain, that's why it's so green. Of course there's heavy industry in places but mostly it's fruit and hazelnut plantations, trees, trees and more trees—'

Turgut's voice broke in. 'He's heading for the coast. Şile.'

'That makes sense,' Forbes responded.

'What sort of place is Şile?' I asked.

'It's a seaside resort, restrained by our standards but the Turks love it. Convenient for Istanbul. Nice beaches. Great seafood. Things to do. There's a Genoese castle. Not a bad place to meet up.'

But PM was not planning on meeting anyone in Şile; he carried on along the coast. For a moment I thought he might be planning on driving all the way to Georgia, but that would be another 700 miles. He must surely stop soon.

Sunset, I knew, was at 7.30, about now, but that was purely academic. With the rain bucketing down, visibility was just a few yards.

'He keeps slowing down,' Turgut told us.

'You think he's seen you?'

'Not in this weather. He's looking for somewhere.'

26

'Ağva!' Forbes exclaimed. 'That's where he's going.'

'Ağva?'

'Another resort. Smaller than Şile. Reasonable beach. Very peaceful. Squashed between two rivers and the sea. Discreet. The sort of place Turkish men take their mistresses. Holiday homes in among the trees. Barbecues in summer. Cuddling up by a wood fire in winter.'

Just then Turgut confirmed that Forbes was right. 'He's turned off towards the sea, on the road that follows the Koca River.'

'More like a creek than a river,' Forbes informed me. 'My wife and I've been hiking around there. There's a couple of nice restaurants on jetties over the water. Very peaceful.'

Turgut's voice came over the radio again. 'He's stopped. There's a private house that seems to back onto the river. No cars in the driveway. He pulled in there. I had to carry on past; 600 or 700 metres on there's a small hotel. I'm now in the car park.'

'Stay there,' Forbes instructed. 'We can't be more than ten minutes away.'

'Will do,' Turgut responded.

Two minutes later he was on the radio again. 'Something's happened. A Ford came down the road past the house where our target stopped. I think there were four men in it, difficult to tell in this rain. When it reached this hotel it pulled into the car park, turned round and drove straight back the way it had come. But I heard it stop after a couple of hundred metres and I think somebody got out of the car. Then they drove off again.'

'Don't do anything,' Forbes repeated. 'Just stay in your taxi, we're almost there.'

Five minutes later we passed a wooden house on the right-hand side, set well back from the road. Sitting in the drive was a Mercedes and, blocking it in, a Ford Taunus station wagon. Presumably the Mercedes PM had hired and the Ford that Turgut had just seen.

We carried on and drew up beside Turgut's taxi. Turgut himself clambered out and climbed into the back of our car.

'What do you think?' he asked. 'Who are the men in the station wagon?'

'It must be the people PM came here to meet. There's no other car there, unless it's around the back. Perhaps they were waiting back near the main road to check that PM was alone.'

'Then why drive past the house and have to turn round?' I asked. 'Do you think there was anyone in the house when PM arrived?'

'I can't be sure,' Turgut replied. 'But the lights were on.'

If there was someone there to let PM in that must mean there was quite a large welcoming party. At least one in the house, four in the Ford that turned up a few minutes later.

Something didn't sound right. Our assumption had been that the theft of the missiles had been opportunistic. Renegade Russians looking for a way to make a quick buck had taken the weapons without much of an idea of where they were going to sell them. PM or his father would not be the first choice for anyone who knew the market. Now the whole operation was looking more sophisticated. Somehow they had identified Forbes and me and disabled our cars. Then four of them had lain in wait for PM or, more likely, having disabled our cars, they followed PM from the airport. That all suggested these men were locals, not a couple of opportunist Russians trying to make contact with someone who could help them dispose of the weapons they had stolen. And there was another anomaly. If Turgut was right they had dropped at least one person off outside the house before going in. What was that for? And where was that person now?

'We have to get closer,' I said. 'We need to be able to watch that house but we can't do that from a car, they would spot us.'

'We could leave Turgut here and just drive back towards the main road and find somewhere to park there,' Forbes suggested. 'Then at least we can observe the Ford when it leaves, maybe follow it'.

'If it leaves. They could be here for days. We need to try to see inside the house, try to work out how many are in there. It's odd there's only PM's car and the Ford in the drive.'

'I've got waterproofs,' said Forbes. 'I'll cut down to the river and then follow that along so I can get a view of the back of the house. See if there's anything parked there. You and Turgut stay here.'

I shook my head. There was no point my sitting around waiting for him to return.

'I'll drive back past the house like you suggested and find somewhere further back to park. Then I'll cross into the trees on the other side of the road and see how close I'm able to get to the front of the house. If they do start to leave I'll race back to the car and try to follow them.'

'OK. But make sure you don't bump into whoever they dropped off up the road.'

I had taken a light raincoat with me when I left the hotel but realised that I'd left it in the car at the airport.

Forbes found an old coat of his wife's in the boot but it was far too small for me. Eventually Turgut lent me his leather jacket. He also produced a pink umbrella emblazoned with the name of the Pera Palace hotel, but that would be conspicuous, even at night. In any case the rain seemed to be easing again, although in this light there was no point in taking the camera Neil White had given me.

We agreed Forbes and I would take our radios but maintain radio silence. In emergencies we could call Turgut but we didn't want anyone calling us. Turgut would go into the hotel and try to contact Forbes' deputy who should be arriving in Istanbul.

'Get him out here as soon as possible,' Forbes insisted. 'We're going to need help. And make sure he brings a radio.'

I drove back past the house again. Nothing seemed to have changed. I thought I caught a glimpse of movement at one of the windows. It was not easy to find somewhere to park where I would not be seen. The vegetation came right up to the road and there seemed to be no tracks leading off into the trees.

I passed a house on the other side of the road which seemed to be the mirror image of the one I wanted to observe, about half a kilometre further on. It was in complete darkness, two large juniper trees guarding the entrance. The house was surrounded by high metal railings. At the front the railings were set back about a metre from the road. That would have to do. I pulled the Renault as far off the road as I could and got out.

I wanted to keep under cover as much as possible, which was easier than I expected. It was not difficult to push my way through the bushes, shrubs and long grass close to the road and further back the trees provided good cover. I would have been much quicker with a torch, especially as the ground underneath was almost marsh-like in places, but I couldn't risk that.

I stayed well back from the road as I approached the house where we had seen PM's car. The lights were now on inside the house. I didn't try to get too close. An oak tree fifteen yards away from the road provided some shelter from the rain which was now certainly easing off, just a few heavy drops falling from the tree above. There was movement inside the house but I couldn't make out what was happening.

The shot when it came was unmistakable.

IV

The sound came from inside the house. The front door was flung open and I realised that I must have missed someone standing guard outside. I could see him, gun in hand, crouching as he rushed into the house. People were moving around inside and then the front door was slammed shut. The guard did not reappear.

My first thought was that Vernon Forbes had got too close to the house. I moved further back and radioed Turgut.

'Is Vernon there?'

'No.'

'I heard a shot. Did you hear it?'

There was a pause. 'No. You think somebody shot at Mr Forbes?'

'I hope not. I'm staying here. I will call again.'

Nothing seemed to happen for ten minutes, except that the exterior lights were switched on. Then the front door opened and a group of men emerged. One of them unlocked the boot of PM's rental car. From this distance it was difficult to distinguish any of their features but none of them seemed to be Forbes or PM. I edged forward.

Then I saw PM, or at least something that could have been Poghos Mkrtchyan, or Vernon Forbes.

Two men carried what appeared to be a body out of the house and threw it into the boot of the Mercedes. Another appeared with a roughly rolled-up carpet, threw that in on top and slammed the boot shut. The body had seemed to be dressed in a jacket, not a waterproof, which I hoped meant it was not Vernon Forbes.

The men all went back inside. I pulled back further into the woods and radioed Turgut again.

'This is getting serious. I think I've just seen a body being carried out and dumped in his car.'

'Mr Forbes?'

'I don't think so.'

Turgut said nothing at first. 'Mr Forbes has not returned yet,' was his only comment. Then he added, 'His deputy is on his way, but he won't be here for an hour.'

And, I thought to myself, like us he wouldn't be armed.

'Let him know what's happening,' I said.

I really needed to get much closer to the house. That meant crossing the road. I moved away under cover of the trees and when the road bent so that the house was out of sight I sprinted across the road and carefully made my way back so that I was less than twenty yards away from the house.

Suddenly the front door opened again and a man emerged. He approached PM's car and seemed to be checking one of the rear tyres. Satisfied, he went back inside. I realised he hadn't been checking the tyre. He had been feeling for a tracking device which he had now removed. So that's how the four men in the Ford had found their way here.

And that probably meant they weren't the people PM had been expecting to meet. So who were they?

I didn't have time to consider the question. The front door opened again and half a dozen men appeared. The rain had stopped now and as they were standing in the light I was able to see that two of them had on some sort of black, military-style kit. I was close enough to see that there were no obvious insignia. The other four were wearing jackets and ties. One of them was a big bull of a man. He turned to one of the men in black and shook his hand. As he moved towards the Ford Taunus he raised his hand in an exaggerated wave. I could distinctly hear his farewell shout.

'*Dasvidaniya.*'

Clearly people were leaving. I needed to get back to the car and try to follow them.

I pushed through the trees until I was out of sight of the house before stepping out onto the road. I then sprinted back towards the car. Just before I got there I heard the sound of vehicles approaching from behind me. I jumped back into the bushes at the side of the road and crouched down, reasonably confident that I would not be seen.

The first car to pass was PM's Mercedes. The driver looked familiar. It was the man who had helped PM at the airport Avis desk earlier. I had thought then that he was American but realised now that it's not difficult for anyone to put on a generic American accent when speaking English. He must have noted the hire car details and alerted someone to fit a magnetic tracker.

The driver swung his head in my direction as he passed but he couldn't have seen me. Nevertheless, I moved further back from the road and flattened myself to the ground behind another large shrub.

After the Mercedes came the Ford station wagon. I pulled the shrub aside to try to obtain a clearer view, hoping that the bush was not what it looked like, wild daphne, which could produce a nasty rash. I couldn't make out the features of any of the three men in the car but I was fairly sure that the bull of a man I had seen earlier was in the back seat. As soon as they'd gone past I rushed out and unlocked the car. As I did so I heard a car coming in the opposite direction and realised that the Ford was reversing back down the road.

I swung the door of the Renault open, cursing when the courtesy light came on. Jumping into the driver's seat I reached for the ignition as the Ford stopped only ten or twelve yards away. Two men jumped out and walked slowly but menacingly towards me. It was like a scene from a bad gangster film. As I switched on the ignition both men reached inside their jackets, pulled out handguns and in one smooth movement took up the classic 'isosceles' stance: both hands thrust forward, gun held high, feet, knees, hips and shoulders square to the target. And I was the target. They've practised that before, I thought.

I could almost sense the mocking smiles on their faces but that was just my imagination. All I could really see were two silhouettes.

And then, at exactly the same moment, both men fired.

Instinctively I ducked down. The car rocked. They had missed me. At that range that seemed impossible. I registered that the windscreen was still intact, no shards of glass showering on me. Without looking over the dashboard I slammed the car into gear, producing a horrible grating from the gearbox. The Renault lurched forward and then the engine stalled. I raised my head to squint through the steering wheel. The men were walking back towards the station wagon. As I watched they slowly climbed into the car and drove off.

It was obvious what had happened. They weren't aiming at me. They were shooting at the tyres and had hit them. Even at that range that was good shooting. The only light on the road had been the red glow from their car's rear lights. These guys were professionals and I was starting to guess whose professionals.

I called Turgut and told him briefly what had happened. Forbes had still not returned.

There was no point in waiting inside an immobile car. I walked back towards the house. It was now in complete darkness. I knew at least two men had remained inside when the others left. As they didn't seem to have a car they would be staying there for a while. I wanted to get back to Turgut but didn't dare stay on the road. Again I pushed into the trees, giving the house a wide berth. I had just regained the road when a vehicle approached from the direction of the sea. It was a Murat Şahin taxi: Turgut. Forbes was in the seat beside him.

'What the hell's happening?' Forbes greeted me, at the same time gesturing to Turgut to drive on as I clambered into the back seat.

'PM is dead,' I replied. 'Four men followed him all the way from the airport into the house and then either one of them or somebody who was already in the house shot him. Then four men came out of the house, shot out the tyres of your wife's car and drove off, taking PM's car with his body in the boot. No doubt that will be dumped somewhere well away from here. Whoever PM expected to meet must still be in there.'

'No,' Forbes responded. 'Everyone's left the house.'

'How? There was no other car.'

'By canoe.' Forbes turned round, looking at me over his shoulder. 'I managed to work my way round to the side of the house. But there wasn't much to see from there. It was pitch black. There's a lawn at the back, leading down to a large shed by the river. I decided to risk crossing the lawn to have a closer look at the shed. In fact, it's a boathouse but I couldn't see anything inside. I did get a better view of the house. There seemed to be a big room at the back with a light on but the shutters were closed so I could only see a few slivers of light. Next to that was a kitchen again with the lights on, but nobody went in there.

'I had just decided to come back to the taxi when I heard the shot. Startled me, I tell you. London didn't say anything about us needing to be armed. After the shot nothing happened for a bit but then the exterior lights came on and the whole place lit up. I heard noises round at the front and I thought they might be leaving. But again, nothing more happened for a while. The exterior light stayed on. I was stuck. If anyone looked out while I was crossing the lawn they were bound to spot me. I must've been there for around ten minutes and then there were more sounds from the front of the house. This time people were leaving. I heard two cars drive off. I know somebody remained inside the house because suddenly all the exterior lights went off. I thought I could get back to the taxi but then some chap appeared in the kitchen and opened the back door. That's when I heard more shots.'

'That must have been my tyres getting shot out.'

'That really shook the man at the back door. He rushed back inside and a minute later came running out with another guy. I could see they both had heavy-looking backpacks. They switched off all the lights in the house and came running towards me. One of them had a torch. If they'd gone round to the left side of the boathouse I'd have been a goner. But they went the other way. They pulled the metal door on to the slipway open and disappeared inside. When they emerged they were carrying a canoe or kayak of some sort. A serious bit of kit, not the sort of thing the tourists paddle up the creek with. A fair-sized kayak with a hatch where they put their backpacks. They put it in the river and just paddled off.'

'You didn't hear anything they said?'

'Not really, they weren't talking to each other. One of them shouted something but I didn't recognise the language. Not Turkish. Could've been Russian. Something about *taimen*. Is that a Russian word?'

'*Taimen*? Yes, that's Russian. It's a fish like a big trout but it's also a brand name. *Taimen* are the folding kayaks used by Soviet special forces. You could cross the Black Sea in that in the right weather.'

'Do you think that's what they're planning to do?'

'No, I'm just saying you could if the sea conditions were good and you had the time. Those guys will want to be well hidden again by day break. I doubt if they'll go more than thirty or forty kilometres, probably a lot less. They could just paddle across the creek. But that doesn't help. We've lost them and we've lost the men who drove off with PM's body.'

'And you think they were Russians as well?' Forbes asked.

'Because one of them shouted goodbye in Russian? *Dasvidaniya*. No. Whoever said that wasn't a Russian speaker. The intonation was all wrong. *Dasvidaniya* is the sort of word foreigners pick up. But what that does mean is that whoever he was talking to was probably Russian.'

'The two men left in the house? The guys in that kayak?'

'That's right, we should try to get into that house to see if anything has been left behind.'

Forbes shook his head. 'Perhaps. But if anyone heard the shots we shouldn't be here. Especially Turgut. The military are throwing their weight around again. They don't appreciate Turkish nationals working with the likes of us, even though we are all supposed to be on the same side. One big happy NATO family. And you should get out of here, too. We don't want any questions being asked about what you're doing in the country. Or what I'm doing in Ağva, for that matter.'

I wanted to see inside the house but Forbes was right, it was too risky. He radioed his deputy and we arranged to meet in Şile. Meanwhile Turgut called a friend who agreed to drive to Ağva that night with a pick-up truck and if possible collect the Renault.

'I'll come back here tomorrow. If there's no police around and everything seems empty I'll try to get in,' Forbes assured me.

On the drive back to Istanbul Forbes gave me his thoughts on what had happened. 'PM came here to meet someone who would sell him those surface-to-air missiles. One of his rivals found out what he was planning and decided they would follow him, find out who had the missiles and make them a better offer, taking PM out of the equation while they were about it.'

That made some sort of sense. 'That's why the Ford drove past the house first and dropped someone off,' I suggested. 'They didn't know who was inside and what sort of reception they would receive.'

'The answer's in Beirut,' Forbes insisted. 'There must be

all sorts of gunrunners there. We need to find out who knew PM was flying into Istanbul and why he was coming here.'

'You don't think it could have been someone local? Or perhaps the Georgian gangsters you mentioned? They may have been on the trail of the missiles and didn't want PM interfering.'

Forbes shook his head. 'If it had been, you would be dead. Those sorts of people don't shoot tyres. And how would they have identified you at the airport?'

They were good questions, but Forbes had missed the obvious answer. The two men who shot out my tyres were professionals, Special Forces or Intelligence. They could have killed me but had been told not to. Why? I could only think of one organisation that had sources in Beirut, that would do anything to stop those missiles getting into the wrong hands and who employed agents with the skill, ruthlessness and sheer arrogance to kill when necessary and play cowboy games when killing was unnecessary. Mossad. Israeli Intelligence.

V

When somebody shoots at you, even if they are only aiming at the tyres of your car, it's natural to expect there to be consequences. And if not consequences at least explanations. But that simply didn't happen. Life carried on in Century House as if nothing untoward had happened except that one of the top-floor mandarins, Clive Dreyton, requested a personal briefing on my adventure in Ağva. As his diary was full, that was two weeks after I returned.

Dreyton first had to attend a Security symposium in Brussels. 'Ridiculous talking shop,' Neil White commented. 'Bloody Europeans trying to play spies when the Americans are out of the room. Can you believe it's being chaired by some guy from the SRE, the Luxembourg security service.' But for Dreyton the symposium clearly took priority over one of our own agents being shot at.

When the meeting with Dreyton did take place it lasted less than fifteen minutes.

I hadn't met Dreyton before but I had once sat through a training session, the low-point of which was his humourless explication of the Treasury's peculiar budgetary virement rules. Since then he had progressed up the ladder to Assistant Secretary and was rumoured to have been in contention the last time the Service's top post became vacant. Gossip had it that the man who had finally been appointed had offered

Dreyton the consolation title of Assistant Secretary Security but Dreyton had turned it down when he realised what the acronym spelt.

Clive Dreyton was like a miniature version of everyone else I had encountered at the top of the Service. Dark suit immaculately cut, crisp white shirt with monogrammed cuff links, dark tie with double stripes which since joining the Service I had learned to recognise as Old Harrovian, and brogues polished so highly that he must have been able to see his own reflection in them. All that on a frame that seemed to have stopped growing in early adolescence, something that could not be said for his waist. Clive Dreyton was a man who clearly liked to lunch.

Neil White accompanied me to Dreyton's office clutching a sheaf of papers, none of which we needed to refer to.

They included a telex from Vernon Forbes who had reported that there was no sign of police activity at the house the next day. The house itself was owned by an Istanbul hazelnut trader renowned for his piety. Although, as Forbes reported, the man's piety did not preclude him renting out his Ağva holiday retreat by the day or even by the hour. Forbes had managed to rent the house himself for twenty-four hours but discovered nothing at all of interest inside it.

The Turkish police found a burned-out Mercedes near the Ömerli Dam and then discovered the gruesome remains in the boot. They had tracked the car down to Avis and learned that it had been hired by one Poghos Mkrtchyan who had given an address in the Hamra district of Beirut. As far as the Turkish police were concerned the trail stopped there.

'Of course you should have stuck with Vernon Forbes in Ağva,' commented Dreyton. 'Gone round to the back of the house with him and seen if you could get anything on the Russians. They're the ones with the missiles. Forbes hasn't produced much of a description. And you forgot your camera.'

'I didn't forget the camera,' I insisted. 'It was pitch black and raining. A camera would have been useless.'

'Perhaps. But there was nothing you could do on your own at the front of the house. And then you park where they are bound to see you when they drive away. Not ideal. Pure luck that you're not dead.'

I could sense Neil White stiffen beside me but he said nothing. We both knew that Dreyton was not a field man. He had reached the top by being able to say, 'Yes sir' in every known language.

'Could you recognise any of the men you saw if they were to pop up again?' he asked.

'Just the one I saw at the airport.'

'Well, we won't be seeing them again,' concluded Dreyton. 'It was obviously the Jews. Just the sort of shenanigans you'd expect from the "chosen people".'

In those days anti-Semitism was not uncommon in the Security Services.

'That will be all,' Dreyton concluded.

'Dreyton's father was attached to our Embassy in Rome in '46 when the Zionists blew it up,' Neil White told me as we waited for the lift, as if that justified Dreyton's snide remarks about the chosen people. 'If the bombs had gone off five minutes earlier Dreyton would have been orphaned. The man's a total prick. His father ended up ambassador somewhere, which is how little Clive got where he is today.'

White at least had the grace to smile at that last remark.

We all knew how much he himself owed to his illustrious father. There was a side to my Desk Officer that could be remarkably catty. In general White was tolerant of other people's foibles, but some people he took violently against. His uncharacteristically bitchy remarks made me realise that Dreyton was one such person.

White had operated undercover in Moscow for five years before having to be pulled out at very short notice for reasons nobody wanted to discuss. He had been in Belfast for the last couple of years. He was a professional and would have commanded universal respect but for the backbiting and jealousies that plague any organisation where the pulls of ambition outstrip opportunities for advancement. Neil White's most valuable skill, I soon discovered, was his ability to sense which way the winds were blowing in the corridors of Whitehall. He might not like Dreyton but he would say nothing to ruffle the man's feathers. I had not been so tactful; I shouldn't have contradicted him about the camera.

My theory that my attackers had been Israelis was generally accepted, although direct approaches to Mossad had met a stonewall and our Station in Tel Aviv remained sceptical. Our Beirut Station, on the other hand, reported that there were so many Israeli agents in the city, especially among the various Christian militias, that it would not be at all surprising if they had picked up news of PM's plans.

I was confident that a Mossad team had followed PM from the airport, perhaps even from Beirut, interrupted his meeting with the Russians who had stolen the missiles, and in the ensuing 'discussion' PM had been shot. The Israelis and the two Russians had then reached some sort of arrangement. Perhaps the missiles would be dumped out to sea under Israeli supervision in exchange for considerably more cash than PM had been able to offer.

News came through from Washington that our friends there were also confident that the Israelis had solved the problem of how to stop the SAM missiles ending up in the wrong hands.

Then it all went quiet. For more than two months nothing at all was heard by anyone. Eventually the missing missiles became yesterday's news.

It was about then that I first heard the name Dr Roger Montacute.

Although Julia had been unhappy about being compelled to resign her RAF commission and leave the Defence Intelligence Staff when our daughter Eveline was born, it had proved to be the right decision. The Exodis consultancy she had then helped set up was becoming a success. The firm's quarterly bulletin, edited by Julia, had recently been quoted on the BBC.

One of the other partners was a friend of Roger Montacute's mother and had suggested that Julia meet him. 'You would be doing me a favour,' Sir Jonathon Craverse confided. 'Just humour him. Roger's a bit odd. But if anything comes of it he does have one thing going for him: unlike most academics I've come across he's extremely rich.'

'What does he want us to do?' Julia had asked.

'I'll let him tell you that. Something to do with the Spanish Civil War.'

VI

All civil wars are vicious and Spain's was no exception. Neither side showed mercy, neither side ever forgave. The assorted idealists, republicans, communists and anarchists, fighting for the elected government when they weren't fighting each other, committed numerous atrocities, but they were dwarfed by the scale of the White Terror unleashed by Franco's Nationalists. Well over 100,000 Spaniards disappeared, their bodies dumped where they were killed. Thousands of mass graves still remain undisturbed; to many they are best left that way.

The discovery of the bones of Juan Manuel Casares and his six companions back in 1976 raised a momentary flutter of local interest because of who he was, but that soon disappeared. Casares became once again nothing but a footnote in the more recondite histories of the period. By the time Montacute first mentioned his name to Julia, and Julia mentioned Montacute's name to me, the Casares affair had returned to obscurity.

'We have a new client,' Julia announced one evening over dinner. I had spent the day trying to sort out a problem the Service had in Rome and wasn't fully concentrating on Julia's news.

'That's good,' I responded, possibly without the enthusiasm Julia expected.

'A man called Montacute. I can't decide whether he's a brilliant eccentric or just totally mad. He wants us to prove that a company in Spain was set up using buried treasure. He says it's immoral and he wants to expose the man behind it.'

'Doesn't sound the sort of thing Exodis would want to get involved in,' I responded.

'I agree but his mother, Lady Constance Montacute, is a friend of Jonathon Craverse. We would be doing him a favour. And business is business.'

'Where is the treasure supposed to have come from?' I asked. 'Did somebody find a pirate map with X marking the spot?'

'Don't be silly! Nothing like that. Much more recent. Spanish gold reserves looted in the civil war.'

'You can't be serious. Not Moscow gold again. That story's been doing the rounds for years.'

Because Spain had stayed neutral in the First World War, trading with both sides, it had the fourth largest gold and currency reserves in the world when the war ended. Twenty years later, during the civil war, the Republican government pulled together their gold reserves and shipped them off to Russia. Since then there had been endless efforts to prove that the gold had never left Spain, or, if it had, it never reached Moscow, but none of them came to anything for the simple reason that none of these beliefs were true. The central bank's reserves, thousands of sackloads of gold coins, had been loaded onto four Soviet ships in Cartagena and shipped to Russia. There Soviet bureaucrats had carefully sifted out any for which collectors might pay extra before melting down the rest. Stalin then had anyone involved in organising the shipments shot.

'Surely all the fairy tales about hidden Moscow gold have been thoroughly debunked,' I said.

'Yes, I know that,' Julia agreed. 'I've spent all morning hearing about it. But apparently the gold wasn't all shipped off to Moscow. Some was sent to France. That's what this is about. It seems a truckload of gold coins didn't arrive. They were intercepted by a gang of anarchists led by a man called Juan Manuel Casares.'

'But the anarchists were on the Republicans' side.'

'Well perhaps they were, but the story is that this man Casares stole the gold and hid it in his home village. He later became some kind of anarchist hero but was badly wounded in the fighting in Barcelona. He and his gang then returned to his birthplace, San something or other, and dug the gold up again.'

'And you've been hired to prove he should hand it back, fifty years later?'

'Not at all. Casares is dead. They found his body in 1976 along with the bodies of his men. They had all been shot. One of the looted gold coins had been stuffed in his mouth.'

I was about to ask how anyone was supposed to have found the treasure if all the men who had stolen it were dead when Julia shook her head and smiled. 'Just let me tell you the story.'

Her client, she explained, was a Cambridge don by the name of Dr Roger Benson Montacute. The Montacute family had owned fifty per cent of a prestigious merchant bank but Roger Montacute had never shown any interest in banking. Nevertheless, as the only son of the late Sir Keeler Montacute he had benefited considerably from the recent sale of the family's stake to one of the American banking behemoths taking over the City at the time.

Aged around fifty, Montacute certainly didn't look like a banker, Julia told me, but neither did he look like an absent-minded professor. The white-gold Patek Philippe Calatrava wristwatch he wore on his right wrist must have cost a fortune; Julia had a knack for noticing such things. Montacute had arrived in Julia's south London office dressed for a day in the country.

'Would you believe he was wearing a half Norfolk in London?' Julia asked, assuming I knew she was referring to a style of tweed shooting jacket. 'I couldn't make him out, even after he'd told me all about himself.'

I was surprised. Julia had a wonderful ability to encourage other people to open up about themselves.

'It seems his father wanted him to go into the family bank but his mother, Lady Constance, encouraged him to follow his passions. That was his expression, although he didn't look like the passionate type at all. It seems one of his passions was religion and he went off to Trinity, Dublin to study theology. I suspect he chose Dublin to get away from his father but he says there was a cousin studying there already. After that he came to Cambridge and has been there for twenty years or so.'

'Still studying theology?'

'Not quite. His field now is wars of religion in the twentieth century.'

'And he includes the Spanish Civil War in that?'

'I don't know,' Julia replied with more than a hint of exasperation in her voice. Then she grinned. 'Stop interrupting and let me get back to the missing gold.'

Because I still had a schoolboy fascination with tales of buried treasure, listen I did.

'Clearly lots of people over the years have tried to find out what Casares did with the gold, but Montacute approached the subject from a very different angle. Or rather someone else did, a Moroccan woman, a Cambridge colleague who has been studying the role played by Moroccan troops in the Spanish Civil War. When the war started Franco was commanding the troops the Spanish had garrisoning their African colonies. They formed the backbone of the Nationalist forces during the war. This woman has been studying one group in particular, from a place called Ifni. They were an elite: Arab troops and Spanish officers. She discovered from records in Morocco that one platoon had been in the very area where the bodies of Casares and his men were uncovered. And they had been there at exactly the time that Casares disappeared with the gold. But the odd thing was that the official records in Madrid didn't match what she had found in Morocco. The Spanish records seemed to show that the Ifni troops were miles away.

'Montacute's theory is that the Spanish officer in charge, a man called Francisco Vilafermosa Cortés, changed the Spanish records to hide the fact that he had intercepted and killed Casares and his men. Montacute believes Vilafermosa stole the gold himself, which he used after the war to set up a very successful business, a business that maintained close links to the Franco regime. He wants us to look at Vilafermosa's business interests. He can find out what's public knowledge about this company, but is there anything that's not public knowledge? Has the company got any secret connections in Spain or this country?'

'Why should it have secret connections here?' I asked.

'Montacute didn't say. He just pointed out that the company has expanded enormously in recent years and asked how that happened. Is there some state involvement or has Vilafermosa found another source of funds? Has some of the gold been hidden away for nearly half a century and is now being dug up? Is there still more out there somewhere? He's leaving for Morocco tomorrow to see what he can discover there.'

The story was intriguing but it still didn't seem to be the sort of investigation Exodis was set up to undertake.

'It's all a bit speculative, isn't it? Haven't you got better things to do?'

'It's business Thomas. Exodis needs the cash. We aren't big enough yet to turn any business away.'

'I didn't mean Exodis has better things to do, I meant you. Exodis was meant to be a part-time role, you don't want it taking over your life.'

'Don't I? You allow the Service to take over your life. What's the difference, please?'

We were on sensitive ground. Julia was not always finding it easy to balance home and office and clearly thought that I could be doing more to help. She may have been right. I felt an overwhelming loyalty to the Service, but I didn't want to become what the Japanese call a 'salaryman' thinking only of work. I had missed Eveline's school play by going to Turkey and, as Julia had pointed out in no uncertain terms, a pot of rose petal jam was not sufficient compensation.

I brought the subject back to her new client. 'What's Montacute planning to do with anything you might find?' I asked. 'Dig up some gold himself?'

'That's what I kept asking. It may be an interesting historical puzzle but I can't see what uncovering anything about the company today is going to add. Montacute seems obsessed with the whole story, irrationally so, like a dog barking at itself in a mirror or chasing its own tail. Or like a bloodhound, he's following a trail and is determined to keep on to the end without really caring whether there will be anything useful when he gets there. He just says the gold was stolen and has to be given back.'

'And how does he propose to do that? Turn up on Vilafermosa's doorstep and say hand it over?'

'Of course not, don't be so patronising. For one thing Francisco Vilafermosa died years ago.'

'Well best of luck,' I concluded. 'It will be a nice holiday for him.' For me Morocco meant not Ifni, which I had never heard of, but the romance of wartime Casablanca or the Beat Generation's drug-fuelled Tangiers.

That was my introduction to Roger Montacute. And to the name Vilafermosa. I didn't expect to hear either name again.

VII

A walk-in at our Embassy in Rome had been keeping me busy. The assistant to the KGB Rezident in the city had obviously seen how the wind was blowing in Moscow and decided the time was right for some free enterprise. He initially contacted our Head of Station with the promise of earth-shattering secrets for sale but then announced that as the KGB knew everyone we had ever had in the Italian capital he would only deal with someone from London. Neil White was sceptical until the man reeled off the names of every Service asset in Italy, declared and undeclared. Neil decided I should go out and talk to him. The idea being that if he was genuine we would pay him a retainer in the hope that he could become really useful when he moved back to Moscow.

It didn't work out like that. After taking three weeks to set up a meeting that I was confident was completely secure, the man failed to turn up. We later learned he had approached the French who had grabbed at the opportunity and made him an offer which he had already accepted. Two weeks later he returned to Moscow and neither we nor the French ever heard anything about him again.

White took me along to Grosvenor Square for his next meeting with our opposite numbers at the American Embassy. He wanted me to explain what had happened. It was the first time I had met the Company's newly appointed Deputy Chief of Station. White had returned from his previous meeting and announced he had been introduced to Bill Merryweather, the new arrival. White clearly didn't like him, which again was unusual. I hadn't come across anyone other than Clive Dreyton to whom my Desk Officer had so plainly taken exception. White usually made a point of suffering fools if not gladly at least politely.

He told me he had invited Merryweather to lunch at his club only to be told that the American 'didn't do lunch'.

'So he's a fitness freak,' I had responded.

'Not at all,' snorted White. 'I should think he starts the day with a mountain of pancakes and bacon drowning in maple syrup, has double hamburgers at his desk for lunch, donuts all afternoon and then stuffs himself every night. He told me three times that he's a Texan, which I'm supposed to think means something special: Texas has the biggest and best of everything, and by extension that applies to him. I checked his papers: he left Texas before he was four and spent his school days moving from one state to another. Probably explains a lot about him. His father was in the Air Force.'

I couldn't help thinking that checking Merryweather's background said a lot about Neil White. A Fettes and Balliol education, along with his father's connections, had given White both the right of entry to the upper ranks of the civil service and the sense of security and effortless self confidence that Merryweather's peripatetic childhood would not have provided.

It wasn't easy to understand why Merryweather had been posted to London. The first thing he told me when we were introduced was that 'heretofore I've always been on the front line,' the implication being that London was well away from the real action. Until now, he explained, his career had been spent in Vietnam and Central America. That, he seemed to be saying, was where the bullets were flying and Company men were risking their lives. I could sense Neil White recoiling. His own periods on the 'front line' in Moscow and Belfast would have been every bit as demanding as Merryweather's, but, unlike the American, White would never flaunt them as a badge of honour.

Merryweather was a big man with a commanding presence and booming voice, even by American standards. I thought at first that I had met him before, perhaps years earlier on a CIA training course in Langley, Virginia. But then I realised it wasn't the man I recognised but the type. He could have stepped out of a dozen TV series. Although he couldn't have been much more than forty he acted like the veteran police captain who knows who the killer is and doesn't need some young wise-ass poking their nose in or the old-time coach who will win the game his own way and isn't going to take lessons from anyone. Like a doctor approaching retirement, Bill Merryweather had seen it all before and consequently had nothing more to learn.

As soon as the meeting started, he made clear that he knew all about our Rome operation and managed to imply, without saying, that if we had only told him about it earlier he could have saved us a lot of time and effort. The Company had been approached by the same man three months ago, he announced, and had turned him down.

'Bad lucky buddy,' he concluded, although I couldn't imagine we would ever be characterised as buddies.

We ran through a couple of other topics of mutual interest.

Whatever Neil White might think about Merryweather, the American was certainly on top of the detail. We had approached the meeting as a general catch-up and had informally run through the subjects we wanted to raise on the way over. Merryweather had a typed list in front of him which became the meeting's agenda. His questions probed for what he wanted to know from us and his answers gave away nothing he didn't want us to learn from him.

Before we left I asked him if he'd had any news about the missiles stolen in Georgia. He seemed surprised by the question.

'No, nothing. We would have heard by now if they were still on the market. Our theory is that if the Israelis didn't get hold of them, either the Russians managed to retrieve them or the guys who stole them took fright at what they'd got themselves into and dumped them somewhere, in the Black Sea perhaps. There are other things to worry about right now.'

I said nothing but as I commented to White after we had left the Embassy, if the Americans had stopped looking for the missiles it meant they knew where they were.

'Perhaps,' he replied. 'One thing's for sure, nobody's going to dump thirty brand new SAM-18s in the sea.'

He was right, as we found out not long after. And when we did find out it wasn't thanks to Bill Merryweather but to a ghost from the 1970s that came back into the Service's world and landed on an island in the Atlantic.

Two months after returning from Turkey I flew down to Madeira, with a passport not in my own name, to investigate a claim that someone there might be trying to sell 'needles'.

VIII

I arrived in Madeira using a passport in the name of Thomas Williams. If I was asked, my cover was 'insurance assessor', but I didn't expect to be asked. If anyone phoned the Birmingham number on my visiting card they would go through to a line the Service maintained for just such eventualities.

I was going to meet an unsung hero.

Julia had told me that some people still regarded Juan Manuel Casares, the anarchist leader whose body had been discovered in San Blas de la Ciduela, as a hero. I was now going to meet someone many in the Service considered a hero but who was a very different type of person. A man from the more recent past. The story of Vasily Kornelyuk was still used as a case study at the Service's training school at Fort Monckton.

When Casares had been executed Vasily Kornelyuk would have been just six years old. He was living in Leningrad with his father Georgi, mother Olga and his little brother Anatoly. It was an unremarkable life for the whole family, surviving in a cramped and shared apartment. Still three years too young to enrol in the Young Pioneers, little Vasily was already a dutiful Soviet citizen waving pictures of Uncle Joe Stalin on May Day. Life was not easy. It would have continued without note but for the arrival of the Germans in 1940.

Vasily remembered his father explaining why he and his school friends had to be evacuated from the city. His mother waved him off at the train station in Leningrad, urging him to look after his little brother and promising that he would see her again soon. He never saw her again. And he never saw his father.

The bitter winds had been bringing the first snow to Yekaterinburg when he was summoned from the classroom and told that both his parents had given their lives for Mother Russia. He never learned the exact circumstances. And he didn't return to Leningrad. When the war was over the two young boys were sent first to an orphanage in Chelyabinsk and then to Vladivostok on the Pacific. They were just two amongst the millions whose lives had been shattered by the Great Patriotic War and would never recover. All they had was each other.

When the time came, Vasily entered the Makarov Higher Naval School in Vladivostok, one of the Soviet Navy's two elite naval colleges. He enjoyed the solitude of the sea and when he was posted to Odessa he realised he had discovered his vocation. He settled down to a career as a naval officer and his quick intelligence soon impressed his superiors.

His brother, on the other hand, was called up to the army and in 1956 found himself in Budapest looking down the barrel of his rifle at Hungarians chanting slogans he could not understand, willing to give their lives for a cause that he found totally alien. Two and a half thousand Hungarian lives were to end on the Budapest barricades, along with the lives of 700 Soviet troops.

When Vasily heard about his brother's heroic death, protecting socialism from Hungarian counterrevolutionaries, the world he had quietly reconstructed in his own mind was shattered again. He went into a deep depression which his brother's posthumous medal did nothing to alleviate. The Soviet naval doctors were more sympathetic than their Western opposite numbers would have been: they had all seen the dreadful effect of war at first hand. Vasily had already been marked out as a rising star and four months later he was back in Odessa. One year after that he was in command of a Yurka class minesweeper.

The medics congratulated themselves on ensuring his full recovery; it was only much later that they discovered that deep inside Vasily Kornelyuk had changed beyond recognition. Any sense of belonging had gone. The unthinking patriot had simply become unthinking. The simple answers of Marx and Lenin had been replaced by the unanswerable doubts of faithless nihilism. Kornelyuk didn't know what he wanted but he knew that whatever it was he had to find it alone. And he knew that wherever he was going it would be somewhere very different. He set himself one simple goal: to find a place where he would never have to confront his ghosts again.

Five years later a British Member of Parliament whose constituency included a large naval dockyard took his wife to Moscow on what he grandiloquently described as a fact-finding mission. While there he was invited to meet senior representatives of the Soviet Navy. The British Naval attaché was to accompany him and before the meeting the two Britons and their wives had lunch in a restaurant near the Kremlin.

'No alcohol for the men,' insisted the MP. 'We need our wits about us today.'

'Nor for the ladies,' insisted his companion, Captain

Jeremy Maguire RN. 'If my wife is to show yours the delights of Moscow this afternoon I mustn't let the commies pull her over for drinking and driving.' His wife smiled sweetly; she was used to her husband talking about her as if she wasn't there.

It was a cold day outside and when they left the restaurant the Naval attaché's wife reached for her gloves. She thrust her hands into the voluminous pockets of the fur coat that had been her first purchase when she arrived in the Russian capital. Her fingers unexpectedly touched something about the size of a postcard. Without thinking she drew it out. It was a photograph of what NATO called a Foxtrot-class Soviet submarine. On the back, carefully written in English in capital letters, was a brief inscription: GIFT FOR CAPTAIN MAGUIRE IN TRUNK.

Mrs Maguire was perplexed but assumed correctly that it was something to do with her husband's work.

'What trunk?' asked her husband when he arrived home. 'We haven't received any trunks.'

Mrs Maguire had the answer to that. Safe inside the embassy compound she directed her husband to what he called the 'boot' of his car. Inside were dozens of the most secret Soviet naval documents British Intelligence had ever seen. There was also a note. 'If you agree to pay $75,000 for these papers, wear a red tie on Thursday. There will be more. Oleg Buriakov.' The following Thursday the attaché wore a red tie all day.

The documents were immediately sent on to London where the Defence Intelligence Staff pronounced that they were without doubt genuine and my Service, MI6, pronounced that the name Oleg Buriakov was without doubt not genuine. Both agencies waited to see what would happen next. How would the man calling himself Buriakov claim his money? What else would he produce?

Nothing happened. For two years London speculated on the identity of their mysterious informant, wondering if perhaps he had been caught before he could pass on anything more. The original papers were copied to Washington, where speculation became even wilder.

Then the owner of a small engineering company in Manchester opened a consignment of parts shipped from Rostock in East Germany. To his surprise, beneath the parts he had ordered he found a large cardboard box addressed to his company. Inside there was a metal container welded shut and a note asking for it to be delivered to Captain Jeremy Maguire at the Ministry of Defence in London. The note was signed Oleg Buriakov. Once again British Intelligence found itself in possession of highly sensitive Russian naval documents. Among them was a copy of a US Navy manual that was supposedly so secret that only twelve numbered copies had been printed. In Washington the FBI, CIA and ONI (the Office of Naval Intelligence), along with assorted agencies few had ever heard of, went into panic mode. They were not helped by the front numbered cover of the manual being missing, something the FBI unhelpfully suggested must be because 'the Limeys had lost it'.

Nothing more was heard from Oleg Buriakov for more than three years. Then something very similar happened again. This time back in Moscow and this time the papers that made their way to the British Embassy included two documents relating to military strategy which could only have come from within the naval high command.

'This is a goldmine,' the Americans told their British colleagues. 'Make sure it keeps coming.'

But it didn't keep coming. In 1972 a tall European walked into the new British High Commission in Dhaka, Bangladesh, announced that he was an officer in the Soviet Navy and asked for political asylum. He had, it seemed, been supervising the clearing of Chittagong Harbour, which had been badly damaged in the recent war with Pakistan. The Kremlin had offered the new nation of Bangladesh the Soviet Pacific fleet's assistance in restoring the port's facilities.

The man gave his name as Oleg Buriakov. As soon as London heard that name bells started ringing and within hours an RAF transport was on its way from Cyprus to Dhaka. Oleg Buriakov was halfway to London before the Bangladeshis, or even the Russians, knew what was happening.

Buriakov was accompanied on the flight by MI6's Dhaka Head of Station who learned only that the Russian's real name was Vasily Kornelyuk and that he was carrying nine rolls of film for which he wanted a further $75,000. Kornelyuk, it turned out, spoke very little English and in any case said nothing more when he reached London. This changed once he had seen evidence that $300,000 had been deposited in a Swiss bank account that only he could access. After that the Russian was completely open. He spent the next three weeks at a discreet country house in Buckinghamshire answering every question fired at him by his British and American interrogators. He only needed to break for food and sleep; never once did Vasily Kornelyuk even leave the house.

The special relationship between the United States and

the UK being what it was, by the second week the CIA were demanding Kornelyuk be moved somewhere safer, meaning somewhere on their side of the Atlantic. The MI6 Desk Officer, Morgan Ellis, protested that Kornelyuk was a British responsibility but the Russian was nevertheless transferred to a CIA safe house in Maryland. As far as the American agency was concerned, he was now their man, much to the satisfaction of the MI6 accounting officer who agreed with his CIA counterpart that a subvention of $350,000 towards the costs MI6 had incurred would be appropriate.

The Americans didn't know what to make of Vasily Kornelyuk. He was obviously motivated only by money but not motivated as they understood it. He had earned his $300,000 but now seemed to have no desire to earn more. He would tell them all he knew but that was it. He had no interest in working for them in any capacity whatsoever. He intended to retire. After six months of attempted inducements and barely concealed threats, the Agency concluded that he was serious and settled him in a Florida condominium under the name of Hans Schmidt and provided him with a US resident visa and a West German passport, although the new Herr Schmidt spoke no German.

Kornelyuk spent his time learning English and sailing out alone into the empty sea.

Six months later he disappeared. By the time the Agency found out, he had arrived in the Bahamas and bought a plane ticket from Nassau to London. The first my Service knew about his plans was when Morgan Ellis's secretary picked up the phone to be told that a Mr Buriakov wanted to speak to her boss.

Kornelyuk's presence in London presented a problem

for the Service, as Ellis explained to the Russian over lunch at his club.

'You can't come to work for us,' he explained. 'The Americans will go mad.'

'I don't want to work for anyone,' the Russian responded. 'I keep telling everyone that. I want to retire to an island in the middle of the sea and never see any of you again.'

'I thought that's what the Americans offered you.'

'No. They say they reserve the right to call on me if necessary. There is no right to call on me. I have been paid for everything I delivered. Our business is over. In any case, Florida is too hot and too uncivilised. And' – here Kornelyuk spluttered with indignation – 'they make me into a German!'

Ellis had to agree. It was clear that he needed to do something and, he concluded, what the Americans didn't know they couldn't cry over.

'We could provide something more suitable,' he suggested. 'A British passport and a place where we have contacts, a place where a British passport still means something. Cyprus perhaps, or Malta.'

'Not the Mediterranean. Our Navy is in the Mediterranean.'

So he still thinks of it as 'our' Navy, thought Ellis but said nothing. 'Where then?' he asked.

'The Canary Islands.' A smile crossed the Russian's face. 'I have sung like a canary have I not?' Kornelyuk's English had improved enormously.

In the event, Madeira, north of the Canaries, proved easier to arrange. The Portuguese had always proved more welcoming to my Service than the Spanish. Vasily Kornelyuk alias Oleg Buriakov alias Hans Schmidt became Basil Rosen and settled into a modest villa in Funchal.

Rosen was given a new registry reference with the suffix X, which signified he was an ex-asset deemed to deserve protection but of no current value. I had once heard a colleague comment that what the X suffix really stood for was expendable.

Before the Russian departed for Madeira, Ellis gave him a card bearing just an address and phone number. 'In case you ever need us,' he explained. 'Just quote my name.'

Kornelyuk looked at him without expression. 'I won't need you.'

IX

The picture postcard of Funchal that arrived some years later
addressed to Morgan Ellis at the discreet address in Camden
that my Service maintained for such purposes was simply
signed 'OB'. The message was just as simple. 'I hear needles
are for sale, not arrows. Suggest you come here.'

We had a phone number for Kornelyuk in Madeira
for use in emergencies only. There was no reason to think
this was an emergency but a phone call was cheaper than a
wasted flight, so we tried it. The line had been disconnected.

The card sent back from our station in Lisbon instead
was just as brief as the one we received. 'Tom hopes to visit
you next week, Ellis.'

'I'm going to search for needles and arrows,' I said to
Julia when I told her why I was off to Madeira.

Despite being warned in my early days in Intelligence
that if ever I felt the need to discuss my work with my wife I
should find a new job, or a new wife, I was always completely
open with Julia. She had after all joined British Intelligence
before me.

'Could the arrows be strelas?' she asked.

'That occurred to me.'

Strela is Russian for arrow. More importantly, as Julia
knew very well after spending three years on the Defence
Intelligence Staff in Moscow, it was also the name the

Russians had given to their ubiquitous SAM-7 man-portable surface-to-air missiles. And as Julia was also aware, the *strely* were being replaced by the *igly*, meaning 'needles', what we called the SAM-18, thirty of which, along with fifteen launchers, had been stolen in Georgia.

Why our Russian friend, effectively exiled to a tiny island in the Atlantic, should have anything interesting to tell us about SAM missiles, new or old, I could not imagine. He had been away far too long to know anything about the men who had stolen the missiles from the base in Khelvachauri and he could have no conceivable connection with the Israelis we were confident had acquired them since. But it needed to be followed up.

As a very, very young boy I had been taken to visit an aunt in Southampton and seen a flying boat take off from Southampton Water. I was told it was the regular Aquila Airways flight to Funchal. From then on Madeira had always seemed a slightly exotic faraway place. But times had moved on. Flying boats had long since disappeared. When the island's first airport was opened in 1964 it was considered one of the most dangerous in the world, perched precariously between mountain and ocean. Fortunately, when I arrived the runway had just been extended by 200 metres, although it still remained much shorter than it is today.

Portugal joining the European Union at the beginning of 1986 was a signal to start planning massive change in Madeira. New roads would knit the island's communities together. The red-light district behind Funchal's waterfront would be cleaned up and made suitable for tourists. A new container port at Caniçal would leave the harbour at Funchal to the cruise liners. But all that was still in the future. I wondered idly what Basil Rosen, as I had to think of him, thought about the modern world reaching his sanctuary.

I might have been able to fly in and out on the same day but I wasn't even sure I would find Rosen. In any case, there was no need to hurry. I just had to make contact, see what he wanted and then fly back. For the same reason Neil White had decided that I didn't need to take any scrambling equipment for calls back to London, any message which needed passing on could wait until I was back home.

The travel people in Century House had booked me into a hotel in the web of narrow streets near the cathedral, probably chosen because of its name. The Hotel Windsor proved to be a wonderful example of art deco architecture. I knew that art deco had been all the rage in Lisbon in the 1930s, but the hotel still looked as if it would be more at home in northern Europe than on a tiny island off the coast of Africa. It stood on the Rua das Hortas, Street of the Vegetable Gardens, a name only a little less incongruous than the names of two streets that ran parallel to it, Street of the Factory and Street of the Agricultural Cooperative of Funchal.

Rosen's villa seemed a relatively easy walk away when I had looked at the map in London. I realised in the taxi from the airport that I couldn't have been more wrong. To describe Funchal as hilly would be a ridiculous understatement. The streets were precipitous. Once I had checked in, I took a taxi across to the old town where Rosen lived. I gave the driver the address of what the map had told me was the Jewish cemetery on Rua do Lazareto. It was two blocks away from Rosen's villa, although block was not a concept of much use in Funchal. True there were streets heading straight, almost vertically, down to the ocean, but roads parallel to the sea were anything but parallel, snaking up and down across the hillsides and twisting alarmingly back on themselves. The driver had looked surprised at my directions and I could see why: the Jewish cemetery turned out to be a small plot on the edge of a cliff surrounded by a high wall. There was a small, arched entrance, bearing the inscription '1851' and above it a shield I could not decipher, and a solid wooden door firmly locked. I waved the taxi away and set off to find Rosen's house.

Rua do Lazareto was spectacular: on one side a sheer cliff descending to the ocean below and on the other houses clung precariously to the almost perpendicular hillside. Rosen's property was on a corner site and I was grateful that the authorities appeared to require every property to clearly display its number. Otherwise I might have walked straight past the single small door that was set into an eight-foot tall wall. There was no sign of a house.

I didn't stop but walked on along the road for five minutes. Alarmingly, the yellow fort at the bottom of the hill seemed to be occupied by the Military Police. I returned on the other seaward side of the street. There was no sign that I was being observed but it was impossible to be sure. I realised that behind the tall wall I had seen earlier, the rock had been excavated to permit the construction of a house set back into the hillside. The steepness of the hillside allowed an extra room or cellar to be built under the front of the house. The result was that Rosen's home had an impressive view out over the wall towards the sea. Rock and soil filled the space immediately behind the wall, turning it into a garden with some sort of climbing plants tumbling over a metal trellis.

The house itself was similar to many of the other houses in the area, although smaller than some. From the road it appeared to be single storeyed: white-painted walls with green shuttered windows and terracotta tiled roof. It was much less grand than the villa I had expected. There was no sign of life.

I carried on along the road again and was eventually able to circle around and descend the steep narrow street that ran down the side of Rosen's house. Most of the homes I passed were built with one storey on the upper side of the hill but two storeys on the lower, and all with the same green doors and shuttered windows. When I approached the bottom of the hill I found a gate padlocked shut and behind it an old Renault. Both the gate and the car looked as if they were hardly ever used. I could see the back of Rosen's home but it seemed that the main entrance was the door in the wall I had seen earlier. Returning to it I found a bell push set into the plasterwork. There was no sound when I pressed it and I wondered if it was working. After a minute or two I pressed it again, harder this time, but there was still no sound of movement behind the door.

I stepped back and sensed a movement above me. I looked up to see a man looking down at me over the wall. He said nothing. It was Rosen.

'I'm Tom,' I shouted, hoping he'd received our card.

Before I could say anything more he raised his hand. 'Wait there.'

A minute later came the sound of a bolt being pulled back and the door opened. Rosen stepped out into the street.

'This way,' he said, motioning me through the door and up the steep steps that lay behind it. He followed, bolting the door behind him. I found myself in a small and neatly tended garden between the house and the parked Renault. I introduced myself simply as Tom Williams.

'Business first,' announced the Russian, leading me indoors.

He was a big man, broad-shouldered with short dark hair just starting to turn grey. His face was exactly as it had been in the photos I had seen in London, showing no signs at all of ageing. I knew he was fifty-eight but he could easily have been ten years younger. He now spoke English with hardly any trace of an accent. He wore an old flannel shirt in a faded check pattern, mud-coloured trousers with a heavy leather belt and what my father would have described as gardening shoes.

The room we entered was comfortably but simply furnished. The walls were lined with bookshelves that must have been added by Rosen himself. Poetry and fiction in English and Portuguese; I could see nothing in Russian. An enormous old-fashioned radiogram took up one end of the room. There was no television. Rilke's *Sonnets to Orpheus* in English lay open on a side table, incongruously on top of the latest Patrick O'Brian novel. To be reading mystical poetry alongside naval adventures from the Napoleonic wars suggested either a voraciously open mind or an alarmingly indiscriminate one. There were no photographs.

'Business,' he repeated when we had seated ourselves. No suggestion of a drink or any small talk. 'You have received my message. Are you authorised to pay for information?'

'I wouldn't be here otherwise. How much depends on what you have to sell.'

'Of course. You understood my mention of arrows?'

'*Strely*? Missiles?'

71

'Exactly. The sale of Russian missiles but not arrows – needles.'

He looked at me but I said nothing.

'That is what we are discussing,' Rosen continued. 'Needles. I will explain. There is a very famous hotel in Funchal: Reid's. Winston Churchill stayed there. Very expensive. Once a year I eat at that hotel. On the anniversary of my brother's death. I order the very best. Anatoly would have approved. This year I went as always. There was a group of five men at another table, discussing business.'

'You heard what they were saying?'

Rosen looked surprised. 'It is not the sort of place where one can eavesdrop. But afterwards, in the bar, that is different. I always have one glass of brandy after I have eaten there. Anatoly would have chosen Georgian brandy but here that is not possible. I drink a toast to Anatoly and my parents. But this time I was not the only one drinking a toast. In the bar were two of the men I had seen in the restaurant earlier. I realised they were Russian. They were drinking vodka, of course, and twice they raised their glasses and their voices. The first time I hear them raise a toast to 'sales' just like any businessman might do. And then one of them toasted *Igly*.'

'You're sure?'

'Of course.'

'*Igly* in the plural, not *igla*, a single needle?'

Rosen nodded.

'What else did they say?'

'The only word I could make out was arrows. I don't know why that word carried, but I heard it clearly. "Needles sell better than arrows." That is all I heard, needles and arrows. I didn't want to be noticed, who knows who might still be looking for me. I moved away. But then I thought: what are two Russians doing here toasting needles? When one of them looked at his watch and they stood up to leave I finished my brandy and did the same. They were not drunk, far from it, but they were relaxed. I followed them out, hoping to hear more. But all I heard was one of them asking the other what the Englishman meant by a grouse.'

The mention of an Englishman startled me but I didn't want Rosen to notice that.

'The other explained that a grouse is a bird. It must have been an English joke, he said.'

Rosen hesitated. 'I did not want to get too close. I missed what they said after that, except that one of them mentioned Americans and they both laughed. They took a taxi and I did the same. At first both taxis were going in the same direction but theirs soon turned off. They went into the harbour.'

That was it. It wasn't much.

'What did the men look like?' I asked.

'Not like businessmen. Like army men. Soldiers. They were young, the oldest was less than forty, the others younger.'

I considered what Rosen had said. It was more than likely that there was a perfectly innocent explanation for what he had heard. Madeira was famous for its embroidery. Perhaps the men were here to sell embroidery needles. Or Rosen had misheard them. But it seemed unlikely. One word in particular alarmed me.

NATO insists on giving codenames to Soviet weapons; Soviet fighter aircraft for example are all given reporting names beginning with F. Surface-to-air missiles have codes beginning with G; the SAM-7 is Grail, the SAM-18 is Grouse. Whatever the men had been talking about over dinner, grouse was not an English joke.

If the two mysterious Russians were really trying to sell surface-to-air missiles, my Service would want to know all about it. That was worth paying for.

Rosen was waiting for me to respond. 'That could be interesting,' I conceded, 'but really we need to know more. Can you describe the other people? You said there were five men dining together.'

'I can do better than that. I can give you the names of two of them. You paid $300,000 before, $75,000 for each package, but inflation has been high since then. And $300,000 does not go as far as I expected. It had seemed an enormous sum of money in the Soviet Union back then, but now, now things have changed. My price is $100,000.'

'That's too much. I'm only authorised to pay fifty.'

'Then you should ask for more authority. The price is $100,000.'

'And what if the names turn out not to be real?'

'They are real.'

I knew that London would let me go higher. 'No more than before,' I had been told by the Service finance department. I could go up to $75,000.

'I'll offer $70,000 off my own bat,' I said. 'I can't go any higher.' That left me $5,000 for one last concession.

'The price is $100,000,' Rosen repeated. '$100,000 for two names, one Spanish, one English.'

He knew that would make me sit up, as I had tried not to when he mentioned an Englishman earlier. If an Englishman was involved in selling missiles we had to have

74

his name. This time it was Rosen who moved. 'I will give you the name of one of those attending. You can check him out. His photo has been in the papers. I am not mistaken. Seventy thousand. Then you can ask London to authorise the remainder.'

I was confident London would give me the authority, but you can never be entirely sure.

'You can phone from here,' he suggested.

'You have a phone?'

'Of course. I am not a hermit Mr Williams.'

And yet he had disconnected the number London had set up for emergencies.

I decided to return to the hotel and phone Century House from there. I wasn't going to risk letting Rosen listen in on my call. I wasn't sure I trusted him.

'One last question,' I said. 'You have been out of all of this for a long time. When you heard the toast to *igly* why did you think of missiles? The *igla* was not even under development in your day.'

'But arrows we all knew. Nevertheless, you are right. All the talk of needles and arrows could have been entirely innocent. In which case you would have ignored my card and I would have lost nothing but the price of a stamp.'

I still wasn't sure I believed him, but it was time to go. I wanted a chance to think but first I wanted a name.

'OK. Give me the English name and I will call London. We will see if they want to pay for another.'

Rosen smiled for the first time. 'No. I will give you the Spanish name. That is sensible. Come back this evening for the other name. I will open some wine and we can toast to never meeting again.'

I returned his smile. 'And the name of the Spaniard the two Russians met is?'

'Oh yes. A powerful man in this part of the world. You will have no trouble finding him. Señor Mateo Vilafermosa.'

X

It had to be a coincidence. Even if Mateo Vilafermosa proved to be related to Francisco Vilafermosa, the man who allegedly established his business using gold stolen during the Spanish Civil War half a century before, there could be no connection between my mission and Julia's own investigation.

The truth is I had lost interest in the whole story of Roger Montacute and Spanish gold by the time I flew down to Madeira. I knew that Exodis had finished the report Montacute had commissioned, but Julia told me they hadn't found anything exciting. It didn't seem to be a secret that the company Francisco Vilafermosa had set up, and named after himself, had powerful political connections. The Spanish fishing industry was the largest in Europe and the Vilafermosa company was one of the most powerful in the industry. Headquartered in Cádiz and operating all over the world, the company not only owned its own fleet but more importantly owned the freezer ships that accompanied Spanish fishing fleets wherever they sailed. The funding of the expansion Roger Montacute had been worried about was perfectly legitimate, if opaque: a well-known bank investing through a Panamanian holding company. Vilafermosa SRL seemed to be a dominant force in the Spanish fishing industry and was now diversifying. A big fish in fishing: not something of any interest to me or the Service.

Time would tell if that judgement was right.

Once back at the hotel I called London. It took some time to confirm that the line was secure before I was put through to Neil White. Even on a secure line I tried to be careful with what I was saying.

'This could be big,' I started. 'The card we received really did mean what we thought it meant. A couple of representatives from the opposition met three men here, apparently to discuss selling the merchandise we talked about.'

'That's bad. That sort of merchandise in the wrong hands spells trouble.'

'It gets worse. One of those present seems to have been British.'

'British or Irish?'

'I was told English but I'm not sure our informant would know the difference. He has a name, though.'

Neil White considered for a moment. 'This is important, Thomas. We need to be absolutely clear and we need to act quickly. Is there any reason to think anyone might be listening at your end? No unexpected little bugs in your room?'

'None.'

'Then we must trust that this line really is secure and go "en clair". I need to know the Englishman's name.'

'I don't have it yet. Our friend wants another 30,000 for that. As I said, the opposition met three people: the Englishman, an unknown and a Spaniard. I've been given the Spanish name. Mateo Vilafermosa. He owns a big fishing business in Spain.'

'I'll check that out. And I'll try to find out if any Russians flew into Madeira around that time—'

'There's reason to believe they came by sea,' I interrupted.

'Perhaps. But the important thing is the English name. Try to discover as much as you can. You think our friend is being straight with us?'

'I think so. I can't see any reason why he shouldn't be.'

'Well, I can think of a hundred thousand reasons,' said White. 'But that's a risk we need to take. Go back and tell him if the name turns out to be genuine, he can have his extra 30,000. And call me back tonight. I'll have the call routed through to wherever I am. If the IRA are in the market for modern Russian missiles, we have a problem on our hands; if they've actually bought anything already, we have a full-blown crisis.'

'You really think that's possible?'

'We'll discuss that when you get back. It certainly doesn't mesh with what we think happened to you in Turkey. Phone me tonight, whatever happens. Any time.'

I knew Neil White well enough to know that if he was taking Rosen's report seriously so should I. There must be something I didn't know about. I considered phoning Julia to see if she could tell me more about Mateo Vilafermosa but decided that could wait. I took a taxi back to Rua do Lazareto, again asking the driver to drop me well away from the house.

Rosen was waiting. This time he led me into the little garden. Two metal chairs sat facing the sea where a glorious sunset was partly visible behind a promontory at one end of Funchal Bay. Reid's Hotel, where Rosen had overheard the two Russians, must be somewhere in that direction.

Rosen clearly didn't believe in polite introductions. 'You have authority now?' he asked, as much statement as question.

I nodded.

'Of course,' he replied and disappeared into the house. To my surprise he returned with a bottle of white wine and two glasses which he placed on a small metal table in front of us. He really was planning a toast.

'Wine not vodka,' he said. 'What would my brother have said to that?'

Without asking he poured out the wine. 'You no doubt know my story. I don't know yours.'

'You don't need to,' I replied. I didn't want to get into a marathon drinking session with a lonely Russian, I just needed a name.

As if reading my mind, he smiled. 'We are drinking wine my friend, as I said. My vodka drinking days are over. I won't keep you long. I just want to know who I am dealing with. I expected Mr Morgan.'

'He's retired,' I explained.

Rosen nodded. 'So now I need to understand you. If I learn anything more, do I send you another card, or do I bank my money and forget we have ever met? So, no vodka.'

It was my turn to smile. 'No vodka. No *zakuska*.'

I was referring to the little bites that always accompany vodka in Russia. Rosen understood. 'So they send a Russian speaker. Mr Morgan would have known that was not necessary. I prefer Portuguese these days, or English. I left my past behind a long time ago.' He examined me dispassionately over his glass, twirling the stem slowly. 'So you speak Portuguese and Russian, an unusual combination.'

He waited for me to comment. Was he trying to find things in my background he could check or just, as he said, get to know me?

'That's why I was sent here.'

He obviously expected more.

'I had a Portuguese grandmother,' I lied. Let him try to check that.

'You have family?' he asked.

I wasn't going down that path. Julia and Eveline were off limits. But I didn't want to alienate him either. 'My mother,' I answered. 'My father is no longer with us.'

'No longer with us. What a strange expression. Your family are always with you, when everything else has gone they remain in your soul. Do you think your father, wherever he is now, is proud of you? Of what you are doing here.'

I took a moment to answer. That was an interesting question. 'My father would not have chosen the route I have chosen but he would be proud of who I am.'

'Then you are a lucky man.' Rosen paused before continuing. 'None of us follow the path we would have chosen. We can only choose where that path will end.'

'And where will your path end?' I asked curiously. 'Portugal could not be more different than the country where you grew up.'

'You think so. The system here is not so different. If you want anything done you must know someone with influence. I have been on this island for more than fifteen years, now I know the right people. But I am at peace here. I have the sea without the stupidity and brutality of my old life.'

'Russia is changing. Perhaps one day it will be safe for you to return.'

He seemed shocked. 'Return? There is no return. My soul is stateless. I would be no Jew returning to Jerusalem for

Aliyah. John Donne was wrong, all men are an island, entire of itself.'

I didn't know how to respond. I had spent four years in our Station in Moscow but had come across nobody like Basil Rosen. All Russians have Mother Russia in their soul. Even Trotsky wanted to go home. The once desolate Leningrad orphan, Vasily Kornelyuk, had grown into someone entirely unexpected. I had seen no photos or pictures inside his house other than, above the radiogram, what appeared to be a painting of a single yellowy rectangle in a cheap black frame. On closer inspection the yellowy rectangle turned out to be a facsimile cover of the first edition of Hermann Hesse's *Siddhartha*, the ultimate novel of self-discovery.

'So you will never move on again?' I asked. 'Find somewhere where you don't have to be so fit, where there are no hills to climb.'

Rosen took me literally. 'No, I will stay in this house. I swim in the sea every day down by the fort. One day I will no longer be strong enough to climb back up here afterwards. On that day I will just keep swimming out into the ocean.'

I looked at him and realised he was serious. The ghosts that had tormented Vasily Kornelyuk held no fear for Basil Rosen.

Rosen refilled his glass and topped up mine. 'You thought me rude. I got down to business without asking about your flight or commenting on the weather. And now you have no time for such things. It is you who is in a hurry. You want me to give you a name. What else do you want?'

'Anything else you can tell me. What the Englishman looked like. And the other one, the third man. Could he

82

have been English as well, or perhaps Russian. How did they dress? How did they walk? How old were they?'

'The other man sat with his back to me. I did not see him clearly. A powerful man. Not tall but strong. Middle-aged. Not English. Not European, I think. Dark. Arab perhaps or Afghan.'

'Afghan! Why do you say that?'

'Just to see your reaction. No, not Afghan. Arab perhaps. Although he walked like a sailor.'

'And the Englishman? You're sure he was English? Could he have just been speaking English? American perhaps, or Irish?'

'No, he was English. Very proper. Beautiful suit and one of those ties with stripes that the English wear to show what school they went to. He sat at the head of the table. He was clearly the host. When I got home that night I thought about that man and about the conversation I had heard. Two Russian soldiers come to Madeira to sell needles. That is very mysterious. That is a mystery MI6 may pay to hear about. Life here is becoming more expensive. But then I thought to myself, have I got enough to sell? Can I learn more? Can I find out who was the man at the head of the table? So the next morning I went back to the hotel. I told them I had spoken to one of the guests the night before in the restaurant and he had mentioned a book he had always wanted to read. When I got home, I realised I had a copy of that very book so I had brought it for him. But stupidly I hadn't taken his name.'

'And the hotel believed you?'

'Yes. I had the book with me. They were very helpful. I look honest,' Rosen added with no hint of irony. 'I told them where the man had been sitting and they were able to tell me who had reserved the table. But, they apologised, he was not staying at the hotel so they could not give the book to him. There was a phone number that he had given when he had booked the table a week before. They gave me that. I have not tried to call it.'

He went inside and returned with a phone number written neatly on a piece of paper. I asked him to write his own phone number below it. After a moment's hesitation he did so. 'This number is for you only. I will change it when our business is complete. I have written the Englishman's name on the other side. It is just as the hotel gave it to me. I had not seen such a name before, with two Fs.'

I turned the paper over. George Ffortiscue.

I hoped the shock didn't show on my face. The previous name Rosen had given me, Mateo Vilafermosa, had been a surprise, but this was entirely different. I knew George Ffortiscue. He had once been spoken of as a future 'C', the Chief of the Secret Intelligence Service. The man the Russians had been meeting had been one of us.

XI

I was put straight through to Neil White when I called Century House again. 'I have the name,' I said, 'and you're not going to like it. George Ffortiscue, Ffortiscue with two Fs.'

There was silence at the other end. I had expected him to say that I was wrong, that what I had said was impossible.

Eventually he just uttered a monosyllabic 'Shit!'

'I suppose it could be a different George Ffortiscue or someone borrowing his name,' I suggested.

'There's only one of him. And someone borrowing his name is just as bad as it being him. You must get back here as soon as possible. We need a conference on this. Make sure you remember absolutely everything that was said.'

'I told our friend I would be back tomorrow with a photograph. I thought you might fax something down. And I was going to chase up the phone number Ffortiscue gave when he booked the restaurant. It must have been a hotel, they may know something. Perhaps he wasn't alone.'

White considered that briefly but then reiterated that I should come back to London. 'Can you fly back tonight?'

'I doubt it. The last flight's probably gone.'

'When were you planning to return?'

'Tomorrow. I should be back early evening.'

'Well come in here as soon as you land. I'll have a car for you at the airport.'

He hung up and I was left wondering why my mention of Ffortiscue had caused such a decisive reaction. There was no obvious reason for hurrying home.

Ffortiscue had left the Service a long time ago. He would be around sixty now, an age when he might have expected to retire into a lucrative but discreet role in the City or in one of the transatlantic think tanks. That had not happened because of his premature exit from the Service. He had made the mistake of authorising an operation which would have severely embarrassed Ministers if they had known about it, caused MI6 to lose face with other agencies and above all hadn't worked.

His name was still occasionally mentioned over drinks in the private bar at Century House where MI6 staff huddled after work to talk dismissively about the latest James Bond film. 'Wonder what happened to George Ffortiscue?' would produce a few knowing looks, with nobody saying anything definite. He had probably, I thought, slipped into that grey world labelled, if labelled at all, as 'private security': a world floating around in the interstices of British and US Intelligence but never officially recognised.

I called Julia.

'How's it going?' she asked after updating me on Eveline's day at school. 'Have you met your friend?'

'Yes, I have. I'll tell you all about it when I get back. It seems we might have friends in common: George Ffortiscue for one.'

'Ffortiscue! What's that bastard done now?'

Julia had family reasons for intensely disliking George Ffortiscue.

'I don't know, his name has just come up along with

86

someone else you know: Mateo Vilafermosa. I may like to chat to that Cambridge professor of yours.'

'Really? That might be difficult. He seems to have disappeared. You remember it was Jonathon Craverse who introduced Montacute to Exodis? Well apparently Lady Constance Montacute called Jonathon this morning to say her son had "gone walkabout". It's happened before, so she's not too worried. She wondered if we'd heard anything.'

'And had you?'

'No, nothing at all. I wasn't expecting to. Jonathon called back later to say that if Roger Montacute hadn't shown up in the next day or two Lady Constance would like to come and see me with a friend. I've no idea what she meant by that. We're not in the missing persons business.'

'Well let's hope he reappears. At least it can't have any connection with my conversations here.'

We bade our farewells after I had explained I would not be home until late the next day as Neil White wanted to see me as soon as I landed. In fact, I was home much sooner than I expected. Ten minutes after I had put down the phone to Julia it rang again. One of the Service dispatchers informed me that I was booked on an early-morning flight from Funchal to Lisbon and that I should only take cabin luggage as the transfer time in Lisbon was 'rather tight'. Luckily that's all I had.

***

A car was waiting for me as promised at Heathrow. The driver took the usual route into London but then decided to cross Vauxhall Bridge and cut down past the Oval before turning onto the A3. I presumed he was avoiding road works until we stopped outside Kennington Tube station and Neil White hopped in.

'Thought we should have a quick word,' he said, after sliding across the screen separating us from the driver.

He looked uneasy. 'I wanted you back right away because any mention of George Ffortiscue was bound to cause waves. I was hoping to have a quiet chat with you first but it's too late. We're summoned to a meeting upstairs as soon as you get in. Don't suppose you ever met Ffortiscue? He left the Service before you joined.'

'I met him briefly when I was on the Defence Intelligence staff,' I replied. I was being more than a little disingenuous. Julia and I had crossed paths with Ffortiscue in our early days, which is why Julia had reacted the way she had on the phone. I wasn't about to explain the details to White.

'I see. Quite an enigma is Ffortiscue. Left under a bit of a cloud. I gather he got us involved in a rogue CIA operation that went wrong, somebody on our side ended up dead. Caused quite a stink at the time. Ten or twelve years ago now. I was in the field and missed out on all the details. The point is there's a view that he was left to carry the can, forced to fall on his sword, as it were. He had friends and still has. Ours is a funny old world. Some people go and you never see them again, others go but never completely disappear. They just drift around on the periphery, ready to be called in if needed. I suppose your wife and her colleagues are a bit like that. George Ffortiscue is no longer in the Service but that doesn't mean he's no longer one of us. But the point is he's stayed close to the Americans. I suspect this meeting is something to do with our transatlantic friends.

That's why I wanted a preliminary chat. Basil Rosen is our little secret. I don't want the Americans knowing his real identity.'

'Will they be at the meeting?'

'I certainly hope not. I'm guessing that's why we're having a meeting. To decide how to approach Washington. Clive Dreyton tends to look after any sensitivities with the Americans. And once upon a time he and Ffortiscue were very close. If Ffortiscue is up to anything and the Americans are involved, I don't want Dreyton thinking he can earn a few brownie points by telling them about Rosen. You understand? Rosen is strictly need to know.'

I nodded. White, a Desk Officer, was asking me to keep information from one of the most senior men in the Service. It was a big ask. For the moment I would go along with it, and not just because I trusted Neil White and wanted to do nothing to jeopardise Basil Rosen. I had encountered George Ffortiscue only briefly but unless he had changed enormously in the last ten years, he remained one of the most unscrupulous men I had ever met.

'So what's my story?' I asked.

'The advantage of Ffortiscue floating around in our world is that people know him. Our story is that the Portuguese were keeping an eye on a Russian cruise ship when they saw two of the crew members meeting Ffortiscue, so they asked us what the hell we were doing on their patch. I sent you down to take a look. You confirmed the meeting. Here's the difficult bit. I want Clive Dreyton to hear about the SAM missiles. That's the tree we have to shake. You'll have to say you managed to get hold of one of the waiters who served Ffortiscue and the Russians and say he reported they were talking business and he heard them mention missiles. Don't get too specific, no arrows or needles.'

'It's still a bit unlikely.'

'Well, it's the best we can do, unless you can come up with something better. And can do it quickly.'

I couldn't.

As we approached Century House another thought struck me. 'If you didn't want anyone upstairs to start asking why I was in Madeira why did you tell them anything at all?'

'That's a good question Thomas. I didn't. I logged your first call mentioning Vilafermosa and asked for another 30,000 dollars. Clive Dreyton signed that off and asked to be kept informed. But I didn't tell him when you phoned back saying our asset had produced the name Ffortiscue. I thought we might keep that to ourselves for a day or two. I put one of our team onto trying to trace George Ffortiscue's recent movements. The next thing I know is that when I get in this morning there's a message from Dreyton's office suggesting we might have a meeting right away.'

When we arrived at Century House we sat in one of the meeting rooms waiting for Clive Dreyton to appear. He eventually came in, hands clasped behind his back. He may have thought that made him look like an admiral pacing the bridge of his battleship, but in reality he looked more like a novice monk trailing behind a non-existent abbot. We were joined by one of Dreyton's team who said nothing but who made occasional notes, usually of something Dreyton had said.

'George Ffortiscue,' said Dreyton by way of introduction. 'Bit of a rogue by all accounts. Not much to do with the Service these days. What's your interest in him?'

'I'm not sure if we are interested,' responded White. 'His name's come up. As you know Thomas Dylan here has just been down to Madeira on what we thought was a bit of a wild goose chase. Portuguese copper reported that a group of five foreigners were heard discussing the sale of missiles in a restaurant. Pretty poor security if that's true. They weren't speaking Portuguese, so we were inclined to assume the copper had got it wrong, but he insisted one of the men was British. So we sent Thomas down. I'm still not convinced there's anything in it but the Portuguese came up with a couple of names. George Ffortiscue is one. That's about it really.'

'Any idea how they got the name?' Dreyton asked.

'The table was booked in his name,' I explained.

'And the other four? You said a group of five foreigners. I assume one was the Spanish businessman Neil told me about, Vilafermosa.'

'I've checked him,' put in White. 'He seems to be perfectly above board, we've no file on him.'

'And the other three?'

'The Portuguese think they were Russian, but as far as I could tell that was pure guesswork.'

I was very conscious that I was now not just embroidering the facts but lying through my teeth. I knew with absolute certainty that two of the men had been Russian, but I wasn't going to say anything that might hint at Basil Rosen being involved.

'Why would there be Russians in Madeira?' asked Dreyton in a tone that he might have used with a dim-witted child. 'That's not their usual stomping ground.'

'That's easy to explain,' responded White. 'You may

remember that back in the 1960s the Soviets commissioned five luxury cruise ships from a shipyard in Wismar, East Germany. They named them after Russian poets. Then they set up a company in London and entered the Western cruise ship market. The ships were designed to demonstrate to Westerners the wonders of Soviet life, but they also had heavy-duty loading gear and specially strengthened hulls so they could be quickly reconfigured as military transports. On top of that each ship has a carefully vetted crew of over 300, any one of whom could be a potential spy. Madeira and the Canary Islands are frequent stopover points.'

Dreyton nodded as if he had known that already, which given his position he should have done. 'And were any of these poetical cruise ships in Funchal at the time?'

'Yes,' White replied. 'One arrived the day this supposed conversation took place.'

There was a moment's silence while Dreyton digested that.

'That's all very interesting,' he concluded. 'But there are a number of problems with the story. First, did this Portuguese policeman really hear what he thinks he heard? Second, if he did so was it really our George Ffortiscue? Was it perhaps someone with the same or similar name or somebody who, for whatever reason, was pretending to be George Ffortiscue? And even if the identities of two of the men are correct, who were the other three? Who was it who was actually buying and selling missiles? Was it the same people you saw in Turkey? I take it you think the Russians were selling, although it sounds more like the Jews to me. But who was doing the buying? There's one obvious answer.'

Before White or I could say anything, Dreyton continued. 'Moroccan guerillas, Polisario.'

He must have seen the look of surprise on our faces.

'Think about it. Just look at the map. Where's the nearest place to Madeira? Morocco. And what's happening in Morocco? All-out war in the Western Sahara. The rebels, Polisario, would no doubt love to get their hands on modern weapons. And if Israel is involved in some way they would love to stir up trouble in an Arab country. Now why would George Ffortiscue get involved with people like that? He's not working for us. But of course he's been very close to the Americans.

'The next stage has to be conversations with our cousins in Virginia. I think you had better leave that to me Neil. I'll handle it from here. I'll talk to our transatlantic friends and I will talk to George Ffortiscue. If this is some sort of US operation we need to avoid any suggestion that we are interfering. Nothing more is to be done for now. Let's keep this very low key.' The meeting was over.

'What do you make of that?' White asked when we made our way down to his office.

'We've been warned off.'

'Exactly. It's now out of our hands.'

'What will happen when Dreyton asks for the details of the Portuguese policeman who supposedly started all this?'

White smiled. 'X-suffix assets are strictly need to know and he doesn't need to know. In any case he won't ask. He wants the whole thing buried. He'll talk to Ffortiscue next and whatever Ffortiscue says Dreyton will accept. There will be no need to look for anything else.'

'You think Ffortiscue was really trying to set something up for Polisario?'

'Of course not. The Moroccans invaded the Western Sahara in 1976. Polisario have been resisting the occupation since then. And nobody gives a damn. The Moroccans are major players in the region; the Sahrawi, the people of Western Sahara, are not and their so-called army, the Polisario, are just a nuisance. Neither the Americans nor the Russians have any interest in supplying them with surface-to-air missiles. Nor do the Israelis. Dreyton must know that.'

'So what was Ffortiscue doing in Madeira?'

'I've no idea,' White replied. 'And I don't intend to try to find out. I still think there could be an Irish connection, but if the IRA are involved that's Dreyton's area not ours. And if he's right that Polisario or some other bunch of guerillas is buying missiles they are not our concern either. We'll let some other Desk worry about that when there's any real evidence. Our Desk is responsible for the Soviet Union and there's a hell of a lot happening there at the moment, the whole stack of cards could come tumbling down. There might not even be a Soviet Union soon, and if in the process someone with access to a shedload of SAM-18s is trying to sell them on the black market our job is to find out who that is. Dreyton has warned us off Ffortiscue but the two Russians on that cruise ship are ours. You concentrate on that.'

Tracing the two Russians that Rosen had seen at Reid's hotel proved surprisingly easy but totally pointless. The Portuguese authorities confirmed that none of the Russian cruise ship's crew had remained in Madeira. But the Spanish authorities reported that at the ship's next port of call, Tenerife, two crew members had been replaced. The departing sailors, named by the Spanish as Pavel Pleshakov and Yuri Datsyuk, had flown back to Leningrad via Madrid.

Neither name was known to us. There was now no chance of us talking to either of them. The Spanish sent details of the documents the two men had been using but they didn't include photographs. Neil White sent the names to our Moscow Station but without expecting any useful response.

Whatever George Ffortiscue had been doing in Funchal, we were effectively out of the picture.

XII

While I had been worrying about George Ffortiscue and stolen SAM-18s Julia had a more immediate concern.

Roger Montacute was still missing and his mother had announced that she was coming into the Exodis office the next day and would be bringing with her the woman who had been researching Francisco Vilafermosa's role in the Spanish Civil War.

After Basil Rosen had mentioned the name of Mateo Vilafermosa in Madeira, Neil White had made some preliminary enquiries. He had learned nothing that Julia hadn't already discovered except that the Vilafermosa company had some sort of low-level relationship with Spanish Intelligence agency, the CNI. The Registry in Century House held no files on him or his company, or at least no files our Desk was authorised to access. White made plain that after our meeting with Dreyton he was not interested in knowing anything more. A Spanish businessman, however important in the fishing industry, was not high on our Desk's priority list.

Before going home that evening I happened to mention to White that Julia had a meeting arranged with Montacute's mother.

'There's nothing more that Julia can do,' I told him, 'but obviously Lady Montacute is pretty determined.'

To my astonishment White nodded. 'Perhaps you should join them, without mentioning your connection to the Service of course. See if they mention Mateo Vilafermosa.'

'I thought we were leaving Vilafermosa to Dreyton.'

'We are but I've just had a call from the Cabinet Office. They wanted to know why I had asked for a background report on Mateo Vilafermosa.'

'What did you say?'

'I referred them to Clive Dreyton.'

'Did they say why they were asking?'

'Possible PQ.'

I was startled. Parliamentary Questions are the bane of every senior civil servant's life. Backbench MPs, or even worse, underemployed peers, riding hobby horses of no conceivable interest to the wider public. An enormous amount of civil service time and energy is spent preparing answers that say as little as possible and under no circumstances offer up any information that isn't directly asked for and which might prompt yet more questions.

'You mean an MP has been asking about Vilafermosa?'

'Something like that,' White agreed. 'Possible question they said. I imagine someone has made some informal enquiries and it's been decided Number 10 should be prepared in case it develops into something more. What I don't know is how the Cabinet Office knew I'd asked for that report. Like I say, it won't do any harm for us to be forewarned as well, but don't let on you're anything more than an Exodis consultant.'

Julia was amused when I told her I wanted to join her meeting the following morning. She had once commented, when I had been temporarily rotated into an unattractive post on the Subsaharan Africa desk, that if a future in the Service became unbearable I could come and work for her: she was always looking for enthusiastic junior staff.

When Exodis was set up, by two old school Defence Intelligence men unused to women doing anything more than making the tea and keeping the files in order, I had expected Julia to last no more than a few weeks in the job. Instead within months she had made herself indispensable. The *Exodis Bulletin*, on which the consultancy's growing reputation was soon built, was very much her responsibility and in no time at all she was bringing in new clients who more than paid for the additional staff Julia insisted on hiring.

We agreed that she would describe me to Lady Montacute merely as her husband and if pressed would say I used to work for Exodis but was now an independent consultant.

Julia had done her homework on both of the women we were planning to meet. Lady Montacute, she had concluded, was clearly a formidable lady. 'She didn't ask for an appointment,' Julia explained. 'She just announced she would be coming in to see me and hoped 10.30 would be suitable. I suggested she might prefer to come in a day or two later when one of the firm's founders, Richard Mendale, could be there, along with Jonathon Craverse. They're both out of town tomorrow. But she insisted that although Jonathon was a friend of hers she knew he would have nothing of value to contribute and as Richard had never met her son there was no point waiting for him to be available. That lady knows her own mind.'

'What about the woman who's coming with her? An academic like Roger Montacute.'

'Yes, and an interesting one. Khadija Jones. She's Moroccan, recently widowed. Lady Montacute is the aunt of a Conservative peer and Khadija Jones's late husband was a Labour MP.'

I could see why the Cabinet Office might suddenly be taking an interest in Mateo Vilafermosa.

Next morning Julia and I went into work together for the first time since our Moscow days. The original Exodis office had been a room in a Chiswick flat rented by one of the firm's founders. Now the consultancy's was in larger, although no more luxurious, offices in unfashionable Lambeth. 'Midway between MI5 and MI6,' Julia misleadingly explained to new customers put off by the thought of venturing south of the river.

Lady Constance Montacute was not quite what I expected. I knew she was nearly eighty but she seemed smaller and frailer than Julia's description had led me to believe. Her heavily lined face was skilfully made up, her expensively coiffed hair subtly coloured; her high-necked blouse and plain grey slacks hid a figure now shrunken but still held perfectly upright. It occurred to me that as she had climbed the stairs to Julia's second-floor office rather than take the lift she was clearly not as frail as she appeared at first sight.

Her companion was taller, unremarkably dressed and half as old. If I hadn't known she was Moroccan I wouldn't have been able to place her. Khadija Jones was just what she appeared to be: a working woman making no concessions to fashion. She wore almost no make-up and her stubby fingers contrasted sharply with Lady Montacute's carefully manicured hands with cherry red nails, doubtless regarded by

Julia as decidedly old-fashioned. Lady Montacute belonged in a stately home, Khadija Jones in a library. The younger woman looked as if she couldn't wait to get back to her study. The deep brown eyes behind her glasses were neither warm nor hostile; they merely observed.

Julia introduced me as her husband. 'He's working with me temporarily,' she explained.

Lady Constance shook hands lightly, her own hand brittle and blue-veined. A massive diamond ring looked oddly incongruous and I wondered how often she had needed to have it resized so that it didn't slip from her finger despite the gold guard ring.

'You have of course both been highly recommended,' Lady Montacute began.

That seemed unlikely, I thought, as she had never heard of me until then.

'May I ask by whom?' asked Julia, her expensive public-school accent becoming more pronounced to reflect the regal tones of Lady Montacute.

'By Sir Jonathon Traverse of course, a very old friend, and by a cousin of my late husband whom I believe is known to you. Justin Brasenose.'

I was less surprised by her archaic use of whom than by the mention of Justin Brasenose who had been a senior member of the Service. Julia and I had known him for a long time, in fact since our early days on the Defence Intelligence Staff. When I transferred to MI6 I worked closely with him. Brasenose had become what in the jargon of human resources would be called my 'mentor'. He had also been instrumental in Julia joining Exodis. Like George Ffortiscue he had once been talked of as a future head of the Service and now had an undisclosed role in the Cabinet Office with the Joint Intelligence Committee.

Lady Montacute was letting us know she had important friends.

'As you know my son has disappeared. He is a male of the species and consequently has never been one for keeping his mother fully informed. But this is unusual. Nobody has heard from him for more than two weeks. He told Dr Jones that he felt threatened in Morocco.' Lady Montacute motioned towards her companion. 'Perhaps we should commence at the beginning, with Roger's so-called research. Context, I find, is always so important.'

We looked across at Khadija Jones who had clearly been prepared for Lady Montacute's suggestion. When she spoke, her voice took on an unexpected authority, as if she was addressing a group of interested but ill-informed undergraduates.

'In the 1920s and 30s the Spanish fought brutal colonial wars in North Africa using what they called the Ejército de África, the Army of Africa. When Francisco Franco rebelled against the democratic government the Army of Africa was airlifted to the mainland in aircraft provided by Hitler and Mussolini. That was the real beginning of the civil war, which of course you know Franco's forces won. I have been researching one small part of the Army of Africa, the Tiradores de Ifni. Do you know where Ifni is?'

I shook my head.

'Sidi Ifni is on the southern coast of Morocco. I will not bore you with its history, which is complicated. The Tiradores were infantry soldiers recruited there and renowned for their bravery, like your Gurkhas. They had Spanish officers.

During the civil war one *goum*, or troop, was commanded by Francisco Vilafermosa. Dr Montacute told you about him before.'

'He's the man alleged to have stolen the Republicans' gold.'

'That's right. The Spanish government decided to send the whole of their gold reserves abroad. Émile Labeyrie, the Governor of the Bank of France, took the gold that could not be sent to Russia to strengthen France's own reserves. One hundred and ninety-three tonnes of gold were exchanged for French francs which the Republicans then used to buy weapons. That's the official story but we know more gold left Burgos than arrived in France. And we know some, a truckload of gold coins, was stolen by an anarchist named Juan Manuel Casares whose body was uncovered thirteen years ago.'

'And,' I interjected, 'you think Vilafermosa and his men in turn stole the gold from Casares.'

'I'm sure of it. His *goum* was right there where Casares' remains were found. He claimed that they were sixty kilometres away but they weren't. I found their original handwritten log in Morocco. Vilafermosa must have bribed his commander, Emiliano Estriquez, to falsify the official records. But Roger wasn't satisfied with the log, he wanted witnesses. Estriquez had emigrated, so Roger went to Morocco. To find Mourad Zineb.'

'Who is Mourad Zineb?'

'Most of the officers in the Tiradores were Spanish but a few were local. Zineb was one. He was Vilafermosa's number two.'

'And you think he could still be alive?'

'It's possible. He was an important man in Ifni, a tribal leader, we thought that his word would count. But what Roger discovered is that Zineb had to leave Sidi Ifni, forced out by his own people.'

'Why?'

'Because he remained loyal to Spain. You certainly won't have heard of the Ifni War. The Forgotten War it's often called. Most Spaniards have never heard of it. The Spanish did not give up their colonies easily. In 1958 there was vicious fighting around Ifni. The local tribesmen were bitterly divided. When it was all over those who had sided with the Spanish had to leave. Mourad Zineb was one. Roger discovered that Francisco Vilafermosa settled him in Lanzarote in the Canary Islands. And even after Spain ceded Ifni to Morocco in 1969, he didn't go back. Roger needed to follow him to Lanzarote.'

Dr Jones paused as if expecting questions. I wasn't sure what point, if any, she had been making. Her story was no doubt interesting to an historian but what had it got to do with Roger Montacute's disappearance?

'You mentioned that Roger Montacute had been threatened in Morocco,' I said. 'Who by? And why?'

'By Hachim Zineb, Mourad's son, who had stayed behind when his father moved to the Canaries. He didn't want anyone poking around in Sidi Ifni asking questions about his family. Hachim Zineb is now a very powerful man. I think Roger was genuinely frightened. He already had the Moroccan secret police following him. He just wanted to leave.'

'Why were the secret police interested in him?'

Dr Jones gave me a pitying look.

'They are interested in everyone down there. Since 1976 the secret police have been everywhere.'

'What happened in 1976?' Julia asked.

Dr Jones's eyes flashed angrily. 'The Moroccans invaded the Western Sahara.'

'My son must have discovered something,' said Lady Montacute. She wasn't interested in history lessons. 'Why else would he vanish? That gold is at the bottom of all this.'

I noticed that Dr Jones shook her head but said nothing.

'When did you expect your son to return from Morocco?' Julia asked.

Both Lady Montacute and Khadija Jones looked surprised.

'But Roger did return,' said his mother.

'That's how I know he was threatened by Hachim Zineb,' added Dr Jones. 'He came to Cambridge and we discussed the whole trip. That's when he decided he had to go to Lanzarote.'

'So he disappeared in Lanzarote.'

'Not at all. Roger discovered that Mourad Zineb had stayed in the Canaries for twenty years. He was very useful there as Vilafermosa's agent, which may be why he never returned to Ifni. However, eventually he retired and moved on. So Roger had to follow him again. To Madeira.'

XIII

Khadija Jones explained that Roger Montacute had a theory about why Mourad Zineb had finally settled in Madeira. When Zineb had been exiled from Ifni it would have been natural for him to settle in Lanzarote. Not only was it nearer to Ifni than anywhere else but the people spoke Spanish and had a way of life Zineb, from his time in Spain, would have understood.

Montacute reasoned that Francisco Vilafermosa would have wanted to protect Zineb after the Ifni war, whether out of loyalty to an old comrade or out of fear of what Zineb might reveal about the stolen gold. At the same time, he wouldn't want people to start asking too much about their shared pasts so bringing him to Cádiz would have been an unacceptable risk. Instead Zineb went to live in Lanzarote and had been given the role of handling Francisco Vilafermosa's affairs in the Canaries. Vilafermosa was still expanding his business empire and had ambitions to control a large part of the fish processing in that part of the world.

However, Spain changed. With Franco dead, questions about the civil war were at last being asked. One of them being how did so many of those close to Franco become so rich? The discovery of the bones of Juan Manuel Casares had reopened the mystery of the missing gold. Then Francisco Vilafermosa developed cancer. He started thinking about passing the company on to his son, Mateo. He, or his son, wanted to clear the decks. It was time for Zineb too to move on again, somewhere outside Spain but not too far away: Madeira.

It sounded plausible but my mind was elsewhere. When I had believed that Roger Montacute had disappeared in Morocco, the fact that both he and Basil Rosen had mentioned the name Vilafermosa seemed no more than a bizarre coincidence. Francisco Vilafermosa stealing gold coins fifty years earlier and Mateo Vilafermosa trading in Russian missiles seemed to have no possible connection. But now I had a connection: Roger Montacute prowling around Madeira asking questions. Had Montacute uncovered something? Had he even witnessed the same dinner hosted by George Ffortiscue that Rosen had reported to me?

'When exactly did you last hear from your son?' I asked Lady Montacute.

'When he returned from Morocco,' she replied. 'But he phoned Dr Jones from Funchal.'

Khadija Jones confirmed that. 'He called me to say he was coming back to England. He had discovered that Moureb Zineb was dead. He had a copy of the death certificate. He sounded deflated. Zineb's death meant there was nothing more to do in Madeira. He had booked a flight back.'

'Which he didn't take,' said Lady Montacute. 'Justin Brasenose was kind enough to make some enquiries for me. It seems my son never boarded the plane. He left my nephew's house but it appears something happened to him on the way to the airport.'

'Your nephew?' Julia asked.

'My sister's son, Patrick, he lives on the island. They're a

106

very old family, been there for centuries. Roger was staying with him. That's where you need to go. Funchal.' She turned to look at me. 'I do hope you will be accompanying your wife Mr Dylan. I will of course pay all your expenses.'

Julia and I looked at each other in surprise.

'I'm afraid there's been a misunderstanding Lady Montacute,' said Julia. 'Exodis does not handle missing persons enquiries. There are specialist companies for that sort of thing.'

Lady Montacute was not to be dissuaded. 'My dear, Justin Brasenose told me all about you. He assured me you are just the people for the job.'

Julia and I had both worked with Brasenose and I was confident he would not have told anyone 'all about' us. I hoped he hadn't even hinted at our backgrounds in Intelligence. He also knew perfectly well that Exodis was not set up for what Lady Montacute had in mind. Either she had misunderstood him or there was something going on that we didn't know about. Either way, we had to say no.

Julia took a softer approach. 'That's very flattering Lady Montacute but I still feel we are not the right people for you. I will talk to Mr Brasenose and see if we can't find someone more suitable.'

'And I am confident that Justin will want you to help. My son is very special, Mrs Dylan. All I am asking is that you go to Madeira and try to find him. Is that too much to ask? I have of course contacted the Foreign Office who assure me they have spoken to the appropriate authorities in Lisbon, who in turn have alerted the police in Madeira. But you know what these places are like. A sense of urgency is so often lacking.'

Lady Montacute might have been talking about her maid failing to bring the morning's post.

'You have met my son. Do not be fooled. Roger is highly intelligent but he is not always at his best with other people, especially people he doesn't know. He has difficulty understanding what others are feeling. He might not pick up on the social cues in the way you and I would. He has in the past caused offence by laughing inappropriately at something someone else says or does. He likes order, Mrs Dylan, a sense of predictability. He hates the unexpected.'

'And yet he jetted off to Morocco on his own and then followed this Zineb man first to Lanzarote and then to Madeira.'

'But that is one of his great strengths. Determination I call it, although others have spoken of Roger's obsessions. Once on a path my son will follow it to the end. As a child he loved jigsaw puzzles, the more complicated the better, and he wouldn't rest until his puzzle was complete. He would refuse to eat, refuse to go to bed, the puzzle had to be finished. He had the most dreadful rows with my husband. Roger in those days had a ghastly temper—'

'He still does,' Khadija Jones interrupted. 'He doesn't display it often but when he does people keep away. There are no greys with Roger. What is not right is wrong.'

'I have a picture of my son,' said Lady Montacute, producing a black and white photograph from her bag. It was a studio portrait, head and shoulders with her son turning to one side, his chin proudly raised. She passed it to me. I saw a man with overlong hair neatly brushed into place, tie perfectly knotted, matching jacket and waistcoat. Here was a man in his fifties clearly trying to demonstrate that he was on his best behaviour; I suspected that Lady Montacute had been present when the photo was taken, giving instructions to both the photographer and her son.

'Is this picture recent?' I asked.

'It was taken three years ago but Roger has not changed.'

She produced another photo. 'This was taken more recently.' It showed Roger Montacute seated in an open sports car.

'A Caterham 7,' commented Julia who had raced kit cars herself in former times.

'Roger has no sense of fear,' responded Lady Montacute. For a second she seemed lost in her own thoughts.

Julia spoke softly. 'I understand how you must feel, Lady Montacute. If I could help I would. As I said I will speak to Justin Brasenose and see what he says.'

Lady Montacute's response sounded something like 'Hmmff' but Julia was not going to budge. As she told me when the two women had left, Justin Brasenose had a lot to answer for. I left Julia to phone him while I returned to Century House.

Neil White was waiting for me. 'How did it go?'

I repeated most of what Lady Montacute and Dr Jones had told us. White was non-committal. 'I don't suppose it will come to anything.'

I hadn't mentioned Justin Brasenose's involvement: dropping the name of the Joint Intelligence Committee in Century House was never a wise thing to do. The conventional wisdom in the Service was that the JIC served more as ornament than instrument. Being close to Brasenose had stood me well when he was on the inside; it was not so helpful now.

'You say the name of the woman with Lady Montacute was Jones, Khadija Jones?'

'That's right. Apparently her late husband was a Labour backbencher.'

'Rings a bell,' White responded. 'Look her up. Find out what she's been researching, but don't spend too long on it. Things are hotting up around the Baltic. Gorbachev has well and truly let the fox into the henhouse.'

It didn't take me long to discover that Dr Khadija Jones was not the mild-mannered academic I had assumed. And she wasn't Moroccan, or at least she usually insisted that she wasn't. Khadija Jones's academic interest might be the Spanish Civil War but her primary interest was human rights. In particular she was passionate about the rights of her own people, the Sahrawi, the inhabitants of what we called Western Sahara, occupied by Morocco for more than twenty years. Her brother was a senior commander in the 20,000-strong army that, until recently, had been fighting against that occupation, Polisario. The same Polisario guerilla force that Dreyton had suggested were the likely buyers of SAM-18 missiles.

'That might change things,' commented White. 'I'd better tell Dreyton.'

He disappeared upstairs half an hour later. When he returned he reported that Dreyton had taken Khadija Jones's involvement as evidence that his theory that Polisario were the customers for the Russian missiles was correct.

'What else did he say?' I asked. 'Does he still think the Americans could be involved? Did he mention George Ffortiscue?'

'No, he was being very cagey. He did say he was taking the

Montacute matter very seriously. Told me not to say anything to the Cabinet Office, he would handle any Parliamentary Questions. Apparently the request I received from the Cabinet Office about Vilafermosa originated from Justin Brasenose. That's a proverbial red rag to a bull for Dreyton. You know that both he and Brasenose were after the Chief's job. In the end they were so busy stabbing each other that it was decided that neither would get it. But there's always a next time, the Chief's not well.' I sometimes wondered what Neil gave in return for the gossip he picked up.

'Dreyton also said he would be going to Madeira himself.'

'I didn't think he was a field man.'

'He's not. Strictly a desk warrior. I can't imagine what he thinks he's going to do down there.'

If Dreyton went to see the Portuguese police I could be in trouble. They would certainly reveal that it hadn't been one of their men who had overheard Ffortiscue's conversation with the Russians; the little subterfuge White and I had cooked up to hide Basil Rosen's identity would be exposed. But surely Dreyton wouldn't go all the way there just to check on what a Portuguese policeman might have overheard. So why was he going? The Russians were no longer there and there was no reason to think that Ffortiscue might still be. I suppose it was possible that Vilafermosa could be on the island, but what would Dreyton expect to learn from him? That just left the fifth man at the dinner Rosen had witnessed, the man he suggested might be an Arab and who walked like a sailor. But if we hadn't been able to discover who that man might be how could Dreyton be expecting to find him?

XIV

'We are going out tonight,' Julia announced that evening. 'Justin Brasenose has invited us to dinner. Maria will look after Eveline.'

To the unspoken but clearly conveyed disapproval of my mother we now had what she insisted on calling a 'servant'. Maria, who had been our Spanish au pair, had become our unqualified but much-loved live-in nanny.

'I adore Julia,' my mother explained, 'and it's lovely that you've married someone with all that money, but having servants in the house is not how you were brought up.'

The truth is that my mother still had difficulty understanding that Julia had a real job. Julia often seemed to think, unfairly, that I had the same difficulty.

'Eveline needs her mother,' insisted my mother. 'Don't let this nanny get too close to her.'

Eveline in fact had become close to Maria, even mimicking her accent, but that I was sure didn't mean she was any less close to us. And Maria's presence in the house allowed us time to ourselves, time to go out to dinner.

'Brasenose will be on expenses,' I commented. 'I hope he's taking us somewhere special.'

'Not at all. Our local Indian. He said he wanted it to be discreet, so I suggested he come over to Wimbledon.'

I couldn't imagine Justin Brasenose dining in an obscure

Indian restaurant in south London, however good the food. His idea of great food, he would often tell us, was the beef Wellington his parents' cook used to serve. I had discovered that Brasenose had no sense of humour when I made the mistake of remarking facetiously that my mother made wonderful pork Wellington, but she called it sausage roll. It was a cheap crack and Brasenose was not amused.

Julia explained that when she had phoned Brasenose to remonstrate about him recommending Exodis to Lady Montacute he had listened patiently and then suggested we have dinner somewhere well away from Whitehall.

'To discuss what?' Julia had asked. 'Shouldn't you be pressing the Madeira police to step up their efforts if you really think something has happened to Lady Montacute's son? You know Exodis isn't some kind of missing persons bureau. We really can't help.'

'Perhaps,' Brasenose had replied. 'Or perhaps Thomas could help. I will explain over dinner.'

And that was all he would say.

'Let him do all the talking,' Julia insisted as we walked to the restaurant. 'He is plotting something and I'm not sure we should get involved.'

Julia and I had first met Justin Brasenose in our early days on the Defence Intelligence Staff. In those days he had been an arrogant sod and we had not hit it off. I had just graduated from Durham and didn't take well to being patronised by one of MI6's rising stars. But when I moved over to MI6 myself, we both seemed to have changed. Brasenose was now a risen star and his tone had become more patrician than patronising. No doubt my own rough edges were not so evident and he had certainly helped my career along. But now our positions had changed again. I was the Deputy Desk Officer on one of the most important Desks in the Service whereas Brasenose was technically no longer part of the Service. As Neil White had told me, Brasenose had been a candidate for the top job and had received the Cabinet Office Joint Intelligence Committee role as a consolation prize. I suspected he still thought of me as his pupil, someone from whom he could expect unquestioning loyalty, but Julia was right, whatever games he was playing weren't necessarily games I was paid to play.

When we arrived we discovered that Brasenose had made an effort to dress down. He had replaced his suit jacket with an expensive blue cashmere jumper which sat oddly with his pinstripe suit trousers. The jumper bulged at the wrists where it was hiding his usual double cuffs and discreetly crested cufflinks.

His driver sat outside in a black Jaguar, a step up from the Vauxhall that had been his official car before he moved over to the Cabinet Office.

Brasenose was in earnest conversation with the restaurant's owner. I thought he was asking Mr Alam what a biryani was, but as I drew closer I realised that in fact he was debating with the owner whether the name biryani came from the Persian word for rice or from the way the dish was cooked.

When we sat down we discovered that Brasenose had already agreed with Mr Alam what we would order. 'Add anything else you fancy,' he offered, 'but I think you'll find this selection rather good.'

I was happy with his choice but Julia didn't like being taken for granted and on principle added pani puri to the order.

'It's good to see you both again,' he said. 'I do hope you are well. And your daughter, Eveline, isn't it? Settled in well at school, has she?'

Before we could do anything more than nod he continued, 'I expect you're wondering what we're all doing here. Well, it's about channels. There are one or two little mysteries that have been intriguing me and I'm not sure the usual channels are best placed to resolve them. You know what Whitehall is like. People are always happy to help as long as it doesn't involve providing actual assistance. Departments will tell you whatever you need to know, but you must let them decide what it is you need to know. All very sensible of course. "Need to know" is the golden rule in our business but you can't solve a mystery if all the clues stay hidden.'

He paused and looked across the table. Neither of us said anything because neither of us had any idea what he was driving at.

'Mystery number one you know about. Roger Montacute has vanished. Lady Montacute is worried, more worried than she appears. I've known Constance all my life, she's a real grande dame. She's not a worrier. The fact is she thinks her son is dead and I'm inclined to agree. Roger simply isn't the sort of man to take himself off without telling anyone. So what, we need to ask ourselves, was he doing in Madeira? Researching some hoary old story from the Spanish Civil War. Here we come to mystery number two...'

'The Spanish gold,' I interrupted. 'You really think he might have been on to something, might even have found it?'

Brasenose looked surprised. 'No, no. There won't be any hidden treasure. If it ever existed it will all have gone by now. No, the mystery is the man Roger thought had stolen it.'

'Francisco Vilafermosa.' This time it was Julia who interrupted. 'You think there's something mysterious about him? Why would that matter? He died years ago.'

Then a thought struck her. 'Did you send Roger Montacute to Exodis in the first place? Was it you who suggested to him that Exodis might be able to find out something about Vilafermosa? I thought that was Jonathon Craverse's idea. He said Lady Montacute was an old friend.'

Brasenose just smiled. 'What did you discover about Vilafermosa?'

'Nothing. The company had expanded recently and Roger Montacute thought that might have been financed using the Spanish gold. It was nonsense. They raised money from a Panamanian bank and bought a small reefer business.'

'What's a reefer business?' I asked, assuming it was something to do with marijuana.

'Reefer vessels are cargo ships carrying refrigerated cargo,' Brasenose explained, always happy to remind people of his family connections with the shipping industry. 'No doubt Vilafermosa bought the reefers cheaply, there's not much of a future in that sector. Refrigerated containers are going to make reefers completely obsolete.'

'Well Vilafermosa thought it would complement his own fish processing business, let them move frozen produce,' said Julia. 'I reported that to Montacute. There was nothing else to find.'

'Really? I hope Roger didn't pay you for saying that.'

'Did we miss something?' asked Julia.

Brasenose looked around before answering. 'If I didn't know both of you so well we wouldn't be having this conversation. I don't need to remind you, Julia, that you are still bound by the Official Secrets Act. The fact is that Vilafermosa is an asset we want to protect.'

I was shocked. Neil White had just gone through the files and found no mention of Vilafermosa. 'You mean Francisco Vilafermosa's son, Mateo, works for us.'

'Not Mateo specifically, the company, Vilafermosa SRL. I understand that the Vilafermosa trawlers are providing a valuable service for this country.'

'Doing what?'

'That you don't need to know. Indeed I don't know. That's the next little mystery. They appear to be regarded as a protected asset by your Service, Thomas. They are not to be interfered with. And nothing should be done that might reveal them to be our asset. Put simply there's a large keep-off sign over Vilafermosa SRL. And the paint on the sign is still wet, which is perhaps why your informants had heard nothing, Julia. I myself only discovered your Service had an interest in the company quite recently.'

I was struck by how Brasenose, after a lifetime in the Secret Intelligence Service, could have moved so effortlessly from referring to it as 'the Service' to it becoming 'your Service'.

'But if there's a metaphorical keep-off sign and Roger Montacute was asking questions about something he shouldn't have been why didn't you stop him?' Julia asked. 'Why send him to me?'

Brasenose clearly wasn't going to admit he had suggested Exodis to Roger Montacute. 'When I say that I learned that Vilafermosa was a protected asset quite recently, I mean I heard about it this morning, whereas Roger first discussed his research project with me months ago, at a family gathering.

I've always tried to pretend an interest in Roger's work. He's the black sheep of the family you know and every family needs a black sheep. He mentioned the name Vilafermosa. It meant nothing to me at the time. But now that he's disappeared it occurred to me to ask one of my people to follow up the name. She came across a note from Dreyton to Defence Intelligence saying that the Vilafermosa trawlers were a protected asset and the Navy should keep away. What did unsettle me is that I wasn't aware of Clive Dreyton doing anything that might involve Spanish trawlers.'

'So why didn't you ask Dreyton what was going on?'

'Good question.'

A waiter arrived with a bottle of indifferent Australian red which Brasenose, without bothering to taste, told him to pour out. I wasn't sure if it was the curry or our company that made him dispense with his usual wine snobbery.

'The Joint Intelligence Committee is an odd creature,' he explained. 'We really are just a committee. We are there to coordinate not control, support not supervise. I'm in a rather peculiar position. A bit like Walter Bagehot said of the monarchy: I must be consulted but in return I can only encourage or warn. I can't really intervene.'

The food arrived, which gave me a chance to think. Brasenose had never been one to worry about demarcation lines before.

'I was rather hoping that as Roger had turned to Exodis you might have uncovered something that could explain Dreyton's interest in Vilafermosa,' Brasenose continued.

'How could we do that?' Julia asked, but then suddenly realised the answer. 'Unless you thought I might ask Thomas.'

'It crossed my mind,' Brasenose conceded. 'I remember

you and Thomas don't keep any secrets from each other.'

'Then you remember wrong,' I objected sharply. 'I would never use anything secret to help Julia's business and Julia would never ask me to.'

I was more than annoyed that he would think I would use my position at Century House to play detective for Julia's clients. And, in fact, Brasenose knew Julia and I well enough to know that wasn't going to happen. There was something he wasn't telling us. On the one hand he was insisting he had only just discovered that the Vilafermosa company was a protected asset and on the other hand it seemed obvious that he had sent Montacute to Exodis weeks ago, knowing that Montacute would ask Julia to investigate Vilafermosa.

'I hear what you say about the role of the Joint Intelligence Committee and your own position,' I said when the food had been served, 'but it would still have been much easier to simply talk to Dreyton.'

Brasenose helped himself to a naan before responding. 'Well, that brings us to the next little mystery. And now I really am telling tales out of school. This is where it becomes serious.' He looked at me. 'How well do you know Clive Dreyton?'

'I've met him.'

'You see there is what might be quite a big mystery, a question I've been asking myself for some time. What is Clive Dreyton up to? And following a quiet conversation I've had with Bill Merryweather at the American Embassy, there's now a further question: What is Dreyton up to with George Ffortiscue?'

XV

'Let me explain,' Brasenose said.

'I think you should,' I agreed, perhaps sounding sharper than I intended.

Brasenose concentrated on his food for a moment before continuing. 'Clive Dreyton is ambitious. Nothing wrong with that of course. He wants the top job and he knows that if he doesn't get it the next time it becomes vacant he'll have missed the boat. He's deputy to the Chief now so he should be well placed. The problem is he's never done anything outstanding. Until he was made deputy he'd been an administrator: personnel, estates, accounts, that sort of thing. Nothing operational.'

I knew what Brasenose meant. The Secret Intelligence Service has always had a deliberately created aura of mystery. We like to think of ourselves as an exclusive elite, separate from, and superior to, the rest of the civil service. And within the Service there is a group with a sense of being extra-special, those who, in the jargon of the Service, had spent time 'in the field'. Dreyton, however high he had risen, was not one of those. And I have no doubt that the Justin Brasenoses and Neil Whites, who had served out in the cold, would find subtle ways of reminding him of that fact.

'We were both at one of these ridiculous Brussels security symposiums recently,' Brasenose continued, 'all cloak and dagger stuff. Dreyton waving his cloak like a magician while looking for an opportunity to put his dagger in someone's back. He said absolutely nothing of interest. Your chief has given him a roving brief, whatever that means. The nearest he's been to an overseas posting was his time in Washington negotiating information exchange protocols. He needs a success, an operation he can take credit for. He tried to get close to Oliver North in Washington, set up some kind of operation in Belize, but that's rather blown up in his face now the Iran-Contra fiasco is public knowledge. Then he tried to get involved in Northern Ireland but stepped on too many toes.

'Deputies are either rubber stamps or filters. Dreyton has become a filter. Operational intelligence isn't reaching the Chief and it's not reaching the JIC. God knows what he was trying to do in Northern Ireland, the last thing we needed there was yet another cowboy outfit getting in everyone's way. Now he's doing something in Spain. What? He's not brought anything to the JIC. It smells.'

I smiled. 'It smells' was one of Brasenose's favourite expressions, and he was usually right.

'And it smells even more now. There's a woman from the US Drug Enforcement Administration, the DEA, over here at the moment. Police stuff mainly but Bill Merryweather was anxious that she brief Clive Dreyton and me while she was here. We spent an hour at their Embassy yesterday. The DEA are really taking the US drug problem seriously at last, but of course the Company until now have had conflicting objectives. They've been using the drug routes to get weapons to the Contras in Nicaragua, drugs going one way and guns the other. Easier for the Company than building clandestine airstrips themselves, and welcome business for the gangs organising the smuggling.'

Brasenose managed to convey a mild distaste for the Company's tactics but I knew him well enough to know he would have done exactly the same. I remember him telling me about the original French Connection. Back in the 1950s, when the French were fighting to keep Indochina, members of the French intelligence service were sending opium from Saigon to Marseilles, where it was turned into heroin and smuggled into the US through mafia intermediaries in Cuba. The point of Brasenose's story was the irony of the main drug route into America eventually being destroyed by the actions of Ho Chi Minh and Fidel Castro. The morality or immorality of French Intelligence had been of no concern.

'I wasn't really sure why Merryweather wanted us there,' Brasenose continued. 'Some of it was interesting, the DEA woman was certainly fired up about it all, but nothing particularly relevant for us. Merryweather said he had invited us over to demonstrate how all the various US Agencies were pulling together, all playing the same tune. But I decided the meeting wasn't for our benefit at all. Merryweather was based in Central America before he came here, Panama, El Salvador, Colombia. I don't know exactly what he was doing there but I can guess. The meeting was to show the DEA that whatever he'd been doing then he was now firmly on side when it came to the war on drugs.

'Anyway, the point I wanted to make is that as we were leaving, Merryweather turned to Clive Dreyton and casually mentioned George Ffortiscue. "You ought to rein that guy in," he said, "maybe bring him back from Panama."

'Dreyton told him Ffortiscue was no longer one of us,

but Merryweather obviously didn't believe him. "Is that so?" he said. "Well, if you see him tell him the game in the region is changing. I told George that myself but he doesn't seem to be listening. He's done good work down there but, like I say, things move on, yesterday's hero is today's villain." Dreyton asked Merryweather what he meant by that but he just repeated that we should bring George Ffortiscue home.'

'What do you think he meant?' I asked.

'I don't know. Panama's President, Manuel Noriega, used to be the Company's man, but because he's so close to the cartels running drugs into the US he's now an embarrassment. I didn't even know Ffortiscue had been in Panama. He'd dropped off my radar. With everything else going on it's impossible to keep tabs on every ex-spook floating around, you know that. And it's nothing to do with my Committee. But Ffortiscue still has knowledge inside his head which we wouldn't want the other side to get hold of. Someone in your Service should be keeping an eye on him, make sure he isn't tempted to sell any little secrets. I asked Dreyton what Merryweather had been talking about and he claimed he didn't know. Said he hadn't seen him for years.'

He hesitated for an instant before adding, 'I'm not sure I believe him,' which is the way a certain type of Englishman calls someone else a liar.

'Merryweather tells me Ffortiscue simply disappeared a couple of weeks ago. I've tried to check Ffortiscue's movements,' Brasenose continued. 'He's visited this country twice in the last couple of months. I asked Dreyton to check the Registry at Century House to see if you chaps have picked up anything. There's nothing recent. The last address on file for Ffortiscue is in Miami three years ago.

Dreyton suggested he could have retired, which is nonsense. I know Ffortiscue from the old days, he's not the retiring type. Merryweather wouldn't have mentioned his name if he wasn't still in the business.'

'You say Merryweather mentioned Panama. What was that about?'

Brasenose smiled again. 'The Americans are having problems down there. The Company have been using the Panamanian leader, Manuel Noriega, to help get weapons to the Contras in Nicaragua. Noriega himself has been on the Company payroll for twenty years and they've been turning a blind eye to him running drugs into the US. But now, of course, the whole Contra business is coming under the spotlight and people are asking what the Company is doing in bed with a madman like Noriega. It's one thing to say you can't see what's happening when everyone is in the dark, it's not so easy when the attorney general in New York is shining a bloody great searchlight in your face and indicting Noriega on drugs charges. For some time now the White House's position has been that Noriega has to go, but the US won't go in and remove him. Bush has been definite about that – so far. But every coup attempt that the US has tried to encourage in Panama has failed.'

'But what's Ffortiscue got to do with any of that?'

'Well according to Dreyton nothing at all. Merryweather must have made a mistake, Ffortiscue is out of the business.'

'But then,' said Julia, 'his name pops up in Madeira.'

'And,' I added, 'when I pass his name on to London I'm immediately called home and Clive Dreyton takes over.'

'Did Dreyton say why he was doing that?' asked Brasenose.

'He said that Madeira could be an American operation and we had better step carefully. He obviously thought he was better placed than Neil and me to handle anything sensitive.'

'Really?' Brasenose sounded sceptical. 'I thought everybody agreed the Israelis were behind your little adventure in Turkey. Did he say why he thought the Americans could be involved?'

'No, but it could make sense. The Americans don't want those missiles floating around on the black market so perhaps they've decided to buy them themselves. Although that's not what Dreyton said to us. He suggested that they were being sold to the rebels in Western Sahara, Polisario. Madeira is not that far away. And now we know about Roger Montacute's connection to Polisario.'

Brasenose's head shot up. 'What connection?'

'Khadija Jones. The woman who first put Montacute on to the story about Vilafermosa and the gold. Her brother is a Polisario commander.'

'So what are you suggesting?'

'I'm not suggesting anything. Montacute was in Madeira at exactly the time that a couple of Russians met George Ffortiscue to sell those needles. Perhaps Montacute was there as a representative of Polisario.'

'Rubbish,' snapped Brasenose. 'Roger wasn't capable of something like that. He could no more negotiate an arms deal than he could climb Everest.'

'But he might have stumbled on to something. Suppose he had met Dr Jones's brother or seen a photo of him and then came across him in Madeira. He might have started asking awkward questions. We just don't know. In any case Dreyton is right, it's just too much of a coincidence that missiles are for sale in Funchal, not a million miles away from Morocco, and the group that might be buying them are connected to someone who disappears from the same place at the same time.'

Brasenose was not at all convinced. 'That's what Bill Merryweather would call bullshit. You look at a map of the world and Madeira appears to be just off the coast of Morocco, but that's misleading. In reality they must be 700 kilometres or more apart, from here to Paris and back. And there is no direct communication. Look at the map again but don't look at Madeira in the ocean to the west of Morocco, look across the desert to the east. That's where Polisario get all their arms: from Algeria. The Algerians and Moroccans have been at each other's throats for years. Polisario wouldn't need to turn to anyone else. And in any case, they don't have the cash and Dreyton knows that. My question is: why does he float such a ridiculous idea?'

'You think he wants to distract us from the truth.'

'Of course, but what is the truth? And more importantly why does he want to distract us from it?'

'You tell me.'

'I can't, but he's up to something. I want you to help me find out what that is. That's why I want the two of you to go down to Madeira. Lady Montacute has influential friends. Her son is missing. We don't want the press or opposition MPs asking what we're doing about it. She's asked Julia for help.' He looked at me. 'I've arranged with the powers that be that you be given leave to go along as well. Just to investigate Roger Montacute's disappearance. Nothing more. Officially you're not to interfere in any way with Dreyton's team who will be following up the mysterious Russian needle salesmen.

But unofficially, if you come across anything concerning George Ffortiscue or Mateo Vilafermosa, report back to me.'

I didn't like it. He might think that whatever Dreyton was doing 'smells' but Dreyton was an important man in the Service and might become more important when the current chief retired. Knowing that Brasenose had hoped for the top job himself, I didn't want to get caught up in personal quarrels and office politics, especially when, in terms of the Service, Dreyton was one of us and Brasenose was now one of them.

To my surprise Julia responded differently.

'You really think Roger Montacute has been murdered?' she asked.

'I think Constance Montacute believes that. She knows her son. And she wants to find the truth.'

'Then I'll go,' Julia said. 'But if I find anything I report back to Lady Montacute. And I won't be wasting time looking for Russian arms dealers. There's no need for Thomas to come. You can't expect him to spy on colleagues in his own Service.'

Brasenose was unconvinced. 'That doesn't entirely resolve the issue. A British citizen has disappeared in a foreign country and the Foreign Office needs to show that it has taken the matter seriously enough to send one of its own people to the island.'

'So you want me to go as a representative of the Foreign Office this time.'

'That's right. It is after all what you are.'

'And would you tell Dreyton I'm going back?'

'I already have. He understands the position we find ourselves in. He knows Lady Montacute is not without influence. And he will inform your Desk Officer, Neil White, tomorrow. I have your tickets here. I understand you employ a nanny.'

Brasenose as usual had done his homework.

'We'd better pack,' I concluded.

It's never wise to fight against fate, especially a fait accompli. Having arrived at the restaurant determined not to become involved in whatever Brasenose was plotting I realised that Julia and I were now not only involved but had been manipulated into taking sides in a Whitehall turf war. Dreyton might understand the position, as Brasenose put it, but he wouldn't welcome the JIC getting involved in his operation.

I didn't believe that Brasenose had only just discovered that Dreyton was up to something with Vilafermosa. It was far more likely that he had known about Vilafermosa when he sent Montacute to see Julia. He had been hoping that Julia would turn up something unexpected. And there was only one way she was going to do that: by asking me to scurry off to Century House to see if I could find a file on Vilafermosa. Brasenose should have known Julia and I well enough to know that wasn't going to happen. I certainly knew him, and I was sure there was something he wasn't telling us. He was posing questions to which he already knew the answers.

Brasenose smiled again, a touch condescendingly. 'By the way,' he said, 'how did you and Neil White hear about George Ffortiscue and the Russian missiles? There doesn't seem to be a record of any communication about it from the Portuguese authorities.'

It was my turn to smile. 'You don't need to know that.'

XVI

For the second time in little more than a week I landed in Funchal. This time I was with Julia and travelling on my own passport. It had taken no great effort to persuade my mother to travel up from Cornwall to help look after her granddaughter. We just hoped she wouldn't upset Maria, our nanny, while we were away.

I was confident that nobody at the airport would remember me as Thomas Williams.

The Embassy in Lisbon had provided the name of a police commissioner in Funchal who was apparently in charge of investigating Roger Montacute's disappearance. As Julia spoke very little Portuguese, she agreed that once we had checked into our hotel I should go to see him while she sorted out the arrangements for the next day.

The PSP, the Polícia de Segurança Pública, is the main police force in Portugal and a *comissário* is an important man. Perhaps that's why he was too busy to see me. Instead his deputy, with just two silver stars on his epaulette, rose to greet me when, after waiting half an hour, I was shown into his office.

Our conversation was brief. The PSP would do everything possible to help but as of now seemed to have done nothing other than confirm that Roger Montacute had indeed failed to board his flight. Nobody at the airport, I was assured, had seen him. His photo would be circulated to every police officer on the island within the next few days. In the meantime, if I discovered anything the PSP would be grateful if I contacted them immediately.

There was nothing more to be said. Just to annoy the commissioner's deputy I asked if I should perhaps contact the Polícia Judiciária, the police force responsible for dealing with homicides and serious crimes. He was clearly shocked. Absolutely not, he insisted, there was no evidence yet that any crime had been committed. Doctor Montacute had merely decided to prolong his stay on the island, which he was entitled to do.

I returned to the hotel; there was a phone call I wanted to make.

Neil White had made it clear, when I phoned him before our flight left, that I was going to Madeira only to help find Lady Montacute's son. As I had expected Clive Dreyton had not been happy to be told by the Cabinet Office that our Service had to be seen to be taking Roger Montacute's disappearance seriously and that I was therefore being sent back to Funchal. I was not to make any enquiries about the matter that had brought me to the island not long before: the possible sale of surface-to-air missiles. All that was being handled by Dreyton's team. I am sure that had I asked if Basil Rosen himself was therefore off limits White would have said that he certainly was. But I hadn't asked.

White didn't need to worry, I wasn't planning to talk to Rosen about anything that might even remotely touch on issues of national security. When I dialled the number Rosen had given me it was something else entirely that I wanted to discuss: Roger Montacute's disappearance.

When we last met Rosen had commented that he was getting to know his way round the island's bureaucracy. Now that the local police seemed so disinterested, Julia and I might need some help and with Lady Montacute's money in our pocket we could afford to pay for it.

The phone rang three times and was then answered with a curt '*Olá*'.

'This is Tom.'

There was a moment's silence. 'This is a local call. You are here?'

'Yes. On a personal matter. My wife has been hired to find someone, I thought you might help.'

'What has this got to do with me?'

'Nothing at all. I just need someone who knows the right people in Madeira. My wife can pay.'

I could tell Rosen didn't believe me. I wouldn't have done in his place but I carried on. 'I have a name of someone here on the island. Ten thousand dollars cash if you can find an address.'

'What is the name?'

'Mourad Zineb?'

'You think that is the man I saw?'

'No. It's got nothing to do with all that.' I could almost feel his disbelief.

'Mourad Zineb. That is not a Portuguese name.'

'It is Moroccan. He has not been on the island long. A few years perhaps.'

'Where are you staying?' I gave him the name of my hotel, the Casino Park. 'If I find anything I will contact you. If I find nothing we will not talk. Do not contact me again.' Rosen put the phone down.

The next morning we were collected from our hotel by the driver employed by Lady Montacute's nephew.

As well as acting as Patrick Mallow's chauffeur it was clear that Tiago Abreu considered that one of his responsibilities was to provide a running commentary for any visitors to the island. On the two-hour drive to Mallow's estate, Quinta Moran, he hardly stopped talking and we learned far more than we wanted about Madeira. He started with the discovery of the uninhabited island by Bartolomeu Perestrelo and João Gonçalves Zarco in 1419 and continued up to the recent elections. He named every tree and flower and crop we passed. He gave us the name of every village on the route, although we were perfectly capable of reading the road signs ourselves.

The road ascended out of Funchal, winding its way from one hairpin bend to another through vertical walls of deep green trees with precipitous drops on the right-hand side. The distinctive smell of the laurel forests prompted Tiago to explain that there are apparently five types of laurel but all are threatened by 'the Australians', by which he meant the eucalyptus that towered up from the steepest ravines. The slightest lapse in concentration by the driver would send us down a 100-metre drop but Abreu still kept up his commentary.

When we reached Serra de Água he was telling us a complicated story about his father who farmed nearby and had to check the water levels in the irrigation canals three or four times each day to ensure that the electricity for his part of the village was generated smoothly. And as we began to descend back down the mountain range that divides the north and south of the island he started to describe the processes for making Madeira wine; it is the only wine in the world that needs heat in the barrel to reach perfection, he told us proudly.

Many of Madeira's leading wine producers have English names; they were founded by British merchants in the eighteenth and nineteenth centuries – Blandy, Leacock, Miles, Cossart, Gordon, King, Moran, Mallow – but of course most of them were not English, they were Scottish or Irish or Welsh.

I already knew that Richard Patrick Mallow had arrived in Madeira in 1831 from Cork where his family acted as agents for some of the leading Madeiran wine shippers. One of those had been Moran and Company, founded twenty-eight years earlier by Charles Moran, the youngest of seven sons of an Edinburgh surgeon. Within four years of his arrival Richard Mallow had married Charles Moran's daughter and four years after that the firm became Mallow, Moran. Richard Mallow proved to be an astute businessman and when, in 1852, oidium, a fungal infection originating in North America, devastated the Madeiran grape harvest he was able to buy up many of his struggling competitors. When he died, Mallow, Moran was one of the leading firms on the island and his descendants, through judicious marriage as much as business acumen, ensured it stayed that way.

The firm was currently headed by Patrick Mallow whose father had married an Englishwoman of impeccable breeding and considerable wealth named Lady Antonia de Wilton Speight. Lady Antonia's family were unimpressed when their eldest daughter married into 'trade' and only slightly mollified when their only other child, her sister Constance, married into banking.

As we approached Sao Vicente our driver suddenly turned off onto a relatively straight road that ran along the hillside and ended at an ornate iron gate. Abreu got out and pushed the gate back; it wasn't locked. After he had driven through, the gate was pushed shut again and we rounded the side of the hill to find a large pale-pink house with a tiled roof and grey-painted shutters. Quinta Moran was almost square, an impression strengthened by the second storey which had four sets of windows placed symmetrically on each side. At the rear of the house four columns held a red-tiled roof over a balcony looking out towards, in the distance, the sea. Next to the main house stood a newer single-storey building, also painted pink, where Abreu parked the car after depositing us at the front steps. The steps led up to an imposing heavy wooden door which now stood open.

'Welcome to Madeira.' Patrick Mallow greeted us from the top of the steps, spreading his arms wide as if suggesting that the entire island was his domain.

I knew he was in his mid-fifties, but he looked younger, with the casually acquired fitness that comes to those whose place in society has always been guaranteed. He was dressed in a slate grey suit, crisp white shirt and plain blue silk tie. A blue Liberty-print silk handkerchief poked fussily out of his breast pocket.

'How do you like the island?'

He led us onto the balcony at the back of the house without waiting for an answer.

'Tea, coffee or something more uplifting? It's always the right time for a little Madeira.'

Without being summoned a maid appeared with a bottle of 1954 Verdelho.

'Try this, I'm sure you'll like it. Nothing to do with what the Spanish call Verdejo, totally different grape.'

Mallow then launched into a speech about the different types of Madeira wine, the fact that Thomas Jefferson used to drink a pint a day and that the toast after signing the Declaration of Independence had been drunk in Madeira wine.

Rather than talk about what brought us to Madeira he next moved on to the way the grapes were grown not in vineyards but on small plots, *poios,* on the terraced hillsides, using what he called *latada.* I recognised what he was talking about as Julia had commented on it on the road from Funchal. The banana trees on the lower slopes had given way to grapes planted on rusty metal pergolas perched on the faces of almost vertical cliffs.

'The *latada* allow the grapes to see the sun and let the winds disperse the condensation,' Mallow explained. 'And of course they provide the farmers with another crop underneath. You know cabbages, beans, sweet potatoes, pumpkins, that sort of thing.'

Despite the fact that he must have repeated the story hundreds of times before, he spoke with a nervousness that belied his assured appearance. 'Mallow, Moran buys in most of its grapes. Nowadays everything is done at our plant near Caniçal but we used to produce the wine not far from here, just down on the coast between Porto da Cruz and Faial, and send it by ship round to Caniçal and Funchal. Of course when the first proper roads appeared in the thirties that all ended.'

He stopped suddenly as if he had only just remembered why we were here, but even then he didn't move directly on

135

to the subject of Roger Montacute's disappearance.

'So you're friends of dear Aunt Constance. How is she? I'm told she is as formidable as ever, still the grande dame.'

'She seems remarkably well,' Julia responded. 'As you say, a formidable lady.'

'All the Speights were that way. My mother was just the same. Devoted to her charities and to her garden. Don't know how my father put up with it sometimes. And now cousin Roger has vanished. Aunt Constance seems to think he disappeared here, on the island, and she's sent you. Private detectives, are you? Tommy and Tuppence?'

I looked blank but Julia smiled. 'I don't think my husband is as familiar with Agatha Christie as he should be. Wasn't the Tuppence Beresford character rather dizzy? I hope I don't resemble her too closely. Tell me, how well did you know your cousin?'

Mallow, who had been standing looking out towards the sea, came back and sat down.

'How well do any of us know each other? At one time I would say we were very close. Spent the holidays together. My parents packed me off to Blackrock College as soon as they could.'

'In Dublin?'

'That's right. My father was a Rockman. I used to spend Easter holidays with Aunt Constance and sometimes Christmas if my mother decided to return to England for the Speight family gathering, although why anyone would want to spend winter over there I could never understand. Roger was just a year younger, and if I may say so he rather hero-worshipped me. I was rather a good sportsman in those days. Roger never really enjoyed any sport other

136

than cricket, and that was only because he could spend half the match with his nose in a book. He never stayed at the wicket long.'

'So he followed you to Trinity College, Dublin?' suggested Julia.

'Yes, he did. He wanted to get away from his mother as well. We had some jolly good times. Spirited times you might say.'

I could detect a hint of Irish in Mallow's accent but no Irishman would surely refer to 'jolly good times'. There was something very old-fashioned about Patrick Mallow, as if time had passed him by. I half expected him to start talking about 'spiffing larks' and 'jolly japes'.

'Then my elder brother died and I had to come back. The prodigal returns. And now here I am, head of the family and trusted with guiding Mallow, Moran into the next century. I'm sorry my wife isn't here to greet you, she spends a lot of time in Lisbon these days, we have a house there. And my son and daughter are both in the United States: Richard playing in a band in California and Maria at Harvard Business School. She's the brains in the family. Who knows Mallow, Moran could one day have a woman at the helm. My father would have been horrified.'

I was conscious that the conversation had once again drifted away from the reason for our being here. Was that deliberate?

'Let's talk about Roger Montacute's disappearance,' I suggested. 'He was staying here?'

'Yes certainly, here at Quinta Moran. In the blue room. That's where he used to stay in the old days, when he came for the summer holidays. Would you like to see the room?

It's not blue now, my wife changed all that. The old place was far too dark for her, quite right of course.'

'Perhaps later,' suggested Julia. 'Perhaps now you could tell us how your cousin seemed. Was there anything unusual in his behaviour?'

'Well Roger has always been a bit different. But no, there was nothing special. Not entirely sure why he was here. I hadn't been expecting him, you see. He phoned from the airport in London, said he was on his way. Had we known he was coming my wife would have been here but she was in Lisbon looking after her mother, poor dear she's getting on a bit.'

'But didn't Roger explain why he was on the island?'

'Explain? I wouldn't say explain. He told us what he was hoping to do here but to be honest it didn't make much sense. Roger's always had a bee in his bonnet about something or other. This time he was trying to find someone for a book or article he was writing. Roger's an historian you know, very well regarded apparently, but you'll know that. He's writing a book on the Spanish Civil War and he was trying to track down a *moor* who'd been involved in some way. Seems this *moor* ended up in Madeira. According to Roger, the chap stole a lorry load of gold fifty years ago and somehow spirited it to North Africa and then presumably to Madeira. Jolly interesting in some ways, buried treasure and all that. If it was true. We all had a good laugh about it. I think Roger was the only one who took it seriously. He got a bit upset with us, he never did have much of a sense of humour. Salt of the earth and all that but, you know, a bit odd. Michael calmed him down.'

'Michael?'

138

Mallow seemed startled by the interruption. 'Michael, yes. An old Trinity friend of ours who was staying here. I'd invited some friends over for dinner on the night Roger arrived. We had *espetada* I remember, beef on laurel sticks cooked over laurel twigs. Delicious. You should try it. And of course quite a lot of wine. Lovely evening.'

I glanced over at Julia. I was becoming increasingly frustrated by Mallow's constant digressions but she was smiling at him as if we had all the time in the world. She was probably right.

'Did Roger find the man he was looking for?' Julia asked. 'The *moor* you referred to.'

'Find him yes, but he couldn't speak to him. Chap was dead. Roger didn't understand how things work here. You have to know your way around. Roger thought you could just turn up at the town hall with a name and the clerks would fall over themselves to help. It's not like that. Fortunately, a friend of mine managed to find a copy of this chap's death certificate, died last year, seventy-six years old. I gave it to Roger. Very disappointed he was, obviously. Bit of a wasted trip. I told him to stay on but he said three days had been enough. Michael was going home as well.'

Mallow changed the subject again. 'I suppose you're staying at Reid's, everyone does. Oldest hotel on the island. Churchill stayed there and that James Bond fellow.'

'Sean Connery?'

'No, the other one, the one who plays The Saint.'

Mallow really did live in a different world. *The Saint* hadn't been on television for more than twenty years.

'Roger Moore.'

'That's right.'

'When we're abroad we like to feel we're abroad,' said Julia. 'Reid's sounds rather too English.'

'William Reid was Scottish,' was Mallow's only comment.

I suspect Lady Montacute had expected her nephew to put us up at the Quinta Moran but Mallow had presumably thought this too much of an imposition with his wife away. I didn't mind as instead Lady Montacute had put us up in what seemed to me really the best hotel on the island.

I tried to pull the conversation back to the reason we were there. 'So your cousin said nothing that might explain why he didn't take the flight back home?'

'Nothing at all. Everything was tickety-boo. Taxi left here after breakfast and that was the last I saw of him.'

That, I thought, was the last anyone had seen of him.

XVII

'You must stay for luncheon,' insisted Mallow, and led us inside where a table had been laid for three. Real silver cutlery, I noticed, each piece marked with a family crest that might have been Mallow's own but was more likely to belong to one of the families into which earlier Mallows had married.

Before we sat down I asked if I could use the phone to quickly call the hotel. Mallow showed me into a sitting room where an old-fashioned black phone sat on an ornately inlaid burr walnut side table. I called the hotel and asked if there were any messages. There were none. The disc in the middle of the phone's dial carried a seven-digit number.

I wasn't really looking at it very carefully when I suddenly realised that it was not only a number I knew, but a number I had intended to call when we returned to Funchal. Basil Rosen had written it down for me on my first visit to the island. It was the number used to book a table at Reid's Hotel in the name of George Ffortiscue. Surely Patrick Mallow could not have arranged the dinner Rosen had stumbled across.

Patrick Mallow was a curious man. At times he acted like an Edwardian aristocrat and I was sure it was not entirely an act. It was as if he modelled himself on a Mallow family photograph which I had noticed in the hall. Probably taken in the 1930s, twenty years after the passing of the Edwardian era in England, it showed the Mallows relaxing, the men standing as stiff as their collars, smiling weakly through their moustaches, the women wearing dresses that would surely have been deemed unfashionably long in London, the children looking far too serious. It occurred to me that the only other photos on display were of Patrick Mallow's own children. Other than that photo in the hall there were no pictures that might be his parents. And none of his brother or even of his wife. The photos of his children were all clearly taken some years ago, back in their school days.

I suddenly thought of Basil Rosen cutting himself off from his past. Rosen was a Russian in a British skin but the British passport we had given him said nothing at all about the man beneath the skin. As he had said his soul was stateless. Inside that skin was something deeply unfathomable. Patrick Mallow I knew carried a Portuguese passport but that said nothing important about him. In some ways he too had the skin of an Englishman, despite having spent almost all his life in Portugal or Ireland. But inside? He had experienced nothing as truly traumatic as the Russian but there were scars there. A mother who loved her charities and her garden above all and perhaps loved him so little that she banished him to colder climes. An older brother destined to inherit, leaving him to do what? And now a wife who was rarely there and children gone away.

Just as Rosen seemed to have invented a private world that only he understood so too had Mallow created a private world. But whereas Rosen tried to shut out the past Mallow had gone the other way by creating a world that he imagined reflected a more welcoming era. When had I last heard the word luncheon? Had anyone I knew ever described something as tickety-boo?

The maid we had seen earlier laid out cheese, cold meats and salad on a side table and we helped ourselves. A round hot plate held a pile of sweet potato flatbreads, *bolo do caco*, each smothered in garlic and butter. Over luncheon Mallow kept the conversation going without once mentioning his missing cousin; we could have just dropped in to pass the time of day.

'You must have some theory about Roger Montacute's disappearance,' I said as the maid cleared our plates away and placed a bowl of fruit on the table in front of us.

Mallow looked surprised and didn't answer right away. 'You should try this,' he said, pointing at an oval yellow fruit. 'Banana passion fruit.' I noticed he didn't try it himself.

There was another pause, as if this was the first time he had been asked to think about what might have happened to his cousin. 'I've just assumed he will turn up,' he said at last. 'If Roger is still on the island he can't have gone very far. He's not the sort of person to have gone off trekking up a mountain. He'll be in Funchal or Câmara de Lobos. Perhaps he's found his treasure. We've tried the hospitals and he's not there. I suppose he just wanted to be alone. Get away from Aunt Constance, I shouldn't wonder, although he should have known she would send someone like you after him.'

Given how long Roger Montacute had now been missing it was difficult to believe he had simply decided to have some time to himself. Mallow was hiding something.

I decided it was time to shake the tree.

'Tell me about George Ffortiscue,' I said.

143

Mallow stopped with a peeled tangerine halfway to his mouth. 'Who?'

'George Ffortiscue. I understand he's a good friend of yours.'

'Who told you that?'

'Must have been someone in London. When I mentioned Mallow, Moran, she said something about her friend George Ffortiscue planning to stay at Quinta Moran.'

I could sense Mallow relaxing a little but his voice was still hesitant. 'That can't be so. I would know if anyone had stayed here. Your friend must be mistaken.'

'And you don't remember George Ffortiscue?'

'Never heard of him.'

I wasn't going to argue.

'Before we leave,' suggested Julia softly, 'may I have a look at the Blue Room you mentioned, where Roger Montacute stayed?'

'Of course,' replied Mallow, rising from the table.

He led us up the central staircase and then to a nondescript bedroom at the end of a corridor. I had been expecting something more grand. A forged iron single bed with brass knobs that needed a good polish sat by the window, and against the wall stood an antique crossbanded wardrobe with a bevelled mirror and three large drawers. The bed was entirely covered by a rough brown blanket; Roger Montacute was clearly not expected back soon.

'He left nothing here?' asked Julia.

'No, nothing at all.'

'So he had all his luggage with him when he left?'

'I suppose so. I don't think he had a great deal.'

'Well thank you so much for your time and your

hospitality, Mr Mallow. You have a lovely house here and such a beautiful island.' Julia was almost gushing in her appreciation when it came time to leave.

'What do you think?' I asked when Mallow went to find his driver.

'There's something he's not telling us,' she replied. 'I intend to find out what that is.'

We shook hands with Mallow and went down the steps to where Tiago Abreu was waiting with the Mercedes. Julia and I had sat in the back on the way there, but now Julia insisted on sitting in the front so she had a better view of the wonderful scenery. Soon she and Tiago were chattering away while I relaxed in the back, paying no attention to their conversation.

In Serra de Água, Tiago suggested we stop for a *poncha*, the potent local mixture of rum, lemon juice, orange juice and honey. Given the condition of the road I was pleased to see that Tiago didn't have one himself.

Back in the car I heard Julia ask if Doctor Montacute had also stopped for a *poncha* when Tiago had driven him to the airport. Tiago explained that he hadn't driven Doctor Montacute to the airport. He had taken a taxi.

'Oh, I thought you drove all of Mr Mallow's guests.'

'Usually I do. I have been to the airport many times recently. But Dr Montacute wanted to leave early, he wanted to visit Santa Cruz. I had to wait for the other guest, Mr Smith.'

'Mr Smith? Oh, you mean Michael Smith.'

'Yes, Mr Smith, he was flying back to America. So I took him to the airport to catch the flight to Lisbon.'

Julia said something about the effect of the *poncha*

before returning to the earlier subject. 'I wonder what Dr Montacute wanted to see in Santa Cruz.'

But Tiago could tell her nothing more. He had phoned his brother, Aloisio, who drove a taxi in Funchal and who had taken Dr Montacute to Santa Cruz.

'Your brother drives a taxi, that must be very useful. I should think Mr Mallow has a lot of guests who need driving around.'

'No, not these days.' Tiago seemed to have no compunction about discussing his employer's affairs. Clearly he thought Mallow had nothing to hide. 'In the old days, when Mr Mallow's children were here and his mother was still alive, there were often guests at the house. But since Mrs Mallow moved to Lisbon nobody visits Quinta Moran.' His job now, he explained, was to drive Mr Mallow to Funchal or Canical and then drive him back home.

'But Mr Mallow was telling us about a dinner only the other evening, when Dr Montacute was here.'

Tiago nodded. 'Yes, that's true but that was unusual, we have had nobody else staying at the house since Mrs Mallow left. We had to rush to get Dr Montacute's room ready for him. The maid had only made up the two guest bedrooms on the other side.'

'Two bedrooms?' responded Julia quickly, perhaps too quickly. Tiago seemed to realise he had moved from tourist commentary to gossip. He just nodded.

The rest of the journey was spent discussing Tiago's children, the oldest of whom had just turned twenty-two but was still not married, and our own daughter Eveline whose marriage prospects were still far too soon to think about.

Sitting in the back of the car I tried to put the pieces together.

Patrick Mallow already had two guests at the Quinta Moran when Roger Montacute turned up. One was their old Trinity College friend, Michael Smith. The other we didn't know. But we did know that the day before Montacute arrived on the island George Ffortiscue had arrived and that evening had dinner at Reid's with four men: two Russians, Mateo Vilafermosa and someone else. Could that someone else have been Patrick Mallow? Rosen had said a foreigner, possibly an Arab. That didn't sound like a description of Mallow. But whoever had made the table reservation had left Mallow's phone number. It might not have been Mallow but if it had been Ffortiscue himself phoning from abroad then surely he would only have left that phone number because he was expecting to stay at Quinta Moran. Had George Ffortiscue been staying in the second guest room when Montacute arrived? Was Mallow involved in the sale or purchase of surface-to-air missiles? Again, that didn't sound right. But Julia was correct, there was something Mallow wasn't telling us.

Then a final thought struck me. When Mallow had said, 'We all had a good laugh' at Montacute's tales of stolen Spanish gold, who was the we? Had Montacute on his first night at the Quinta sat down to dinner with Mallow, Michael Smith and George Ffortiscue? If so, what were they talking about? Arrows and needles perhaps?

However nonsensical Brasenose found the idea, could it be that Roger Montacute was not the obsessive academic everyone described but was in reality an intermediary between the Russians wanting to sell missiles and Khadija Jones wanting to buy them?

But that sparked another series of questions that had

niggled at my mind since my first visit to the island. We had all assumed that the men who had originally stolen the missiles in Georgia had sold them on to someone else, probably the Israelis, in Turkey. If the Russians still had them and were trying to sell them in Madeira, what had really happened in Ağva? Who had so deliberately refrained from killing me, and why?

XVIII

I spent time in Brazil as a student and later in my days on the Defence Intelligence Staff, and fell in love with the work of Brazilian architect Oscar Niemeyer. His designs for the new capital, Brasilia, were, said one admirer, like pearls strung around the neck of a pig. The fluidity, vivid imagination and sheer beauty Niemeyer brought to all his work was obvious in the curving lines of the Casino Park Hotel perched looking out over Funchal harbour to the ocean beyond. I had decided that if Lady Montacute was picking up the bill this is where we would stay. I started to regret the choice when we discovered the inordinately long dark corridors and echoing empty spaces inside. Disappointment increased when the view from our room proved not to be the ocean but the modernist casino next door. There was a global convention of accountants in town and the best rooms had all been taken.

At least we can find a good restaurant, Julia said, after Tiago Abreu dropped us off outside and departed back to Quinta Moran. But there was a message waiting for me. I was to call Clive Dreyton who, I wasn't surprised to learn, was staying at Reid's Hotel.

This time I had brought a scrambler with me and first tried to phone Justin Brasenose, but he was unavailable. I was told to phone back first thing the next morning. I then called Dreyton.

'Sorry to interrupt your night on the town,' he started, in a tone that made clear he was not at all sorry to interrupt anything I was doing. 'I thought you might like to join an operation I'm running. Meet us at the church in Sao Roque do Faial at 10.00.' He spelled out the name. 'And don't be late. We won't be waiting for you. And one other thing, no reporting to London tonight. This is strictly need to know. We can't risk your communications being insecure. You can brief Brasenose when you get back to London.'

'What sort of operation?' I asked. 'Do I need to bring anything?'

'No just be there.'

He put the phone down.

'You'll be dining on your own tonight,' I told Julia. 'Providing I can find out where the hell Sao Roque do Faial is and how to get there.'

Fortunately, the hotel concierge sorted that out. While Julia disappeared down the hill to the city centre to find a good restaurant the concierge managed to provide a map, a quick *bifana* pork roll and a not-so-quick Opel Corsa hire car.

The concierge was clearly disappointed that I had insisted on the cheapest car he could offer me, but I had no desire to stand out. I had already noticed that the Opel Corsa and Fiat Uno were the most popular cars on the island. Nevertheless, by the time the car was delivered to the hotel I was beginning to think that something more expensive might have been delivered more speedily.

Sao Roque do Faial was near the north coast, in the same general direction as Quinta Moran. For the third time that day I travelled up into the mountains and then down the other side. Sao Roque do Faial proved to be a small rural village dominated by a white church that stood out in the moonlight. Two men were seated in the front of a black Mercedes parked near the church. As I drew up beside it the tinted rear window rolled down and Dreyton told me to follow him. The Mercedes moved off in the direction of the sea. We eventually came to a major road with signs showing Faial to the left and Porto da Cruz to the right. The Mercedes drove straight across and down a narrow, pot-holed lane. A rough wooden sign said simply, *cais*, wharf. After a few minutes the Mercedes turned off onto a grass track that curled back towards the main road. A few hundred yards further on the track petered out. The Mercedes stopped and Dreyton and his two companions emerged. I didn't recognise either of the men with him.

'We walk from here,' Dreyton announced. I looked around and realised we were in the middle of a vineyard. The *latada* supporting the vines looked ghostly in the moonlight.

Dreyton turned to look at me. 'I'm expecting to witness a delivery,' he said. 'A fishing boat will come into the pier below us, unload its cargo into a disused warehouse on the dock and then depart. We will inspect the delivery, ensure that it is what we are expecting and then leave. That's all. John and Barry here have already reconnoitred the area. Barry will go back to the lane we've just left to make sure we are not interrupted. You and John will go down to the quay. As Gold Commander I will stay in the car until you signal me that the delivery has been made. I fear we may have to wait for some time but that's the way it is on this sort of mission.'

John and Barry said nothing. Dreyton spoke as if surveillance and 'this sort of mission' was something he did every day. I wondered if in fact he had ever been in the field before. His use of the term Gold Commander, recently introduced by the Metropolitan Police and meaning something altogether grander, was bizarre.

'Are there any other ways down there?' I asked.

It was the man Dreyton referred to as John who answered. 'No just the one lane down to the beach. If anyone is planning to meet that boat they will have to come that way.'

'No way along the beach?'

'No, cliffs at each end.'

With that John started to move off. I noticed that he and Barry had two-way radios; I assumed Dreyton had one as well.

'Stay here,' John told me. 'Let me check that there's nobody waiting for the boat.'

Dreyton got back into his car.

'What are we expecting to be delivered?' I asked Barry.

'Mr Dreyton will tell you that,' Barry answered, before disappearing back up the track.

After that I stood in silence. Eventually John returned. 'Let's go,' he said, leading the way down towards the beach. He carried a torch but didn't use it. The moon was still bright and the stars were far clearer and more numerous than back in London.

We reached a rough stone quay that was clearly no longer in use. Next to it stood a large grey building, its front door padlocked and the windows on the upper floor in various states of disrepair. 'This is the warehouse,' John said. 'No idea why it's padlocked on this side, there's a door missing on the other side. The shipment will be left inside.'

He kept walking and about a hundred yards further on, set back from the sea, was the shell of another dark stone building, doors and windows now long gone. 'Welcome to your observation post,' commented John. 'Purpose built, you might say.'

'What are you going to do?'

'I'll be inside that old warehouse by the quay. Don't worry, nobody will see me. I'll let you know when the boat has gone and it's safe for us to emerge. They're expected here some time after midnight.'

It was no good my asking who. He disappeared, taking his torch with him.

I found myself in a building that was almost completely derelict. In the moonlight I couldn't tell if it had contained offices, or perhaps a shop, or might even have been someone's home. There was an upper storey but what had been the staircase had collapsed and I wasn't inclined to explore any further. I found a rectangular hole that must have once contained a window frame and perched behind it. It wasn't the perfect observation post. The warehouse where John had taken refuge partially blocked my view of the quay. I settled down to wait.

What the hell was happening? What was Clive Dreyton doing here? Barry and John looked more like SAS than MI6. Who was delivering what to whom and why did Dreyton want me to witness it? I thought Dreyton was here to follow up the sighting of George Ffortiscue and his possible involvement with stolen Russian surface-to-air missiles. Surely he wasn't expecting missiles to be landed in Madeira. And if he was, how on earth did he find out?

I don't think I fell asleep but I came close to it. After

nearly four hours in which absolutely nothing happened, I had to stretch my legs. I considered finding a better vantage point, somewhere closer to the quay and the warehouse. But my movements were more likely to be spotted if I did that. Instead I gingerly made my way through the rubble to the end of the building away from the quay. Cliffs towered above me and advanced towards the sea. Bending low I slipped quietly along the base of the cliff until I reached the sea where any noise I made would be hidden by the sound of the Atlantic.

From there I could make out both the warehouse and the quay but was now much further away. That didn't matter as long as there was nothing to see, but as I decided it might be better to return to my original position I heard the sound of an engine. A boat was approaching from the east. Suddenly a shape appeared around the headland, chugging slowly towards the quay. In the moonlight I could only distinguish the silhouette. It showed no lights. I had expected a fishing boat but this was more like a small cabin cruiser.

The boat was also much closer to the shore than I expected. I crouched right down among the rocks, confident that with the mass of the cliffs behind me I would not be seen unless I moved.

The boat was now just a matter of yards away and bathed in the bright moonlight but I could distinguish nothing inside it. The only splash of colour was fresh white paint on the stern. As it passed me, I could read a name, or part of a name. It might have been a woman's name, *Dora*, or perhaps the Portuguese word for love, *Adora*.

The boat continued along the shore, past the warehouse, to the quay. Someone jumped onto the quay and the boat was tied up. Clambering back onto the boat the figure joined another who appeared from the cabin. Between them they manhandled something onto the quay. They were so far away that I could not even be sure that the figures were both male.

The object they had brought ashore was about six feet long. It could have been a coffin. Or perhaps a case containing a man-portable missile and launcher. The two figures carried the object into the warehouse. Whatever it was being brought ashore needed the two of them to lift it.

I considered trying to move closer but almost immediately the two figures re-emerged and returned to the boat. I wondered how many cases they had to deliver. There was no way they could transport fifteen cases that size on that boat. If they were delivering the missiles stolen in Georgia they would have to make at least one more trip. But that's not what they were doing. As soon as the dark figures had clambered back onboard they cast off and were away, this time heading out to sea before turning to go back the way they had come.

I returned to the derelict building, half expecting to be challenged by John asking where the hell I had been. In fact it was five minutes before I saw his silhouette leave the warehouse and come my way.

'The fun's over,' he announced. 'Let's go find the Gold Commander.'

'What happened?' I asked.

'The delivery was made, we can go home.'

'What was it?'

'No idea.'

I didn't believe him. He had obviously been doing something in the warehouse after the boat had left.

'Aren't we going to look?'

'No.'

John was already marching away, this time up the lane that led from the quay to the main road. When we reached the track into the vineyard where Dreyton and I had parked we found Dreyton's car, Barry at the wheel and Dreyton on the back seat. John got in beside the driver as Dreyton spoke to me through the rear window. 'Ten o'clock tomorrow night. Same place. Sao Roque do Faial. Be there. I can promise you a lot more action tomorrow.'

He turned to tap Barry on the shoulder and the Mercedes moved off. I was left to find my hire car and wonder what the hell the evening had been about.

Neil White's judgement had proved correct: Clive Dreyton, I decided, really was a total prick.

XIX

Julia was asleep when I returned to the hotel but woke as I tried to slip quietly into the bed.

'What happened?' she mumbled sleepily.

'God knows. Dreyton's playing games and seems to have decided I should watch. I'll tell you in the morning.'

'No,' replied Julia. 'Tell me now. What sort of games?'

I took her through the evening's events, partly to try to clarify my own thoughts. But that didn't work. There had been a delivery of something, possibly one of the missing missiles but more probably something like drugs. But who had made the delivery I had no idea. If it had been intended for us, why had we left it behind in the disused warehouse? If it was not for us then for whom?

And why had Dreyton wanted me there? I had been given nothing to do. Nobody told me what was going on. I seemed to be there just as a witness, but witness to what? And why would Dreyton need a witness when he had John and Barry already?

'Who do you think they were, Dreyton's minders?' Julia asked.

'The heavy brigade. SAS at a guess or the increment.' The increment were the paramilitaries used by MI6, primarily in Afghanistan, when it was considered too risky to use serving soldiers. A thought struck me. 'Of course the Service mounts joint operations with the military. But they don't just happen. Dreyton couldn't have simply picked up the phone and ordered a couple of special ops guys to accompany him to Funchal. Whatever he's doing he must have started the planning before I ever visited Madeira.'

With that thought I turned over and fell into a deep sleep. Julia was gone when I awoke.

I called London, Neil White first and then Justin Brasenose. Neither could throw any light on the night's events.

My Desk Officer's response was straightforward: 'I've no idea what the devious little bastard is up to. Why would anyone want to smuggle anything into a place like Madeira? Keep your eyes open and don't believe anything you're told. Dreyton is not a man to trust and he's not a man to cross, but he's a survivor. Remember he got to where he is now by manoeuvring Justin Brasenose off to the Cabinet Office. He knows when to stick the knife in. And when he does just roll over and wave your legs in the air.'

'Well, he's got Vilafermosa protected asset status,' I said. 'I'd love to know why.'

'I'll make enquiries,' White responded. 'But there was nothing in the files about that.'

Brasenose similarly told me nothing new. 'Sounds like Dreyton's flying solo. Whatever he's doing it's not come before the Joint Intelligence Committee.'

'Shouldn't it have done?' I asked.

'Not necessarily. If it's an early-stage operation and doesn't involve any other agencies then Clive is well within his rights to keep a lid on it. I'll make some discreet enquiries. If, as you suggest, he's enlisted Special Ops support I should be able to discover something.'

I then phoned Basil Rosen to tell him Mourad Zineb was dead so he could stop looking for him but there was no reply.

I had a shower and turned on the BBC World Service as I dressed. Tensions in Panama were mounting: a group of off-duty American soldiers had been attacked by Panamanian Defence Force soldiers and a US Army lieutenant killed. The next item was more surprising: Liverpool had beaten Chelsea 5-2 at Stamford Bridge. I went looking for my wife and found her talking to the concierge. She was confirming a time, twelve thirty.

'We're going to Câmara de Lobos for lunch,' Julia informed me as we took the lift back to our room.

'You've booked a restaurant?'

'No, but apparently there are some nice ones there. I'm sure we can ask the taxi driver as long as he's as chatty as his brother.'

'His brother?'

'The concierge managed to find Aloisio Abreu, the brother of Mallow's driver, he's coming to pick us up. I want to know where he took Roger Montacute.'

When we went down to the taxi the receptionist waved me over. 'I have just been trying to call your room. A friend of yours wanted to speak to you, Mister Basil. He says he has the information you asked for.'

'Thanks, can I phone from here?'

The receptionist pointed at a phone on a table near the wall. Julia was standing outside beside a taxi and I signalled that I would be quick. Now that Mourad Zineb was dead we no longer needed his address, although I was still morally committed to paying Basil Rosen for the information. That was one advantage in being able to charge Lady Constance for my expenses rather than having to justify them to the Service's accounts department.

Rosen answered immediately. 'I tried to phone you earlier,' I started.

'I was swimming. I have an address.'

'Thanks, that was quick. But as the man is dead, I'm not sure we need it anymore. Don't worry, we will pay you. Let me know how to transfer the funds.'

There was a moment of silence. 'But Mourad Zineb is not dead.'

'He died last year. A friend has the death certificate.'

There was another silence, longer this time.

'Sorry,' I said. 'I must go, there's a taxi waiting. I will call you tomorrow.'

I heard the phone click as Rosen cut the call.

Julia was already in the taxi. We had decided that we would try the same approach that had worked so well before: Julia would take the front seat and strike up a friendly conversation. Aloísio Abreu however proved more reticent than his brother. His English was fairly good, although his accent stronger, but he felt no need to keep up a running commentary. He would take us to the best restaurant in Câmara de Lobos and wait for us nearby.

Julia tried to strike up a conversation but he replied in monosyllables.

'What should we choose to eat?'

'Fish.'

'Did he recommend any particular dish?'

'Scabbard.'

'Is that a Madeira speciality?'

160

'Yes.'

She changed tack. 'We may want to go to Santa Cruz tomorrow. Do you know it?'

'Of course.'

'Do you often take people there?'

I was looking at the back of Abreu's head and there was a definite stiffening of the neck at Julia's question.

'I take passengers wherever they want to go.'

'Did you take someone there recently?' asked Julia. 'Someone you picked up from Quinta Moran.'

This time Abreu's reaction was unmissable, his hands jerking the steering wheel. At first he said nothing. When he finally responded his voice was so low I almost missed what he said.

'Who are you? What do you want?'

'We just want to know what happened to the man you collected from Quinta Moran.'

'Nothing happened to him. I dropped him in Santa Cruz where he wanted. That's all. Then I drove back to Funchal.'

'Where in Santa Cruz?' Julia persisted.

'In the centre. Near the Câmara Municipal.'

'Is that what he asked for? The Câmara Municipal?'

'No, he wanted the Civil Registry Office, it is nearby. That's where I dropped him.'

Abreu pulled in to the side of the road. 'Now you must go. I will leave you here.'

'You didn't wait for him?' Julia asked.

'No. You must go now.'

He was gripping the steering wheel tightly and it didn't take a trained psychologist to realise that he was lying. Nor that he was frightened. Something had happened either

161

before he and Montacute reached Santa Cruz or after they got there, probably the latter. The way he had corrected the reference to the Câmara Municipal sounded too instinctive to be made up. Montacute had wanted the Civil Registry Office, but why and what was he planning to do afterwards? Presumably go to the airport, which was only a few minutes away. Perhaps Abreu had dropped Montacute as he said, and Montacute walked off towards the Registry Office, Abreu had started to drive away and then he must have seen something, something that was making him nervous.

Then it struck me, something was missing.

I had said nothing since we entered the taxi. I leaned over towards Abreu.

'What happened to the luggage?'

Abreu jumped. He had clearly forgotten I was there.

'Luggage?'

'Yes, luggage. Your passenger was about to fly back to London. He had his luggage with him. He wouldn't have carried that into the Registry Office. He must have asked you to wait for him.'

Abreu turned to look at me. 'Who are you? What are you doing here? You're not the police.'

'Would you rather talk to the police? That can be arranged. You can explain to them what you did with the luggage.'

'I did nothing.'

Julia tried playing good cop. 'Listen Aloisio. All we want to do is find out what happened to our friend, Roger Montacute. He is not a well man. We need to find him and take him home. That's all.'

Abreu wasn't convinced. 'I dropped him in Santa Cruz. Then I drove away.'

'You drove away with his luggage,' I said accusingly. 'You stole it!'

'No!'

'What really happened?' asked Julia softly.

I thought Abreu was not going to answer but then his shoulders started shaking. 'His friends were waiting for him. A Mercedes. Right in front of the office. He got into the car and they drove off.'

'What did his friends look like?'

'I don't know. One was a big man, that's all. He stood by the car. The driver I didn't see.'

'Would you recognise the big man if you saw him again?'

Abreu shook his head. 'He had dark hair. I didn't see his face.'

'What about the car. Would you recognise that?'

Abreu was happier with that. 'Mercedes 190. Grey. About three years old.'

'Thank you, Aloisio,' Julia said gently.

Abreu looked relieved.

'What about the luggage?' I demanded. 'What happened to that?'

He spun around again and his face fell. 'It is in my house, I will show you. There is nothing valuable.'

'You've opened it?'

'It was not locked. I thought perhaps his address was inside and I could return it to him.'

I said nothing. If Abreu had wanted to return the luggage he could have given it to his brother to return to Quinta Moran. It was obvious he had not told Tiago what had happened. I wondered how long he was planning to keep the case before he decided Montacute was not going to reappear to claim his lost baggage.

'Let's go and see it now,' said Julia.

For a moment it looked as if Abreu was going to argue but then he turned the car around and headed north towards Monte.

'Do you do much work for Senhor Mallow?' I asked.

'No. This was the first time my brother had called me since Senhora Mallow left. Tiago usually does all the driving.'

'Does Tiago enjoy working there?'

Abreu looked surprised. 'Of course. Senhor Mallow is an important man.'

The houses became smaller and poorer as we headed upwards. Eventually Abreu pulled into the side of the road. 'I will fetch the case.' He disappeared into a house that looked as though it could tumble down the hillside at any moment and returned with a single leather suitcase. A woman's face peered anxiously from the doorway.

'Is this all?' I asked.

'Yes. He had a smaller case that he carried with him. He needed that for the Civil Registry.'

'How do you know that?'

'He told me. He checked something, a document of some sort, when we arrived in Santa Cruz. Then he put it back in the case. "I mustn't lose this," he said.'

We got back into the taxi and I put the suitcase on the seat beside me. We could look inside when we were back at the hotel. Nobody spoke on the way back.

'What now?' Abreu asked when we reached the hotel. 'Will you tell the police?'

'Not unless we have to. And don't you say anything either. Not to your brother. Not to the man he works for.'

I carried the case up to our room and put it on the bed. As

Abreu had said, Montacute's case was unlocked. We slowly emptied the contents, Julia carefully arranging them on the bed. It felt as though we were intruding. Roger Montacute's life sat displayed before us. There was nothing at all suspicious. We learned that he packed neatly, wore expensive clothes until they were well past the point most people would have considered acceptable, and was fastidiously clean judging by the amount of soap and toothpaste he carried with him, although as Julia pointed out, there was no sign of aftershave or deodorant. There were no papers in the case but in a zipped pocket on the outside we found a single piece of paper torn from a notepad. On it was handwritten an address in Santa Cruz: 37 Rua Santa Bernardina.

'At last a clue,' said Julia. 'Let me ask my friendly concierge for a map.'

She returned five minutes later, a puzzled expression on her face. 'There is no Rua Santa Bernardina in Santa Cruz. In fact there is no Rua Santa Bernardina in the whole of Madeira. What's more, according to the concierge, there has never been a saint called Bernardina, so there won't be a street called after her anywhere.'

What we had thought might help us find Montacute had turned out to be a dead end. But why would Montacute have written down a non-existent address?

'What do you make of it all?' I asked Julia. She took a moment to answer.

'The key question is, did Montacute go willingly? If he really met a friend it's possible they went off somewhere and he's now sitting by the sea sipping a whisky and wondering what all the fuss is about.'

'That doesn't seem likely.'

'No it doesn't, so we have to assume Montacute was taken unwillingly, in which case, to put it baldly, he's probably dead.'

It was not a pleasant conclusion but I had to agree. 'Why would he leave his case behind in the taxi if he was going off with friends? He obviously didn't even contact Abreu later to try to retrieve it.'

'And he didn't cancel the flight back.'

We were both silent for a minute.

'If he's been kidnapped the question is, who by?' I said. 'Is it something to do with all that buried treasure stuff? Did he discover something in Morocco? Why did Hachim Zineb threaten him when he was there, and if it was something to do with Hachim's father, Mourad, was Montacute killed when he tried to follow Mourad from Lanzarote to Madeira?'

'But Mourad is dead,' Julia reminded me. 'It can't be anything to do with him. Montacute must have stumbled into something here, at the Quinta Moran possibly. Something to do with Mallow and Ffortiscue and that meeting your Russian friend witnessed.'

That seemed even less likely than Hachim Zineb following Montacute all the way from Morocco. 'I think we can rule out any connection with what you call my Russian friend.'

We had an early dinner before returning to our room and then it was time for me to set off for Sao Roque do Faial. Just as I was preparing to go there was a knock on the door.

'Who is it?'

'Service.'

I walked across the room and opened the door. Outside stood Vasily Kornelyuk, now known as Basil Rosen.

XX

'We should not be meeting in public,' said Rosen as he pushed into the room, closing the door behind him. 'This is your wife,' he added, looking across at Julia.

'Yes. Julia, this is Mr Basil Rosen.'

Rosen held out his hand. 'You wished to hire me? Ten thousand dollars for one address.'

As I had tried to explain that morning the address of the man Roger Montacute had come to Madeira to find was now academic as Mourad Zineb himself was dead, but I had made a deal with Rosen that I would honour. Julia was thinking along the same lines.

'I presume you've found something,' she said, 'although now Zineb is dead I'm not sure what I will do with your information.'

Rosen looked her in the face. 'I do not understand. Mourad Zineb is not dead.'

'Mourad Zineb died last year—' Julia started to explain.

'No, he didn't,' interrupted Rosen bluntly.

I wondered why Rosen was so adamant. Patrick Mallow had given Roger Montacute a copy of Zineb's death certificate. I said nothing.

'Mourad Zineb lives in Porto Moniz,' Rosen continued. 'He has a house there. And I believe a boat. I have seen him.'

He stopped and waited for us to respond but for a moment neither of us knew what to say.

'Are you sure?' Julia asked.

Rosen looked at me. 'Has my information ever been wrong?'

I was conscious we were all standing staring at each other. 'Let's sit down,' I suggested. I motioned Rosen and Julia towards the two easy chairs while I pushed Montacute's belongings to one side and sat down on the bed.

'Tell us what you've found.'

'Porto Moniz is a fishing village right up in the north-west of the island. That is where you will find Mourad Zineb.'

I was still sceptical. I remembered Mallow telling us how difficult it would be for Montacute to track Zineb down in Madeira. 'You managed to find him in just twenty-four hours?'

'I found him in less than twenty-four minutes. Foreigners need a permit to move here, what the Portuguese call an authorisation of residency. I have one. It must be renewed regularly, so I know the functionaries. You never know when you might need new documents. It was not difficult for me to obtain your friend's details.'

'But you say you've actually seen him?' Julia queried.

'I believe so. I was curious. Why do the British want to know about this man but they fear to simply ask the Portuguese authorities. I am a suspicious man—'

'And,' I interrupted, 'you thought you might be able to discover something we would pay more for.'

'You too are a suspicious man Mr Dylan. I am suspicious by necessity. You, however, are suspicious by profession. But you are right. I thought there must be some connection between this man Zineb and the conversation I overheard at Reid's Hotel. Perhaps Zineb is one of the men I saw.'

He turned back to Julia. 'Your husband tells me that this is not the case. But your husband's occupation is based on deception. Truth in his world is to be bartered, not donated. Then he tried to tell me this morning that Zineb is, as you say, no longer with us. In what sense is he no longer with us? Is the man in Porto Moniz a ghost? Did a dead man renew his authorisation of residency only a few weeks ago? So I decided to go to Porto Moniz myself. I have been there before.'

Rosen was in a philosophical mood. He spoke as if we had all the time in the world. I wondered if he had been at the vodka.

'We all move on one day. I will move on. Mourad Zineb must move on. Porto Moniz must move on, what we call progress comes to us all. Today Porto Moniz is a simple fishing village but the tourists are already arriving, when the motorways come it will never be the same again. Old traditions, old values will disappear and the world will be poorer.'

He paused as if expecting us to respond. Neither of us did. 'If you go there look upwards. Above the harbour the cliff rises into the sky, and high up, perhaps 200 metres, you can see a single wooden shack. That was once the most important structure in Porto Moniz, that was where a man would sit for days just staring at the sea, waiting. Can you imagine that? Waiting for a sign, a fountain rising briefly in the ocean, a signal that he would relay to those below who would launch their boats and rush out to hunt the whales that provided their livelihood. That hut is not used today because whale hunting has been banned. That too was progress and people were worried that it meant the old values and old traditions would disappear and the world would be poorer.'

'And you disagree?' Julia commented.

'You miss the point. You didn't let me finish. Whaling wasn't some ancient tradition. Whaling came to Madeira in the Second World War when the demand for whale oil took off. Whaling here lasted only forty years. Progress came and then went again. Nothing is constant. None of us can stay as we were. The world evolves. I move on, you move on. Mourad Zineb moves on. But for how long?'

Julia was beginning to see that, as I had already discovered, Rosen's mind followed its own path. We might know where his body had taken him but where his mind travelled I had no more idea now than when I first met him. I wanted to get back to the point and Rosen seemed to realise that.

'Zineb's house proved very easy to find,' he said. 'This is not a man in hiding. His home is below that cliff I mentioned, before you come into Porto Moniz, on the hillside above the road. It is a pleasant house, not big but comfortable. Not a peasant's house. Grey stone walls. Two stories. The land between the cliff and the road at that point is wider, and it is flat. It is possible to grow vegetables. A chair by the door, one of those chairs that rocks. He can sit there and look out to sea or east across the harbour to the Fort of John the Baptist. There was no sign of life when I drove past. Across the road is another grey stone building, backing onto the sea. It has been there for a very long time, the roof is in need of repair. It has plain wooden doors. There seem to be no windows. It could be a boat shed but I didn't see a door big enough to admit even a small fishing boat.'

'You didn't stop?'

'No. I am not being paid to take risks. As I said, I drove past. I parked near the fort. As I did so a man came ashore, an old man with a lined face. I paid no attention to him. I know the harbour, it is just like every other tiny harbour on the north coast. A few small fishing boats. The old man had come from an old motor boat which looked as if it belonged there, anchored at the bow and with two long ropes at the stern tied to the harbour wall. The boat, I should say, was at least twenty years old. It had once been white but its hull was now almost grey and the metal rails and wooden cabin needed painting. Only the radar mast looked modern. The engine I don't know, but it might get you to Tenerife or even Morocco. There was nothing else unusual.

'As I was leaving, I noticed that the old man I had seen earlier had walked around the harbour and was approaching Zineb's house. He went inside and when I drove past a few minutes later there was a light on at the back of the house.'

'Would you recognise him again?'

'I doubt it. He was just a peasant, or a fisherman perhaps. Nothing special. He did not stoop. He is an active man. It was not the man I saw with the Russians.'

There was a silence while we mulled over what Rosen had told us. The most likely explanation was that Zineb had died the previous year and his home in Porto Moniz had then been passed to someone else, the man Rosen had just described. But when I put that to him Rosen was adamant.

'That is not possible. Zineb's residency permit had just been renewed. He is not dead. The details he gave for the residency authorisation listed his date of birth. 1917. The man I saw was the right age, he is the man you asked me to find, Mourad Zineb.' As far as Rosen was concerned the matter was closed. 'Now you owe me $10,000.' He stood up. 'You have cash?'

Julia shook her head.

'I'll have the money transferred, as we did before,' I said, but now Rosen shook his head.

'That account is closed. I know a man at the casino who will accept your credit card. Shall we go?'

There really was no more to be said. Rosen wrote down Zineb's address, although he assured us it was unnecessary, we couldn't miss the house.

Julia and I prepared to walk the short distance from the hotel to the casino.

'The boat you mentioned,' said Julia. 'The one in the harbour. Did it have a name?'

'Yes. On the stern was a brown wooden plaque, very faded. But the name was clear, it had been painted recently. *Atiradora*, Funchal.'

I said nothing but I was suddenly certain I had seen that boat just the evening before. Not *Dora*, not *Adora*, but *Atiradora*. I had sat in a derelict building for hours waiting for it to arrive.

And I knew something else. Rosen had indeed found Mourad Zineb. The boat's name itself gave him away. *Atiradora*, the feminine of *atirador*, Portuguese for shooter or rifleman. In Spanish *tirador*. The boat, I was sure, had been named after the Tiradores de Ifni, the troops Montacute claimed had killed Juan Manuel Casares and his men, and stolen their gold.

Surely that wasn't what Dreyton was waiting for last night: Spanish gold?

XXI

I arrived at Sao Roque do Faial a few minutes before ten. Dreyton and his two minders were already there, Dreyton standing just away from his car puffing on a cigarette.

I approached him. There were no words of greeting. 'The mission is at a critical stage,' he announced.

'Are you going to tell me what the mission is about?' I asked.

'In due course. Need to know has always been my guiding principle.' He produced a weak smile that merely persuaded me that he lacked the intellectual subtlety to distinguish aphorism from platitude.

As he spoke, a black, four-wheel-drive Nissan Patrol drew up on the other side of the square. Dreyton walked towards it, his hands clasped behind his back in that curious walk of his. John followed. When I moved to do the same Barry whispered, 'I think Mr Dreyton wants you to stay here.'

I ignored him.

Two men emerged from the back seat of the Nissan, one wearing a suit, the other black military fatigues with no insignia. Dreyton and John obviously knew them. The men shook hands and, as I approached, they turned towards me.

'Mr Dylan is a new member of my team,' said Dreyton without bothering to introduce the men to me. I suspect his instinct was to send me back to wait with Barry but was afraid that would appear unprofessional.

The two men could have been from any one of the various Portuguese police and Intelligence agencies although the younger one had a distinctly military bearing with the same self-conscious masculinity as John and Barry. The AP prefix on their vehicle's number plate was used only by the Portuguese Navy.

The younger man spoke perfect English. 'My men are in place as agreed, beside the road and at the wharf. We also have men offshore in case the target comes by boat.'

'I don't think that's likely,' Dreyton responded. 'We all know our positions. Let's go.'

We moved into what was clearly a well-rehearsed plan. John removed what looked like an American 'third generation' night vision device from the boot of the Mercedes and joined the two Portuguese in the Nissan.

'Follow us,' Dreyton barked in my direction as he returned to his car. We moved off in convoy with my Opel bringing up the rear. When we reached the lane down to the wharf the Nissan headed that way but the Mercedes followed the main road eastwards; I saw Dreyton twisting his head to make sure I was following. After a few minutes Barry turned left onto another lane leading towards the sea and shortly after pulled up beside a low stone wall.

We got out and I realised we were near the edge of almost vertical cliffs. Way below were the quay and warehouse I had observed the previous evening.

Barry removed another night vision scope and two radio handsets. He gave one of the radios to Dreyton and then disappeared into the gloom leaving Dreyton and me alone.

'Now we wait,' Dreyton announced.

'For what?'

'Patience Mr Dylan. All in good time.'

He fiddled with the radio. 'Gold Commander to Unit One,' he intoned.

John's voice responded immediately. 'Unit One in position.'

'Any news on our target?'

There was the sound of a muttered conversation in Portuguese before John replied. 'Target is behind schedule but is under surveillance now, he's approaching Machico.'

Dreyton clicked off.

'So I'm not going to be told anything until this is all over.'

'As I've said before, you don't need to know. Elementary tradecraft.'

'Elementary tradecraft dictates that team members are fully briefed.'

Dreyton smiled. 'But are you on my team Mr Dylan? Aren't you perhaps still on the team of our former colleague Justin Brasenose? Why, I wonder, is he so keen to have you here on the island? I can only imagine it is because he wants you to report back on this mission and I am making every effort to ensure that you are able to do just that. Tomorrow morning you may report back on everything you have seen.'

'But not on what it's all about or what arrived here by boat last night.'

'Justin will quite rightly expect you to be scrupulously accurate in your report. Give him your observations unclouded by conjecture, whether yours or mine.'

'So I'm going to see someone tonight, you know who it is, but I won't be able to tell anyone who I've seen.'

'Whom you've seen,' Dreyton replied pedantically and turned away.

Was he serious? He reminded me of a strait-laced teacher at my school in Cornwall. There had been a pop song at the time with the French refrain: *'voulez-vous coucher avec moi ce soir?'* Mr Simmonds wanted the song banned not, he insisted, because of its apparent immorality, but because of the grammar: that degree of familiarity required the use of *veux-tu* rather than *voulez-vous*.

But Dreyton wasn't trying to be pedantic. He was trying to deflect what he clearly considered impertinent questions. I wasn't taking that. He might be a big wheel in Century House but he wasn't going to roll over me. I had heard something in that snatch of Portuguese on the radio that changed everything.

I hadn't been able to make out all of the background conversation, but it was enough. Dreyton had been asking John, in English, about the target and someone had repeated his question in Portuguese but using a different term for target: 'o irlandês', the Irishman. The Irishman, another voice had said, was now near Machico.

In itself, reference to an Irishman told me nothing, but an Irish connection in those days usually meant only one thing: terrorism. Almost certainly Republican. And if that assumption was correct the IRA would not be sending someone here to search for Spanish gold or smuggled booze. This was about weapons and I could think of one weapon in particular.

Another thought struck me. If the Irishman was on his way here and was now near Machico he was probably coming from the airport, not Funchal. It was time to rattle Dreyton's cage.

'Well, let me tell you what I think is happening. Last

night something was offloaded from a ship somewhere offshore and brought into the quay just below us. My guess is that something was a Russian surface-to-air missile. That missile is for sale and an hour or so ago a potential purchaser arrived on the island by plane and is now on his way here.'

'Really? And who do you think is doing the selling and more importantly the buying?'

'I don't know who is doing the selling but I do know who is buying. And it's not Polisario guerillas in Morocco. As you and I both know very well it's the IRA.'

Dreyton didn't respond right away. I was hoping I had stung him into saying something that would confirm my guess, but that wasn't going to work.

When Dreyton did respond his voice was coldly unemotional. 'I don't know what you and Brasenose are up to but you're playing a dangerous game Dylan. To be effective the Service expects loyalty. It demands loyalty. You need to think about that. If you have information that would help my mission, whether from Justin Brasenose or from your enquiries here in Madeira, your duty is to pass it on. Making up stories about Portuguese policemen overhearing conversations in restaurants is not helpful. I shall be speaking to your Desk Officer about that.'

So Neil White was wrong, Dreyton had bothered to check the cover story I had hastily invented to hide the role of Basil Rosen.

Dreyton was not being totally unreasonable. I was withholding information from him, and I wasn't really sure why. If Basil Rosen had seen the same boat in Porto Moniz that I had seen the night before then I should tell Dreyton all about it. And that meant telling him all about Mourad

Zineb and why Julia was looking for him. But I wasn't in the mood to tell the little git anything. In any case he probably knew far more about Zineb than I did. He knew enough to have been waiting for him last night.

That made me realise something else. Zineb's boat, the *Atiradora*, had not been under surveillance. Dreyton had made no attempt to follow it when it left. Of course it would have been difficult to follow a boat at sea, but Dreyton had the means. Another word I had heard on the radio was *fuzileiro*. The Corpo de Fuzileiros are the Portuguese marines. That's who the men we had met tonight were, the men who were now keeping the quay under observation and who had told us they had a patrol at sea in case anyone approached that way. Why hadn't Dreyton had them here the night before?

'You haven't told the Portuguese how the missile got there, have you?' I asked. 'You let them think that we had been keeping track on a terrorist target and that he's heading here. And then today you tell them you've just discovered he's planning to collect surface-to-air missiles from an abandoned warehouse on the coast. When our Irish visitor arrives at the warehouse the Portuguese will pounce. I bet you'll let them claim all the credit. No mention at all of us being involved. That way your source in the IRA is protected. And the only people who will know it is really your operation will be the mandarins in Whitehall who you are desperate to impress.'

Dreyton shook his head. 'I see Brasenose has you firmly trapped in his fantasy world. Not a world with much of a future.'

He turned back towards his car and opened the rear door. 'It's getting a little chilly I feel. Time for the spies to come in from the cold. I suggest you return to your vehicle, young man, and await developments.'

It was a long time since anybody had referred to me so condescendingly as 'young man' but there was no point in arguing with him. The first rule of office politics is that you never win a battle where you are fighting upwards. I did as I was told.

I was sure I was right about the IRA connection. Disrupting an operation like that would give Dreyton enormous kudos in London. If the stolen Russian missiles were in that warehouse, it did however make rather a mess of my theory about the Israelis being involved; there was surely no way they would be selling weapons to the IRA.

I sat in my hire car and tried to make myself comfortable. After an hour or so I took a leaf out of Dreyton's book and moved to the back seat. It didn't make much difference. The Opel was not designed for comfort, especially not for someone of my height. The night was dark and cold, with not a sound, not even an owl. At some stage I must have dozed off because I was suddenly aware of Barry standing by Dreyton's car. I looked at my watch. 6.25. Barry walked away again but forty minutes later he was back.

This time I got out. As I approached Barry turned towards me. 'We're off,' he muttered.

'What's happened?'

'Nothing.'

Dreyton emerged from his car and as he did so the black Nissan Patrol appeared. Dreyton strode towards it and I followed. John and the two men I had seen in Sao Roque do Faial clambered out. The younger was clearly a Marine officer, the older I still could not place.

'What happened?' asked Dreyton without any preamble.

'The target's going home,' replied John. 'He went back to the airport. Senhor Teixeira says he's checked in on the first flight to Lisbon.'

'But why?' demanded Dreyton. 'Why's he leaving without coming here?'

Nobody said anything. Dreyton answered his own question. 'He must have spotted the surveillance.'

'No,' replied the young Portuguese officer angrily. 'The surveillance was discreet. My men stayed well back from him. There was no need to get close, we thought we knew where he was going, that he was coming here.'

'But he shook your men off,' insisted Dreyton. 'He would only have done that if he realised you were there.'

'We don't know that he lost us deliberately. He left the route we expected. He didn't come here but he went somewhere. We will discover the place where he stayed the night. We have a description of the man who collected him from the airport, and we have the number of his car. We will find the owner. He will tell us what happened.'

'Perhaps,' Dreyton responded unenthusiastically. 'We must decide what to do now.'

The older man in the suit spoke for the first time. 'This is now a national matter.'

Dreyton looked surprised. I could see that at first he misunderstood the other man. It was obvious this was a matter for the national authorities, not just the authorities here in Madeira. But that's not what the man meant. National meant not international; Dreyton was being told that this was now a domestic matter. Dreyton would decide nothing. 'I believe I explained that in Brussels,' added the other cryptically.

It was clear that the two Portuguese had already decided what should happen next.

'My men will maintain observation here for another forty-eight hours,' explained the young marine, 'to see if anyone else comes to collect the missile.' That was the first time I had heard anyone confirm that the case we had seen arriving the previous night was indeed a SAM missile.

'You are welcome to join us. If nobody approaches the warehouse in that time we will seize the missile and take it to Alfeite.' Alfeite is the principal Portuguese naval base across the Tagus from Lisbon. 'The appropriate civil authorities will assume all other responsibilities on the island.'

His companion took over. 'The driver who collected your target from the airport will of course be interviewed. But I must tell you that unless we can link him to that warehouse there is little the police in this country can do. The driver has committed no crime here. And neither has the Irishman.'

'The driver should not be interviewed,' Dreyton insisted. 'That will warn him off. Place him under surveillance, at least for forty-eight hours.'

'We will consider that of course. It is a matter for the police. I will talk to them.'

'I'm sure they will do as you ask Senhor Teixeira.'

Senhor Teixeira did not reply. The marine officer saluted and the two men were driven away.

Dreyton was still fuming that his operation had gone wrong. 'What the hell happened to Byrne?' he demanded angrily. 'Why didn't he come straight here?'

John replied as I registered that I now had a name for the Potuguese civilian, Teixeira, and the Irishman, Byrne.

'It's obvious. Something happened between his landing

181

at the airport and the time he was supposed to arrive at the old warehouse. He wouldn't have flown down here if he wasn't planning to inspect the weapon. Either the locals aren't as clever as they think they are, and he spotted the surveillance, or something else gave us away. He knew we were waiting for him. Something spooked him.'

'Something,' replied Dreyton, looking in my direction. 'Something or someone. You're going home Dylan. Today. I'll have a flight booked for you. Be in Century House first thing tomorrow.' Dreyton advanced towards me. 'And don't try to play the Brasenose card. That man has no authority inside the Service, however many Parliamentary Questions he can conjure up. You work for us and that means you work for me. Or you work for no one.'

XXII

After two nights of discomfort I was looking forward to some rest before the flight home. Dreyton had acted quickly: when I got there the hotel reception handed me a ticket for an early evening flight. But Julia had other ideas.

She greeted me with, 'Let's go to Porto Moniz and see if your mysterious Russian knows what he's talking about or has just conned us out of $10,000.'

The last thing I wanted to do was head off to Porto Moniz to find Mourad Zineb. I had driven across the mountains between Funchal and Madeira's north coast far too often recently. Whatever reason the missing Roger Montacute may have had for pursuing Zineb, half a century after the Spanish Civil War was over, it was definitely less important than the IRA trying to buy sophisticated weapons today. The sad truth was that Dr Montacute was almost certainly dead and finding out how and why he died was not my top priority. That wasn't why Dreyton wanted me back in London.

Julia was not happy when I told her I was being sent home. 'Well I shall stay here and we've still got this morning. I hope you've had some sleep. Although don't worry, I'll drive.'

'Why don't you go on your own?' I suggested. 'I'll grab a few hours kip here.'

'I don't speak the language,' Julia replied. 'If we find

Zineb we need to persuade him to talk to us. That will be difficult enough if he speaks English but we've no reason to think he does. Trying to communicate with an Arab who must be nearly eighty in pidgin Portuguese might be one thing you could do better than me. You can sleep in the car.'

There was no point arguing with Julia when she had made up her mind, especially when she was almost certainly right. I was going to Porto Moniz, although one thing I could be sure of is that I wouldn't be sleeping on the way there. The narrow winding road with precipitous valleys to one side was exactly the sort of route that Julia would relish. I was grateful we had left her sports car at home.

'I must phone London,' I insisted. 'You go and have breakfast.'

'I've had breakfast thank you. What do you need to tell London?'

I was too tired to explain everything to Julia when I knew I would have to repeat it all to Neil White and then to Justin Brasenose.

'Listen in,' I told her as I dialled my Desk Officer's direct line. 'It's all a bloody mess.'

When Neil answered I said the same to him. 'Dreyton has some sort of Irish sting going on. An Irish guy named Byrne flew in last night.'

'Would that be Conor Byrne?'

'It could be,' I conceded. Nobody had mentioned a first name. 'Who's he?'

'Conor Byrne is a Provisional IRA armourer. Dangerous man. And a careful one.'

'Well,' I continued, 'I spent the whole night with Dreyton and a detachment of Portuguese marines waiting for Byrne.

184

We were at the warehouse where I saw the case delivered the night before. Apparently the case contained a missile.'

'One of those stolen in Georgia?'

'I've no idea. Possibly. But in any case, Byrne didn't turn up. Nobody came. We don't know what Byrne was doing on the island and he flew off to Lisbon first thing this morning. Dreyton was really pissed off, God knows what he plans to do now. He's not telling me anything.'

'Well, I can tell you what he's doing right this minute,' said White. 'He's sitting on a plane somewhere between Funchal and London. I've just received a message from his secretary. He'll be back here this afternoon. I've been summoned to a council of war upstairs. Our Head of Station in Lisbon is being sent down to Funchal to take over.'

'Why's he doing that when I'm already on the spot?'

'You tell me. I gather Justin Brasenose at the Cabinet Office is making noises about the Service not following the right procedures. You seem to have been caught in the crossfire between Dreyton and Brasenose.'

'I certainly got that impression. Dreyton obviously thinks I'm Brasenose's spy, which is nonsense. I've hardly seen Brasenose since he left Century House.'

'Perhaps,' responded White noncommittally. 'But Brasenose pulled rank to get you sent down to Madeira. Dreyton wouldn't have liked that. A word of advice: if you have to choose sides remember Dreyton is today's man, he's inside the Service pissing out, Brasenose is outside now, trying to piss back in. Dreyton isn't the forgiving sort. He's an apparatchik, a bureaucrat who's spent his career oiling the wheels. A lot of people upstairs owe him: thanks to him people have been promoted, budgets approved and expenses and subventions authorised. Whatever Dreyton's been doing in Madeira, the rest of the top brass will know and they'll back him. In the old phrase: Dreyton is instrumental, Brasenose is merely ornamental.' It was an expression I had heard before.

On that note White phoned off and I called Brasenose. For once I was put straight through. I repeated the story of last night's events. Brasenose made no comment.

'What do you think is going on?' I asked.

'I don't know. Dreyton is running an operation in the field that hasn't been sanctioned by the Joint Intelligence Committee. Which he's entitled to do of course, in the right circumstances, but it's unusual. He warns off our navy but is working with the Portuguese. The man you mentioned, Teixeira, is senior, SIS.'

By SIS Brasenose didn't mean he was working for us, the Secret Intelligence Service. He meant Teixeira was an officer of the Portuguese equivalent of MI5, the Serviço de Informações de Segurança.

'Dreyton needs his wings clipping,' Brasenose concluded and ended the call.

'Come on, let's go,' said Julia. 'We're here to find the ghost of Roger Montacute, not some Irish version of the Flying Dutchman.'

I started to argue but Julia was right, there was nothing more I could do about Dreyton. And, I reminded myself, if the boat I had seen had been the *Atiradora*, owned by Mourad Zineb, we suddenly had a direct link between Dr Montacute and whatever Dreyton was up to on the island.

When I explained that to Julia she reminded me that we already had a tenuous link between Dreyton and Roger

186

Montacute: George Ffortiscue. Brasenose seemed sure that Dreyton was plotting something with Ffortiscue, and we had good reason to believe Ffortiscue was staying with Montacute's cousin Patrick Mallow when Basil Rosen spotted him having dinner with Russians selling needles.

On the way north Julia started asking herself the same questions I had been asking myself, and she came to the same conclusion.

'Why is Dreyton here?' she asked. 'You told me he was here to investigate whether Ffortiscue had been trying to sell needle missiles. If that's true then he must be the greatest investigator since Sherlock Holmes. Within hours of getting here he discovers that at least one of the missiles is about to be landed at an abandoned warehouse on the island and that a known IRA man is flying down to collect it. That's just not possible. Dreyton must have known about that warehouse before he got here; he was expecting that boat to turn up and leave a missile in the warehouse. What's more, he knew that last night Conor Byrne was going to arrive in Madeira to collect it.'

I agreed. 'And he had a detachment of Portuguese marines available to grab Byrne when he turned up. That can't have been arranged at the drop of a hat.'

'And you know what else is odd about that?' Julia continued. 'The marines weren't there the previous night. Why not? If Dreyton knew a boat was going to land weapons on that quay why didn't he arrange for Portuguese surveillance then? You said the marines had a boat offshore last night when they were expecting Byrne to arrive by road, why not the night before when it would have made more sense?'

We drove on in silence, lost in our own thoughts. Julia was in an odd mood. She wanted to focus on Roger Montacute but my mission with Dreyton kept impinging, causing her mind to shoot off in the strangest of tangents.

'What is the collective noun for needles,' she mused.

'What do you mean?'

'Well, the older missiles were arrows so we could talk about a quiver of arrows. How do we describe a collection of needles?'

'A pincushion,' I suggested absentmindedly.

Julia wasn't convinced. 'Haystack might be more appropriate.'

Later I discovered Dreyton had had the same thought.

It wasn't until we reached Serra de Água, where we had stopped for *poncha* after our visit to Quinta Moran, that I spoke again.

'You know, there's a fundamental question we haven't asked about all this. Why here? Why Madeira? Nothing happens here. It's not en route to anywhere. Nobody would come to Madeira to buy or sell guns. The island's miles away from everywhere.'

'Except Morocco,' Julia said.

'But even Dreyton doesn't believe his old theory about the missiles going to the Polisario guerillas in the Sahara. Now he's decided they're going to the IRA. But we come back to the same question: why would Russians selling weapons to an Irish terrorist choose to do it here? How did Byrne expect to get the needle back to Ireland? He could hardly take it on the plane and it's a hell of a long way by sea. If we're really talking about selling one of those missiles stolen in Georgia, there are a lot of places in Europe or the

Mediterranean that would have been much more convenient for both buyers and sellers.'

'And why only one launcher and one missile?' Julia asked. 'What happened to the other twenty-nine missiles and their launchers?'

'The Israelis hung on to them,' I suggested. 'Perhaps they've discovered they can make money by selling them one at a time.'

Julia shook her head dismissively. I wasn't yet willing to discard my theory that it was the Israelis who had attacked me in Turkey, but I had to admit that the thought of an organisation as professional as the Israeli Mossad getting involved in small-time arms trading seemed thoroughly improbable.

The more I thought about it the only person that Madeira suited was Dreyton. 'If he really is running some private but semi-official operation this place is perfect,' I concluded. 'He's not stepping on anybody's toes. Nobody in Century House will have any interest in an operation here, he didn't even need to pass it by the Joint Intelligence Committee.'

Again Julia just nodded noncommittally. 'Perhaps.'

The final ten-kilometre stretch, winding along the coast from Seixal to Porto Moniz, was spectacular, the sea on the right and vertical green mountains on the left. The first we saw of Porto Moniz was the house Rosen had told us was Mourad Zineb's. A two-storey grey stone building that looked as if it had been there for centuries. It nestled below the cliffs on a rare parcel of flat land that also provided space for a vegetable patch, just as Rosen had said. On the other side of the road a windowless structure in the same weathered stone stood almost in the sea, again just as Rosen had described.

Julia had been looking out for the house and slowed down as we reached it, but the only place to park off the road was already occupied by a black Peugeot 405.

'Let's look around the village and then walk back to the house,' I suggested.

We parked below the fort not far from the small harbour. There was very little sign of any activity. A brightly coloured fishing boat was tied up at the quay. It was empty. But a little further out was a boat that was far more interesting. I recognised it instantly even though it had been dark when I saw it previously. I had no doubt that the *Atiradora* had delivered the missile to the abandoned warehouse two days before, although I could see now that it was not the sleek cabin cruiser it had seemed to be. The silhouette was as I remembered but the boat was probably twenty or thirty years old and the only recent paint was the name itself on the stern.

There was movement inside the cabin. As we watched an old man appeared on the deck. He glanced over at us and seemed to be trying to decide what to do. Then he clambered into a small rowing boat with surprising agility and pulled energetically towards stone steps at the other end of the quay.

'Time for a chat,' I said to Julia.

We reached the top of the steps at the same time as the man who had just rowed ashore. He was a tall man, not bowed with age, but I would guess well over seventy. Almost black eyes were sunk deep into leathery skin, tufts of grey hair escaped from below a denim cap. His clothes and boots were well worn and workmanlike with the exception of an incongruous Paul & Shark yachting sweater worn beneath an old jacket that had seen better days.

'Senhor Zineb?' I said, blocking his way. 'We would like to talk to you about Roger Montacute.'

The man said nothing, pushing past me and coming face to face with Julia.

'Just five minutes,' she said in English, but he gave no indication of understanding.

'Is there a problem Mourad?' asked a voice behind us, this time in Spanish.

We turned to find a broad-shouldered man in a narrow-shouldered suit staring at us. Zineb started to reply but the newcomer put one hand on the older man's arm and guided him away. When Julia started to follow the stranger turned and blocked her way. Despite being a couple of inches shorter than her the man conveyed an almost theatrical sense of menace.

There was a momentary stand-off then the man turned back to Zineb. '*Váyase ahoritica mismo,*' he murmured.

Julia again started to follow but I stopped her. 'We won't learn anything from them.'

'But that was Mourad Zineb. He's alive. We must find out what he knows about Roger Montacute's disappearance.'

'There's no way those two will tell us anything. You can see that. We have no authority here, we need to get the police to act.'

As we walked back to the car I had another thought. 'The interesting question now is why did Montacute think Zineb was dead? Who gave him that death certificate?'

'Patrick Mallow.'

'Quite. And that death certificate was fake.'

'Because Zineb is not dead.'

'Exactly. And more than that I bet it had a fake address

for Zineb on it. That non-existent address we found in Montacute's case. Montacute was obsessive. He would have wanted to check where Zineb lived. When he found the address didn't exist his next step would have been to take the certificate back to the Civil Registry Office. But he made the mistake of telling someone that that's what he was going to do, presumably Mallow, who in turn told whoever had given him the forged certificate.'

'And they grabbed Montacute when Aloisio Abreu's taxi dropped him at the office in Santa Cruz.'

I nodded. 'Next stop Quinta Moran.'

Earlier I would have been happy to stay at the hotel in Funchal and catch up on my sleep but now I was energised again. We were getting somewhere. We drove back the way we had come, passing Zineb and his companion walking in the direction of Zineb's house. 'Stop here a moment,' I said as we reached the house.

We hadn't seen any other traffic since reaching Porto Moniz and Julia pulled up in the road alongside the Peugeot. We couldn't break into the house with Zineb only a minute or two away but I had hoped there might be windows on the front of the stone shed on the other side of the road. There weren't. Just heavy wooden doors and, high up beneath the eaves, slits that must have been the only way sunlight ever entered the building. The building was an old boat shed but there was no sign that it was still in use. There was no reason to hang around.

I heard a shout as I returned to the car; Zineb's friend was gesticulating as he ran towards us. It was obvious that running was something he didn't do very often. I waved in his direction and we drove off.

Only a minute or so later Julia told me to look behind. 'We're being followed.'

It would have been more accurate to say we were being chased. The black Peugeot was approaching rapidly. As it drew closer I could make out Zineb in the passenger seat and his stocky friend behind the wheel.

There was nothing that Julia loved more than driving at speed but there was no way our Opel Corsa was going to outpace the car behind us.

'Stop,' I said. 'This is our chance to talk to them, try to find out what's going on.'

'You think so?' Julia responded doubtfully.

The Peugeot was right behind us now. As it pulled alongside Julia suddenly slammed on the brakes. The Peugeot shot in front and then it too braked to a halt. The driver's door started to swing open but now it was Julia's turn to edge alongside, stopping the door opening fully. I wound my window down so that I could speak to the Peugeot's driver. But it was suddenly clear that this was not the time for talking.

'Go!' I shouted at Julia. 'He's got a gun.' She reacted instantly and we shot forward again.

The driver of the other car was startled and for a moment we left him behind.

The road corkscrewed its way along the coast, the sea on our left. One minute the waves seemed to lap the roadway, the next the shoreline disappearing behind the rocks. On the right-hand side cliffs rose precipitously above us, pierced by gullies and ravines. I couldn't remember any roads turning off on either side before Seixal.

The Peugeot was on our tail again. 'He's shooting at us,'

Julia exclaimed in disbelief. I looked back. She was right. The man behind was steering with one hand while in his left he waved a pistol. There was no way he could aim a gun like that but one lucky shot was all it might take. The road curved and we lost sight of our pursuer. When the Peugeot reappeared the driver had both hands on the wheel and the gap between us had narrowed.

Theoretically our Opel could reach 150 kmph. Julia pushed her foot right down but the engine produced more sound than speed. 'That bastard's firing bullets,' Julia snapped, 'and all we're likely to fire, if I push this much more, is piston rods. We have to do something. Wish we had rear-wheel drive, I could fishtail. Hang on.'

'What are you going to do?'

Julia didn't reply. She straddled the middle of the road and suddenly slammed on the brakes again. The Peugeot did the same, pulling to the left, but Julia's reactions were quicker and we were off again. We had gained perhaps a second or two. That would soon disappear.

We caught up with an ancient van emblazoned across the rear doors BARROSO IMPORTAÇÃO E COMERCIO DE FRUTA. The Peugeot dropped back.

'Perhaps we'll just have to follow this guy into Seixal,' I said.

'Unless he turns off somewhere,' Julia suggested.

Infuriatingly, even as she spoke the van slowed right down and the driver waved us to overtake him, smiling cheerfully to us as we did. The road curved again and the Peugeot was now stuck behind the van. It wouldn't be there for long.

Sure enough the Peugeot was soon on our tail again. 'We

have to do something,' Julia said. The road ahead curled back towards the sea. Julia hurtled towards the bend. 'Get ready to jump.'

As we reached the bend Julia jammed the car into second gear and somehow flicked on the headlights. Out of sight of the Peugeot she maintained the turn, slammed her foot on the clutch and grabbed the handbrake to lock the rear wheels. The car shuddered and skidded almost out of control. The Opel Corsa wasn't designed for trick driving but, as Julia clearly intended, we found ourselves facing back the way we had come with the car slewed across the road.

We jumped, flinging ourselves into the undergrowth at the foot of the cliff.

The Peugeot should have rounded the bend immediately after us, but it didn't.

'Where the hell is it?' In Julia's voice excitement was tinged with fear.

There was a moment's silence. Eventually we heard the other car approaching and I prepared for the sound of the crash as the Peugeot ploughed into our car. But the driver's reactions were quicker than I expected. Rounding the bend he had been confronted with a car apparently coming straight at him and had wrenched at the steering wheel, desperate to avoid a head-on collision. The Peugeot skidded off the road, the bonnet smashing into a jumble of rocks at the edge of the sea. Hitting the Opel might have been a safer option but I realised that the driver had acted exactly as Julia had hoped.

We rushed across the road to the wrecked Peugeot. The two men had swapped seats. Mourad Zineb had been driving, presumably so the gunman could concentrate on his shooting. Both men were alive if not well. Zineb was bracing himself against the steering wheel. The other man was barely conscious with blood seeping from a wound on his face that was probably from the shattered windscreen.

Julia pulled the driver's door open and started to help Zineb out. He didn't seem to know what was happening.

'Leave him,' I said. 'That van will be along in a minute. We mustn't get involved with the police.'

Julia nodded reluctantly and crossed back to our car. 'We're lucky our tyres survived,' was her only comment. She picked up something in the road and then slid into the driver's seat again. 'Put this in the glove box,' she suggested, passing me a Smith & Wesson Model 39 with a four-inch barrel. I balanced the gun in my hand. I would guess less than 800 grams due to its aluminium frame but still deadly. Why would somebody be carrying a weapon like that in an out of the way fishing village?

Julia was thinking along the same lines as she started the car and slowly turned away from Porto Moniz again. 'Who is that man? Why did he start shooting? He was Spanish, wasn't he? Was he the man Basil Rosen says he saw with Ffortiscue and the Russians?'

'Vilafermosa? No, he's not at all like the photographs. You think he was Spanish because he spoke to Zineb in Spanish?'

Julia nodded.

'You may be right,' I agreed. But there was something odd about the gunman's Spanish. I'm no expert but Spanish is sufficiently close to my languages, Portuguese and Italian, for me to pick up on some of the nuances. I had visited Spain often and had never heard the phrase he'd used, *váyase ahoritica mismo.*

196

'I don't think a Spaniard would say *ahoritica*,' I told Julia. '*Ahora* means now, *ahoritica* must be the diminutive, little now or right now. If I'm correct I would guess that's a term only used on the other side of the Atlantic, in somewhere like Panama.'

XXIII

My priority was to call London. If Dreyton had still been on the island, I would have tried to phone him but White had told me Dreyton had already left. We found a place to phone from in Seixal.

White's secretary told me to phone back later as he was just going off to a meeting but I persuaded her this really couldn't wait.

'What is it?' White snapped.

I instinctively looked round to make sure nobody could overhear. 'Someone took some pot-shots at us. We located Mourad Zineb, the man Roger Montacute had been trying to find, and a friend of his chased after us with a Smith & Wesson in his hand blasting away.'

White was obviously shocked, although not half as shocked as I still felt. The exhilaration I had felt when the Peugeot crashed off the road had been replaced by the sober realisation of what could have been. 'Are you OK?'

'Yes. They crashed their car into a rock. We got away.'

'Are the local police involved?'

'Not yet.'

'Good. Get out of there. We don't need that sort of excitement at the moment, both of you. See if you can get an earlier flight. We need to discuss this calmly. I really must rush now. I've been called upstairs. Stay in touch. Phone me when you land and come in here first thing tomorrow.'

'Dreyton's already told me that.'

He called off and I phoned Brasenose. He was out of the office. I didn't feel like leaving a message.

'Come on,' I said to Julia. 'We've got to get back to the hotel, pack our bags and make sure we can book a seat for you on the flight home.'

Julia gave me the look she gives Eveline when our daughter puts on an exaggerated smile and then deliberately does something we've just told her not to do.

'I'm not going home. We haven't found out what happened to Roger Montacute yet. The answer is with Patrick Mallow. I need to see him. I'll drop you at the airport.'

I was appalled. 'You can't stay here. We've no idea who that man was back in Porto Moniz. He wasn't just trying to scare us off. He wanted to kill us. And you heard what Neil White said, we both need to get off the island.'

'I don't care what Neil White said, I don't work for him. I'm employed by Lady Montacute and I'm going to do what I told her I would do.'

'That's ridiculous. If they tried to kill us once they could try again.'

'Well they won't catch me a second time. If you'd hired a car with a bit of oomph they wouldn't have caught us last time. I'm going to see Mallow. You can come with me or I'll drop you off where you can get a taxi to the airport.'

I glanced at my watch. With no luggage to check in we should be able to get to Quinta Moran, talk to Mallow and still be at the airport with time to spare. Perhaps then I could persuade Julia to come back to London with me. What we wouldn't be able to do was to pick up our stuff from the hotel in Funchal but we could sort that out from London.

'Let's go,' I conceded reluctantly. 'Mallow better be there.'

He wasn't.

We had driven east along the coast to Sao Vicente and then inland until we found the carriageway leading to Mallow's house. The ornate iron gate was closed, as it had been when Tiago Abreu had brought us here before. The gate wasn't locked. I pushed it open and Julia drove through. After closing the gate again we drove along the hillside and soon arrived at the familiar pink house with its grey-painted shutters. There were no signs of life.

The Opel looked even smaller parked at the foot of the imposing front steps. The heavy wooden door was firmly shut and Julia jerked impatiently at the ancient bell pull set into the wall. The bell echoed inside but nobody came. I pushed at the door; it was locked. Julia tried the bell again. Still no response.

'Let's look around the back.'

Quinta Moran was almost perfectly square and we went the whole way round peering through windows on the sides and the balcony area at the rear. There was clearly nobody at home. Next we tried the newer single-storey pink building where Abreu had parked the car. Again, there was no sign of life. The garage itself was closed with a metal shutter and it was impossible to see if there was a car inside.

'The bird has flown,' I said.

'Then we'll wait.'

'What for? The maid's not here. The driver's not here. It's obvious Mallow is away. Perhaps he's gone to see his wife in Lisbon.'

'The shutters would all have been closed in that case,'

insisted Julia. 'Let's give it half an hour and see if someone turns up. We've still got time to get you to the airport.'

'Remember we have to get you a ticket.'

'No we don't. If Mallow doesn't appear soon, I'm staying in Madeira. There's more to find out about Mourad Zineb. And that Peugeot was a hire car, there was a sticker in the rear window. I must be able to get a name for the man who shot at us.'

'And then what will you do? You can't go after him on your own.'

'I'll think of something.'

'No. I can't let you.'

Julia turned to look directly at me. 'It's not up to you to let me do or not do anything, I let myself. And I'm staying here.'

'If you stay, I stay.'

'Don't be ridiculous. Dreyton gave you a direct order. Your job could be on the line. I won't do anything stupid. Phone me when you get home.'

I could have argued but there was no point, she was wrong but she was not going to give way. We stood in silence in the shade of a row of jacaranda trees. After twenty minutes Julia suddenly walked to the car. 'Let's go.'

We drove back towards the main road, closing the iron gate behind us. Neither of us spoke. As we turned south, towards Funchal, a police car came from that direction and turned onto the driveway leading to Quinta Moran. From the back seat a man stared quizzically in our direction. We recognised each other; we had both spent the previous night waiting for an Irishman who hadn't turned up. It was Teixeira, the Portuguese Intelligence officer who had brusquely informed Dreyton that from now on the presence of surface-to-air missiles on the island was a matter for the Portuguese to investigate. What was he investigating at Quinta Moran?

XXIV

I had a brief stopover at Lisbon's Portela airport and tried to phone Julia at the hotel but there was no answer.

'What are you going to do now?' I had asked her before leaving Funchal.

'Well, the first priority is to get rid of this bloody car and get something that can overtake the average snail. Lady Constance owes me that.'

I tried one more time to persuade her to come with me. 'It's too dangerous here, Julia. You told Lady Constance that Exodis didn't do missing person stuff and now she will understand why. If you must stay here just tell the police what that taxi driver told us about seeing Montacute being taken away and then go and swim in the hotel pool.'

Julia raised her eyebrows quizzically and gave half a nod, which was her way of saying, 'Yes dear' when she meant, 'No dear.' My advice was recognised rather than welcomed and would certainly be ignored.

I planned to phone her again from Heathrow but to my surprise someone was waiting for me as I disembarked.

'This way,' said Justin Brasenose, bypassing the immigration area. 'I'll have your luggage collected.'

'I don't have any.'

He said nothing more until we were outside the terminal and seated in the back of his official car. As the driver pulled into the traffic Brasenose turned to me. 'What the hell happened? Who's been shooting at you this time?'

'How did you know about that?' I was surprised that White had told anyone outside the Service before I had been debriefed.

'Your wife phoned Lady Montacute and she naturally called me. Why didn't you tell me?'

'I tried. You weren't available.'

'Well I am now. What happened? Start from the beginning.'

I did exactly that. It clarified my own thoughts to go through the events again. Brasenose was a skilled interrogator, probing for detail without interrupting the flow of my narrative. The only thing I missed out was the encounter with Rosen. Brasenose didn't need to know about that. Fortunately, he simply accepted that we had been able to obtain Zineb's most recent address from the Civil Registry.

I had phoned Brasenose from Funchal and told him about the two nights staking out the deserted warehouse, but now he insisted on going through it all again. When I had finished he had only one further question.

'You didn't see the missile yourself?'

'No, but one of Dreyton's men was concealed inside when the *Atiradora* arrived. I'm sure he inspected the delivery before we left. What I don't understand is why Dreyton wanted me there.'

'Oh that's easy: he expected you to report back to me. He wanted everyone to see that he was running an operation in the field but he didn't want me to know enough to interfere. That's why he made sure you didn't actually see what was being delivered. But you can be sure his man would have taken

204

photographs. Expect them to be on display when we meet tomorrow. Your Service is due to have a new chief and Dreyton is determined it will be him, that's what this is all about.'

'And you're determined it will be you,' I replied.

'I'll pretend I didn't hear that. Tell me about Porto Moniz.'

'I'm sure Julia has already told you.' I didn't bother to keep the edge out of my voice. Brasenose had manoeuvred me into his private power struggle.

'Your wife did explain that you'd hired a ridiculously underpowered car and that she had managed to extricate you from the mess your penny pinching had created.'

'Julia phoned you just to tell you that?'

'I phoned your hotel after Lady Montacute called me.' His expression almost melted into a smile, not something that happened very often. Julia had clearly responded well to his call. My wife had a knack for dealing with men of a certain age whose regard for others had gone down as their regard for themselves had gone up. He didn't feel so warmly towards me. 'Come on. Let's hear your version. You were there on official Foreign Office business, we can't have diplomats being shot at.'

It was soon clear, however, that I had nothing to add to what he had learned from Julia. He quizzed me on three issues in particular. Was I sure that the boat I had seen at the warehouse was the *Atiradora*? Yes. Did the two men in Porto Moniz appear to be expecting us? No. Was I sure the use of the word *ahoritica* implied that the gunman was from Latin America? No, but Brasenose should be able to easily check.

'You shouldn't have left Julia there,' Brasenose concluded. 'It's not safe.'

'You think I'm not worried sick? You know Julia, she won't change her mind. I very nearly phoned Teixeira and told him everything, bugger the Official Secrets Act.'

'There might come a time when that's what one of us will have to do. In the meantime, I told her to stay in the hotel until you get back.'

'You think I will be going back?'

'Well, somebody will have to. I shall see to that. Dead or alive, Roger Montacute must be found. I have a duty to Lady Montacute and now I have a duty to you and your wife. And as you know I allow nothing to stop me from discharging my duties.'

That's true, I thought, nothing but ambition.

Before dropping me off Brasenose elaborated his earlier comment. 'Shooting at a member of the Foreign Office investigating the disappearance of a British citizen changes everything. This is now far too important to be left to your Service alone.'

I discovered what he meant when the phone rang just after seven that evening. I assumed it was Julia calling from Madeira. It wasn't.

'Change of plans,' announced a clearly unhappy Neil White. 'Your friend Brasenose has pulled rank again. We're now all meeting at nine sharp at the Foreign Office. Apparently a diplomatic representative being shot at makes this a JIC issue. Anything I should know?'

'No.'

'I hope not.'

With that parting shot my Desk Officer ended the call. I suspect his irritation merely mirrored that of Clive Dreyton who would have been outraged at being summoned to

Whitehall, even though our Service is nominally part of the Foreign and Commonwealth Office and he would therefore theoretically have home team advantage. While Brasenose would merely pop next door from the Cabinet Office to the Foreign Office, Dreyton would have to cross the river with all the social and psychological inferiorities that implied.

I hadn't been completely honest with Neil White; there were a couple of things he should know. But there was one Whitehall maxim I had learned: keep your powder dry. If there was going to be a bust-up with me caught in the middle it would be nice to have something unexpected to lob in.

After I had reached home the previous evening I had called Julia and this time she was at the hotel.

I assured her that my mother had confirmed that Eveline had of course been missing her parents and she had loved her friend Annabel's birthday party. With that out of the way I asked how she was getting on.

'Well, I've hired a new car, a Mercedes, from the same company. It was their sticker that was on the Peugeot. It seems our attacker is named Carlos Iván Moreno from Medellín, Colombia.'

'The hire company told you that?'

'Well, not right away. But when I told the charming young man that I had seen a wrecked Peugeot near Porto Moniz and that's why I wanted something more solid than the Corsa my husband had hired it all came out. The police had told him about the accident but he hadn't seen the car yet. And he hadn't seen the driver either, although the police reported he hadn't needed hospital.'

'Well done. You didn't tell Brasenose.'

'Of course I did. He'd never heard of him.'

It was typical of Brasenose that he hadn't mentioned the name to me, but the lines to Colombia would be humming now. Mention of Colombia usually meant one of two things: guerillas or drugs, or both.

'Is there anything you didn't tell him?' I asked Julia.

'Well I didn't mention Basil Rosen obviously, I knew you wanted to keep that secret. And there was another name that didn't come up, but perhaps I should have mentioned. Michael Sheehan.'

'Who's he?'

'It's a name Lady Constance produced. I think she was really shocked when I told her what had happened. Told me to come straight home, leave everything to my husband. Seemed a bit put out when I said you'd already flown home. I told her I had a few more enquiries to make on the island. She accepted that, in fact she accepted it right away. Whatever she might have said about me coming home she wants the hunt for her son to go on. She obviously called Justin Brasenose as soon as I had put the phone down.'

'And Michael Sheehan?'

'Oh yes. Just a bit odd. You remember Mallow had a friend, Michael Smith, staying with him when Roger Montacute pitched up at Quinta Moran? Mallow said the three of them, Montacute, Smith and himself, had been friends at university. I mentioned that to Lady Constance and she corrected me right away. Not Michael Smith, dear, she insisted, Michael Sheehan. They were inseparable at college. But Michael went to live in America a couple of years ago.' Julia paused before repeating her earlier remark. 'It just seems odd. Lady Constance insisted Roger didn't know anyone called Michael Smith. Mallow must have made the name up when we started asking questions.'

'But Mallow didn't mention the name. He mentioned a guest called Michael, an old Trinity College friend. It was the chauffeur, Abreu, who mentioned the name Smith. So Mallow wasn't just hiding his friend's identity from us, he was hiding it from everybody. Why? That's one question I will be asking tomorrow.'

***

I always feel a sense of reverence entering the magnificently ornate Foreign Office building, designed to epitomise the glory of empire. The glory was somewhat tattered at the moment. Workmen were struggling to restore the banqueting suites where the Locarno Treaties had been signed in 1925 but which had since been converted to offices.

Brasenose was already there when I arrived, no doubt to make sure that he took the chair at the top of the table. He was reading a message that had just been passed to him by a smartly dressed young man who now sat next to him, notepad at the ready. I chose a chair opposite the only other person in the room, Neil White. Dreyton arrived, without apologies, five minutes late, but his entrance was soon upstaged by the arrival of Bill Merryweather, the CIA's Deputy Station Chief. Dreyton and White had clearly not been warned that he would be attending but were too British to say anything.

'I invited Bill to sit in to take his mind off the situation in Panama. Seems to be getting really tense there. And of course because Bill might be able to help with our Colombian connection,' Brasenose began.

'What Colombian connection?!' Dreyton couldn't stop himself exclaiming.

'All in good time, Clive, we'll come to that.' Brasenose was clearly pleased to have landed the first blow. 'Let's just remind ourselves of the seriousness of what's happened. Dr Roger Montacute, a distinguished academic with rather distinguished connections in the Palace of Westminster, disappears in Madeira. At my request Thomas here is sent, as a representative of Her Majesty's Government, to assist the local authorities in their investigations. He manages to locate a potential witness but before he can speak to him is attacked by an armed assailant who, we must assume, had every intention of killing him. Despite what Hollywood might have us believe that in itself is sufficiently unusual, and indeed disturbing, to warrant the attention of the Joint Intelligence Committee. But here we come to a further complication.

'It would appear that, unbeknownst to my Committee, Century House is conducting an operation on Madeira at the very same time, codenamed Operation Haystack. Furthermore, despite my specific instructions that Thomas was to be on the island solely to assist in finding Dr Montacute he is brought into that operation, presumably due to a lack of other resource.'

I could sense Dreyton stiffen but there was nothing he could say. Neil White had told me I was in Madeira only to pursue Montacute's disappearance, an instruction he had delivered at Dreyton's own insistence.

'The question we therefore have to consider,' Brasenose continued, 'is why was Thomas attacked? Was it because of his search for Dr Montacute or could it have something to do with Operation Haystack? Shall we start there? Clive, perhaps you could illuminate us, what exactly is Operation Haystack? I only heard the name myself a few minutes ago when I was informed that an old friend wants to discuss Operation Haystack with me: Colonel Teixeira of the Portuguese Serviço de Informações de Segurança.'

Brasenose sat back, evidently pleased with himself, despite having just massacred the Portuguese language.

Dreyton didn't immediately respond. I thought for a moment he was going to repeat the 'need to know' mantra and say nothing more. This was clearly not how he had intended to reveal the success of his Operation Haystack to the world.

'You will understand,' he started, 'that certain operational details must remain confidential but the outlines are simple. I learned from a reliable source within the IRA that a terrorist attack on an aircraft of the Queen's Flight was being considered, the intention being to target Her Majesty herself. Naturally I was sceptical but my source claimed the IRA were close to acquiring a new Soviet surface-to-air missile from an unknown middleman. I immediately told him to make gaining further intelligence his top priority. He was able to report that funds were being collected to pay for this weapon in North America but the weapon would be handed over in Madeira.

'Handed over by whom?' demanded Brasenose.

'By the Israelis, of course. They've seen an opportunity to make some money and they've taken it. What do you expect?'

'That's nonsense,' Brasenose responded. 'That's not how they operate. The Israelis are utterly professional.' It seemed to me Brasenose was being deliberately provocative.

Dreyton was indignant. 'What do you mean, they don't work like that? Those people don't have any principles. They hate us. Arming Irish terrorists would be right up their street. God almighty, it's not long since a terrorist leader, Menachem Begin, was Israeli Prime Minister – the man who ordered the kidnapping, torture and murder of British soldiers and then booby trapped their bodies.'

'That was forty years ago,' Brasenose replied, his voice rising. 'We've all moved on. Don't you think there are things we did forty years ago that nobody's proud of today? Times change. If the Israelis have got those missiles they'll keep them for themselves. They could use them for some sort of false flag operation – plant them on some dead Palestinians and claim it's evidence that they were terrorists planning to bring down civilian airliners – it would scare the peaceniks at home and more importantly terrify the Americans.'

Dreyton wasn't going to be browbeaten. 'Don't you know what's happening in Washington? The Iran-Contra affair. The Israelis have been supplying arms to the Iranians, to the Iranians for God's sake.' He turned to Merryweather for support. 'You know all about that Bill, tell him. The Israelis will do anything.'

Not surprisingly, Merryweather was not going to be drawn into that can of worms. He had clearly decided to put a stop to things. 'Gentlemen, throwing insults at each other won't help. For what it's worth our Agency's view is that the missiles stolen in Georgia ended up in the hands of the Israelis. What happened to them then we have no idea but it certainly seems likely that at least one of them ended up in Madeira. Let's concentrate on how it might have got there. Mr Dreyton what do you think happened?'

212

Dreyton looked grateful for even this degree of support. 'We know that the Israelis had fifteen missile launchers and their missiles. They clearly had plans for them but somewhere along the line somebody decided to make some money on the side by selling one of them to the IRA. The missiles ended up on a ship heading out of the Mediterranean and south down the Moroccan coast. Maybe the Israelis were going to give them to the Polisario guerillas in southern Morocco. Maybe they were going to ship them all the way down to South Africa for the South Africans to use against the Cubans if they don't pull all their aircraft out of Angola. It doesn't matter. The point is we believed one was going to be offloaded in the Atlantic off Madeira. That's all we knew. That and the date and the place.'

Brasenose interrupted again. 'And how did you know the place and the date?'

'Because the IRA weren't going to hand over any money until they knew exactly what they were buying. So they arranged for Conor Byrne to fly down to Madeira and inspect the product. Our man managed to find out when he was flying and the directions he had been given for what to do when he got there. The plan was that he would be picked up by taxi, driven to inspect the missiles and then taken to a hotel near the airport. He would then call New York to release the money.'

'Really?' said Brasenose sceptically. 'And then he was going to put the missile in his pocket and take the plane back home, was he? Or was he just going to hand it over to a passing Irish fishing boat and say here, put this in your kitbag and take it home to Tipperary, will you? This is absurd.'

'It's not me being absurd,' Dreyton retorted. 'Obviously

they had a plan for getting the missile to Cork. They had a sympathiser on the island. That's why Madeira was chosen in the first place. And that sympathiser was perfectly placed to smuggle the case containing the missile and its launcher to Ireland.'

I knew exactly what Dreyton was talking about. That IRA sympathiser was a man living in his own fantasy world, all alone except for occasional visitors like George Ffortiscue and Michael Sheehan.

'Patrick Mallow,' I said. 'He was going to pick up the missile from the derelict warehouse, a warehouse he probably owned, and put it on a ship bound for Europe along with cases of Mallow, Moran wine.'

'That's right,' agreed Dreyton. 'But of course we wouldn't let it get that far. The plan was to nab Byrne and the missile together. At the quayside. That was the whole point of the operation. Mallow is a lightweight, we don't need him. We wanted Byrne caught in the act, irrefutable evidence. And if it was an independent service that got him, like the Portuguese marines, so much the better. There was no need for anybody to know that we had any involvement in it at all.'

'Just as long as the powers to be realised that it was all down to you and your private enterprise, Operation Haystack,' said Brasenose softly. 'People here had to know that.'

Brasenose's snide remark passed me by. I really wasn't interested in him and Dreyton jockeying for position. My mind was racing ahead. What must have happened is that Roger Montacute somehow got wind of Mallow's plans and that had been his death warrant.

'The plan would have worked,' Dreyton was saying, 'if it

hadn't been for Thomas Dylan.' He looked directly at me. 'If you hadn't gone to see Mallow and alerted him, Byrne would have taken a taxi to the quay where we were awaiting and the trap would have been sprung. Somehow Mallow must have warned Byrne that we were waiting and he just turned round and went home.'

'I didn't alert Mallow to anything,' I insisted. 'At the time I knew nothing at all about your operation. I went to see him about Roger Montacute's disappearance.'

'But you must have said something, it's the only explanation for Byrne aborting his mission. You must've mentioned that you were MI6, just to impress Mallow perhaps, or to try to get him onside. Perhaps your wife said something?'

'Well she didn't and neither did I.' I was confident that there was only one thing I had done that could have alerted Mallow: I had mentioned the name of George Ffortiscue. That, I realised, was the piece that was missing in all of this. Suddenly it was all very clear.

'That's it,' I said, almost to myself. 'That's why Montacute had to be disposed of. He must have heard Mallow discussing the purchase of the missile with George Ffortiscue.'

Before anyone else could say anything, Merryweather exploded. 'What's Ffortiscue got to do with this?'

'He was staying at Quinta Moran when Roger Montacute disappeared,' I explained.

'Ffortiscue was in Madeira? Why weren't we told?' The American's anger was obvious although why he was angry was far less clear.

Dreyton also seemed startled by my remark. 'Nobody's mentioned that. What makes you think Ffortiscue and Mallow ever met?'

'When Ffortiscue booked the table at Reid's for the meeting with the Russians he gave Mallow's phone number. He must have been staying at Quinta Moran.'

'That doesn't follow,' said Dreyton, without explanation.

'Let me get this clear,' said Merryweather. 'This Irish deal was brokered by George Ffortiscue?'

'Not at all,' insisted Dreyton. 'This is all news to me. Ffortiscue has nothing at all to do with Operation Haystack. I told you at the Embassy, Ffortiscue no longer has any connection with the Service.'

'Then what was he doing in Madeira?' Merryweather persisted. 'What's this about a meeting with the Russians?'

'We don't know that he was in Madeira. Dylan went down there to investigate a claim that the Portuguese police had overheard Russians offering to sell missiles. He claims Ffortiscue's name came up. But the Portuguese police hadn't heard anything. I discovered that Dylan and his desk officer had made up the whole story. And now he's claiming some sort of link between Ffortiscue and Patrick Mallow, I've no idea where that comes from. Perhaps Justin can enlighten us.'

Before Justin Brasenose could say anything Merryweather again interrupted. It was noticeable that the American was effortlessly taking over the meeting.

'Is that right?' he asked. 'You think Ffortiscue's been in Madeira? What makes you say that?'

He was looking directly at me but it was Neil White who answered. 'We have an asset in Madeira.'

'What!' exploded Dreyton. 'The Soviet Operations Desk has an asset in Madeira and it's not been flagged up to my team? Nobody mentioned it when my operation was set up. Does our station in Lisbon know?'

216

'You didn't need to know, just as you've never briefed us on Haystack. This has nothing to do with your operation. And Lisbon don't need to know either.'

'I'll decide what I need to know. What's this man's name?'

'I've told you, you don't need to know,' White repeated. 'We're talking about an X suffix.'

'X suffix? What's that?' demanded Merryweather.

'It means someone who used to be an asset but isn't any more,' explained Dreyton. 'In which case he's expendable.'

Now it was White's turn to explode. 'It means the exact opposite,' he almost shouted. 'This man has risked his life to serve this country, he's provided intelligence we would never have discovered any other way. We owe him. If the other side found out where he is, even after all this time, there would be a KGB death squad at his door the next day. That's why nobody knows where he is.'

'If he's that important we have to give him protection,' agreed Merryweather. 'But right now we need to know what he really saw. Afterwards we could find him somewhere secure in the States.'

'We know what he really saw,' he told Thomas. 'And the last thing he needs is the Agency offering him protection in America.'

There was an awkward silence eventually broken by Brasenose. 'I take it that as this man has not been active in any way for years whatever he saw in Madeira has nothing to do with his earlier activities.' White nodded. 'Well in that case none of us needs to know anything about his background, we just need to interview him again. I suggest Thomas does that. And Clive' – he looked at Dreyton – 'you can send one of your people along if you don't feel you can trust Thomas.'

'Which I certainly don't,' responded Dreyton. 'Remember we would have had Conor Byrne by now if he hadn't been frightened off by Dylan poking around. I shall go back to Funchal myself. And I want to know what name this X suffix asset is now using.'

'Then that's settled,' said Brasenose smoothly. 'That just leaves one little matter outstanding. Our reason for being here. Who shot at Thomas and why?'

XXV

'We have one clue,' said Brasenose. 'Thomas heard the man use the word *ahoritica*, a Spanish word that Thomas believes is never used in Spain. I've checked overnight. He's right. It's a slang word used in Central America. Very common in Colombia but used right up to Mexico. It's a start but what we really need is a name. Hopefully the Portuguese will help us there.'

'I have a name,' I said, shamelessly taking credit for Julia's discovery. I looked directly at Dreyton. 'The gunman's car was hired by a Colombian named Carlos Iván Moreno.' I had hoped Dreyton would show some sign of recognition but there was nothing. I was looking in the wrong direction.

'You appear to know that name, Bill,' said Brasenose, looking at the burly American.

There seemed to be a moment's hesitation before Merryweather replied. 'No, not unless you're talking about that terrorist guy, Carlos the Jackal. Don't think I've come across a Carlos Moreno. Although I guess Spanish names can sound similar. Let's go back to the beginning, you gentlemen have the advantage over me. Who is this Montacute you mentioned and how does George Ffortiscue's name come up?'

I replied quickly; I didn't want a rambling discussion about Basil Rosen or, more importantly, about Julia and Exodis.

'We're investigating the disappearance of a Cambridge historian in Madeira. Dr Montacute. He'd been staying with his cousin Patrick Mallow and researching something to do with the Spanish Civil War. Apparently he'd come across the name of a Moroccan veteran living in Madeira who might be able to help. What I think I've established is that Ffortiscue stayed with Mallow at the same time as Montacute.'

'Or someone using a name that sounds like Ffortiscue,' put in Dreyton.

'Perhaps. But I do know that Mallow had friends to dinner at Quinta Moran, no doubt with a lot of alcohol given – Patrick Mallow owns a wine business – and that Montacute and someone I'm told was Ffortiscue were there. I think Montacute heard something that evening which led to his disappearance.'

'Rather flimsy,' declared Dreyton. 'We need evidence. Let's see if we can't find Ffortiscue and find out if he's ever really been to Madeira.'

'Ffortiscue's keeping his head down,' Merryweather added. 'Probably in Central America somewhere nursing a bottle of tequila. Whatever he's doing he's not using his real passport anymore.'

'Well we must keep searching,' said Dreyton. 'In the meantime, we need to find out what this X suffix asset actually saw. And we must talk to Mallow, although he's not going to admit to anything.'

'There was a fourth person at the dinner at Quinta Moran,' I said. 'An old Dublin friend of Mallow and Montacute who now lives in New York. Perhaps we can track him down. Mallow told me his name was Michael Smith but I think his real name is probably Michael Sheehan.'

This time there was a very clear reaction, but again from an unexpected direction.

'Sheehan!' exclaimed Neil White. 'Michael Sheehan! That can't be.'

My Desk Officer suddenly turned on Dreyton. 'What the hell have you been doing? Don't tell me the source for your Haystack operation is Michael Sheehan.'

'I'm not discussing my agents,' Dreyton shouted back. 'Haystack is top secret. We shouldn't be discussing it at all.' He turned on Brasenose. 'Have you set this all up? You called us here to talk about the attack on Mr and Mrs Dylan as they investigated Dr Montacute's disappearance, not sensitive operations being conducted by a Service to which you no longer belong. I have more important matters to consider. If we have finished with the matters in hand the meeting is over. White, Dylan, I will see you back at Century House at 2.30 sharp. In my office.'

With that Dreyton stood up and pushed his chair back. Had he been a taller man he would have strode out of the room; as it was he walked petulantly to the door.

Brasenose didn't try to stop him. I realised Brasenose hadn't called the meeting to learn anything, he just wanted to embarrass Dreyton. He'd succeeded much more than he could have hoped.

'I guess I'm off as well,' said Merryweather. 'Interesting meetings you folks have.'

'Underwood will show you out,' Brasenose told him, pointing at his assistant who had said nothing throughout the meeting but now jumped up and bounded after the American.

Merryweather turned as he reached the door and waved. 'So long gentlemen.'

'What was that about?' Brasenose asked White as soon as Merryweather and Underwood had left. 'The name Sheehan rings a bell. One of your ops, wasn't it?'

'Not an op exactly,' White replied. 'It must be the same man. Michael Sheehan was a Catholic from Belfast, fancied himself as a Republican intellectual. But nobody took him seriously. He drank too much. Attached himself to the fringes of the Republican movement but never really hardcore. But he could be a charmer, guided American pressmen around and made sure they only saw what the IRA wanted them to see. I tried to reel him in. He had a lot of wealthy friends but he was always broke. He would sell odd snippets of information but they never turned out to be of any value. You know how it is, double agents who aren't really anyone's agents. The other side were using him to feed me inconsequential crap thinking that one day they could use him to feed me something big. And I was paying him thinking that one day I could use him to go after something I really wanted.

'Then Dreyton was suddenly given some sort of nebulous responsibility over there, intermediate penetration operations in Northern Ireland, whatever that means. Because I objected, I was suddenly hoicked out of Belfast and told that my field days were over and I was to fly the Soviet Operations Desk in London. Pilot Officer White at your command, reports written on demand.'

'And what happened to Sheehan?' Brasenose asked.

White considered that for a moment. 'The truth is I don't exactly know. What I heard is that Dreyton tried to push him too hard and he took fright and decamped to America. Used his contacts with sympathetic journalists to keep spreading the Republican message. But nothing operational of course. He's a fantasist, has been since his student days. Some might say a romantic idealist, others realised he was away with the fairies. If the IRA are really planning to blow the Queen out of the sky they wouldn't involve Sheehan. It's unthinkable.'

'Everything about Operation Haystack is unthinkable,' said Brasenose. 'If Conor Byrne hadn't actually flown down to Madeira I would have thought the whole operation was fantasy.'

'Including the needle missile?' I asked. 'We've assumed that's what was in that warehouse but I didn't actually see it.'

'That I don't know but it's certainly something Colonel Teixeira will be able to confirm.'

At that point Underwood reappeared. 'Find me an office with a secure phone,' Brasenose instructed him. 'You two stay here, I'll go and call Teixeira.'

'You realise we've burnt our bridges,' White said when we were alone. 'Dreyton matters. He's devious and vindictive but at the end of the day he's loyal to the Service. Whatever he's been up to he'll be convinced that it's the right thing to do, not just for himself but for the Service, indeed for the country. If the Portuguese had been able to nab Conor Byrne with a needle missile in his hands a lot of people would have been able to sleep easier in their beds. If we, or Brasenose, have somehow buggered that up we deserve to be out on our ears.'

After fifteen minutes Brasenose was still not back. I had been mulling over events when it struck me that there was one thing Brasenose had not mentioned. He was no doubt keeping some powder dry.

'Did you discover anything about Dreyton putting a

protected asset notice on a fleet of Spanish fishing boats?' I asked White.

'That's not exactly what happened,' White replied. 'I've had a long and incredibly boring conversation with a chap at the Foreign Office. It's all about fishing. Spain and Morocco have been squabbling about fishing rights for years.

'Apparently the Atlantic shelf off Morocco is one of the richest fishing grounds in the world and the Moroccans are keen to exploit it. Fishery exports are now worth hundreds of millions of dollars a year to them. But most of the industry consists of wooden boats that only stay out at sea for a day or two and don't have things like fish finding equipment. They end up with low value stuff – anchovies, sardines, mackerel and so on. The Spanish fleet on the other hand is the largest in the EU. It has modern, better equipped vessels but it doesn't have a well-stocked shelf of its own. Sixty-five per cent of the Spanish catch comes from international waters, overwhelmingly Moroccan waters.

'In 1981 Morocco declared a 200-mile coastal fishing limit. A new fishing agreement has been signed recently but that won't last.

'The point is that the CNI, Spanish Intelligence, issued a protected asset notice on the Vilafermosa boats a couple of years ago when things were really hotting up. They are obviously using those trawlers to keep an eye on what's happening in the disputed waters.

'But you know what these national notices are like. They're not like formal person of interest notifications. A protected asset notice is more a polite request to friends than an official commandment. If push came to shove, we would probably ignore it and the Americans certainly would. We'd only keep away if it was a NATO notice.'

'So is that what Dreyton did?' I asked. 'Got an existing Spanish notice ratified by NATO?'

If Dreyton had managed to get a NATO notice issued Vilafermosa's fleet would be out of bounds not just to the Royal Navy but to other navies as well, the US for example, and the Portuguese.

White smiled. 'NATO did ratify it but not because of anything we did. That's what I wanted to tell you. It was the Americans who got it NATO-ratified. They put in a request and Clive Dreyton merely added his name in support, although there's nothing in the Registry downstairs about that. And here's the killer: the request came from the US Embassy here in London and was signed by Bill Merryweather. It went in nearly a month ago.'

It took me a moment to take in what White was telling me. British, American and Spanish intelligence agencies were effectively telling NATO navies to keep away from Mateo Vilafermosa's fleet. And that had been done roughly around the time that Basil Rosen heard Mateo Vilafermosa and George Ffortiscue discussing the sale of Russian missiles. What were the Vilafermosa boats doing that had to be kept secret? I could understand the Spanish trying to protect whatever spying operation they were running but why would the Company and my own Service be involved?

The only answer possible as far as my own Service was concerned was that Vilafermosa's boats were connected to Operation Haystack. The more I thought about it the more obvious it became that the missile I had seen unloaded from the *Atiradora* had been brought to Madeira on a Vilafermosa vessel. What's more, Dreyton knew that but didn't want anyone else to find out. That's why he hadn't arranged for the Portuguese marines to be there on the night the missile arrived.

Is that what Roger Montacute had stumbled across? Any mention of the name Vilafermosa in any context would have made Montacute's ears prick up. Is that why he had to disappear? Was it why somebody decided that Julia and I had to go when we started prowling around Mourad Zineb?

There was one other question to ask. I knew how Brasenose worked. He was thorough and he loved detail. He was clearly obsessed with Dreyton. He can't have taken a month to discover that Dreyton was requesting a protected asset notice. And once he had learned that he would have wanted to find out everything about it. He must have quickly discovered the part Merryweather played.

I decided to put that to Brasenose. I would also ask him when he really found out about the protected asset notice. His claim that when he took Julia and me to dinner he had just learned about it seemed very unlikely.

When he returned I didn't have the opportunity to ask him anything.

'Did Teixeira confirm there really was a needle missile in that warehouse?' White asked.

'Yes he did,' Brasenose replied curtly. 'But that's not important now. You're going back to Madeira, Thomas, right away. You've just got time to get to the airport. My driver will take you.'

'What's the rush?'

'Colonel Teixeira wants to interview you. I've said yes. The protocol team will have to sign it off, you know how nervous they get when foreign police want to interview a

226

Brit with a diplomatic passport. But that's a formality this time. You're to cooperate fully.'

'That sounds alarming. What does he want to interview me about?'

Brasenose looked me right in the face and I heard Neil White's sharp intake of breath as he answered: 'Your wife has been arrested in connection with a triple murder.'

XXVI

I love my husband deeply, but there are times when Thomas is the most frightful male prig.

After the attempt on our lives at Porto Moniz, Thomas was naturally concerned to ensure that it didn't happen again. So was I!

I appreciated that he didn't want to leave me in danger and the best way of ensuring my safety was for me to fly to London with him. From his point of view that was a sensible proposal. Had he simply mentioned it as a suggestion I could have explained why I felt committed to the search for Roger Montacute and therefore was determined to stay in Madeira.

But Thomas didn't merely suggest I travel with him. He told me I would be going with him. 'I won't let you stay,' he said. That was the sort of remark that Rupert used to make, which is why I never seriously considered marrying my former flame.

One of the things that attracted me to Thomas was that, unlike Rupert, he never tried to make decisions for me. Of course we disagreed. I remember Thomas wanted a quiet wedding and then a honeymoon on a beach somewhere, not terribly romantic, but in the end we both agreed on a proper wedding in Worcester Cathedral and a honeymoon in Rome. As it happened Rome was not the city of romance I had expected, but that's beside the point.

I wouldn't have been so upset with Thomas if 'I won't let you stay' had just been a one-off remark. It wasn't. Thomas had made other decisions recently without considering my reaction. He must have known, for example, that I would have hated that bloody hire car. That of course was a trivial matter but there were also far more important decisions, decisions about our futures, which I, quite reasonably, expected to be joint decisions. Not whether our future would be together, that was a given, but about how and where we would spend it. Thomas had his career and I understood that; the demands of the Service had to come first. At any time we could be posted abroad again, as Thomas clearly hoped. But would he simply accept any posting that came up? What about my life if that happened?

In Moscow we had both had Embassy posts of similar status. If Thomas was posted somewhere else now things would be different; I would merely be what someone once disparagingly referred to as a 'trailing spouse'.

I was making a go of Exodis. The business was starting to thrive. We now had a reputation to maintain. Whatever role Justin Brasenose had played in pushing Lady Montacute in our direction she had chosen us to investigate her son's disappearance. And that's just what I was going to do.

When Neil White suggested that Thomas join my meeting with Lady Montacute I was quite amused but it was still my meeting, my investigation. Exodis was being paid to find Roger Montacute and at the end of the day the success or failure would be mine. Neither MI6 nor Thomas himself was going to decide how I went about it. It was not up to them to 'let me' go or 'let me' stay.

I watched Thomas disappear into the departures area

with mixed feelings and turned away to find the car rental desk. There I lined up behind an elderly Austrian couple who proudly told me that they had come to the island to visit the tomb of Karl, their last emperor, exiled to Madeira after the First World War.

The young man behind the desk seemed surprised when I told him I wanted to trade the Opel in for something faster.

'Most of our vehicles have been reserved,' he pointed out. 'And a faster car will cost more.'

'Don't worry about price,' I told him, and in my mind I could almost hear Thomas wincing.

The rental clerk failed to realise he was being presented with a salesman's open goal. 'The roads are not so good here,' he told me. 'And there are speed limits. I have one car left in the same class as the Opel Corsa, a Fiat, blue.'

'No,' I said. 'What's your most expensive car? I want something solid, something safe.'

'All our cars are safe,' he insisted unsmilingly.

'Well I saw a horrible crash not long ago. Near Porto Moniz. A Peugeot had spun off the road and hit the rocks by the ocean.'

'You saw that?' The young man suddenly took an interest. 'Was the vehicle black?'

'Yes, it was.'

'It was one of ours,' he replied, telling me what I already knew. 'The police have only just phoned me. An accident on the road between Porto Moniz and Seixal. We will have to collect the car, it cannot be driven.' He waved at some papers on his desk. 'It will be a lot of work for us. You cannot imagine the bureaucracy.'

'Was the driver hurt?' I asked.

'The police said yes, but he is not in hospital. He is foreign.'

'Not English, I hope.'

'No.' He picked up one of the forms and read out a name. 'Carlos Iván Moreno. From Colombia. Medellín.'

I could see that the form he was reading from had a lot more details about the driver, but they were upside down and I couldn't make them out. I was incredibly lucky to get a name.

'Well I need something stronger than a Peugeot,' I told him.

We eventually agreed on a C-Class Mercedes, underpowered for its weight but the best they had. He passed me the keys so that I could transfer my case from the Opel. Fortunately he didn't offer to help; I'm not sure how I would have explained that the only belonging I needed to transfer was the gun wrapped in a scarf in the Opel's glove compartment.

The paperwork for the wrecked Peugeot still lay on the desk. While the clerk was completing the paperwork for the Mercedes I craned my neck to try to read the driving licence details on the other form. Thomas could send that to the Service's station in Colombia and perhaps we could learn some more. There was a heading, *Endereço*, printed on the form, which I thought meant address, but the entry was too short. I couldn't make the scrawled words out until I realised that I wasn't looking at driving licence details but at the driver's address in Madeira. It was simply the name of a hotel, ours.

I passed on the name of Carlos Moreno that evening when Thomas phoned. I certainly didn't tell my husband that

Moreno was staying at our hotel; there was no need to alarm him unduly. I also recounted my conversation with Lady Montacute, although that hadn't added much. She had been her usual imperious self, instructing me to return to London if I felt in danger, while clearly not expecting me to do so, and insisting that her son knew nobody called Michael Smith. The implication was that he would never have a friend with such a common name. 'You must have misheard,' she said. 'It was Michael Sheehan.'

Half an hour later Justin Brasenose phoned and I went through the day's events with him. Like Lady Constance he was shocked, like her suggested I should come home, and like her was clearly relieved when I told him I was not planning to do so. At least my husband had been genuine in his desire to fly me away from danger.

The knowledge that the man who had tried to kill me, Carlos Moreno, might well be a guest in the same hotel was disconcerting. I hadn't told Thomas but I should perhaps have told Brasenose, he was in a position to do something about it, but he wasn't on my list of close friends at the moment. I couldn't help thinking he had manoeuvred us into the situation we were in.

I had brought the gun up to my room and slept with it by my pillow, where Thomas's head should have been.

When I woke up I had a plan. I would try to track down Carlos Moreno, find him before he could find me again.

Before we left London I had asked Thomas what the weather would be like in Funchal. He advised me to bring summer attire, which turned out to be entirely inappropriate for December in Madeira. The previous day for Porto Moniz I had abandoned the shorts I had mistakenly worn to meet

Patrick Mallow and instead put on some pale trousers, my primrose yellow linen shirt and a simple string of beach pearls. Today I needed something completely different and chose a swirly pleated cotton calf-length skirt from Monsoon with a matching top in greens and blues. I discarded the sunglasses I had been wearing in Porto Moniz and put my hair back with a wide navy-blue velvet hairband passed on to me by my cousin Susan when her children started putting it on the dog. If Moreno had the usual male disregard for all but the superficial in a woman, he would not recognise me. I intended to have breakfast in the restaurant and then sit in a chair near reception until he appeared. Then I would follow him and see what I could learn.

As I left my room it occurred to me that it might be useful to try to find his room number. I certainly didn't want him tracing my own, so I couldn't phone him from my room. However, I found a phone at the end of the corridor. I called reception and asked to be put through to Senhor Moreno's room. That would not be possible, I was told. Senhor Moreno and his colleague had just checked out. They were now on the way to the airport.

That was bad news. I thought of calling Brasenose to see if he could have Moreno arrested at the airport but decided against it. Instead I phoned Thomas. His mother answered.

Thomas had already left, he had an important meeting at the Foreign Office. I could speak to our daughter, Eveline, but must be quick, they were just off to school. I told my daughter I missed her and that she should be good; she replied that Daddy had been home last night and had already told her to be good.

I noticed that Thomas's mother, rather than Maria, was

taking Eveline to school. I had been nervous about leaving Maria and my mother-in-law, Edith, together in the house. They were both lovely people but very different: Maria tactile, always rushing to hug Eveline if something was wrong; Edith equally warm but expecting boundaries to be observed. The contrast of Southern Europe and Northern Europe, perhaps. Eveline was the joy of my life but there was no time to worry about her right now.

Plan one having failed I decided on plan two. If Moreno was leaving the country there was no point in my skulking around the hotel. Another visit to Quinta Moran was called for. It would be a much more pleasant drive in a decent car, although I longed for my old MG.

When I got there nothing seemed to have changed since the previous day. I parked the car by the jacarandas and marched up to the front door. Again the bell jangled inside the house but nobody came. The door was firmly locked. The house seemed to be completely deserted. I tried the windows one by one. They were all closed tightly. There was nothing unusual to be seen inside.

The door onto the balcony at the back was locked top and bottom. I could see a small table bearing two empty glasses and what looked like an empty whisky bottle. Had that been there the day before? I couldn't remember.

There seemed to be no way in. I stepped back and surveyed the upper floor. Most of the windows were shuttered. There was no way to climb up.

There was something melancholic about the silence. I had been a champion tree climber as a child. My last memory of my mother was of her standing beneath the walnut tree outside her parents' chateau in Normandy frantically urging me to come down. That was just before they left for the skiing holiday from which my parents never returned.

There was a single drainpipe at the side of the house, with a much larger diameter than drainpipes back home, and now only loosely attached to the wall. I tentatively grasped it, but it certainly would not support my weight. Better to try the smaller building where the driver Tiago Abreu had his quarters. That too was as silent as the grave.

I banged on the metal door to the garage; the sound echoed briefly and then faded away. A small wooden window on the ground floor revealed a tiny kitchen and barely larger sitting room. The door at the side had a heavy patterned glass inset that let in the light but distorted my view of the inside. I pushed against the door and to my surprise felt it move. There was a heavy-duty deadbolt lock two thirds of the way down the door but it had not been locked. The door was held closed by a modern lockable door handle at waist height.

I looked around. There was still no sign of life. I had seen a man supposedly break into a house using just a credit card on a TV police show. I wasn't going to risk breaking my credit card but in my handbag I had an annoying number of plastic membership and store cards, many no doubt no longer valid. I found one and, pushing hard against the door, pressed it into the gap between the door and the strike plate and wiggled it around. Nothing happened. I bent the card towards the door handle and wiggled it again. It slid further in and suddenly I could feel the latch give. The door swung open.

I stopped. What was I doing? There was no sound but anything could be waiting for me inside. I considered going back for the gun I had left in the car. Instead I shouted Tiago's name.

No response.

I tiptoed inside and shouted again. Still no response. I entered the sitting room. Nothing out of the ordinary. In the kitchen a dirty plate, knife, fork and glass stood beside the sink waiting to be washed. Did that mean Tiago had left in a hurry?

I returned to the stairs beside the front door. I climbed slowly up, the creak of the stairs sounding unnaturally loud. At the top the door to an empty bathroom stood open.

I found Tiago Abreu on his bed. He was wearing grey and blue striped pyjama trousers. It looked as though he had been swinging himself out of bed when the bullet caught him in the middle of his forehead. His eyes were open and had the dark lines across the cornea known as 'tache noir' which appear a few hours after death.

There was no point checking for signs of life. There clearly wouldn't be any.

I instinctively stepped back, striking my foot on the door frame. I looked round but there was nothing to see. The body crowded out everything else. I had to get out.

Outside I gulped in fresh air. I realised my hands were shaking. I told myself to relax. A bee buzzed noisily past my face. Somewhere close by a bird burst into song. Further away there was the sound of a car. The jacarandas swayed in the wind. I walked towards them.

As I reached my Mercedes a car swung into the courtyard. I looked up. A police car drew to a stop at the base of the steps where I had parked the day before. The police who had arrived yesterday as Thomas and I were leaving had clearly decided to return, hoping to find Mallow at home. A man got out of the back seat and turned towards me. He hesitated a moment before walking in my direction and saying something in Portuguese.

I shook my head. 'Over there,' I said, in English. 'In that little house. There's a body.'

'A body?'

'Yes. It's Tiago Abreu. He's been shot.'

For a second the man just looked at me. Then, turning on his heel, he told me to stay there as he marched back to join the two uniformed policemen who were standing by their car. The three of them then crossed to the house I had just left. Almost immediately one of the police officers came hurtling out, ran to his car and grabbed the radio. He was followed out of the house shortly afterwards by his two companions who crossed over to Quinta Moran itself and, without even glancing in my direction, started banging on the locked door. There was of course no answer. Just as I had done earlier the three then circled the house and tried all the windows without success.

The civilian then approached me. 'Do you have keys?' he asked. I shook my head. 'Stay there,' he repeated.

He returned to the house and stood aside as one of the policemen smashed a window with his gun and with the help of his colleague clambered inside. The niceties of a search warrant were obviously deemed unnecessary. Almost immediately the front door was swung open and all three disappeared inside. I thought of following after them but decided that the less conspicuous I made myself the better. I was suddenly conscious of the gun I had left in the car.

Just two or three minutes later one of the policemen emerged and again ran to the car to use the radio. He then crossed quickly to me and for the third time in ten minutes I was told to stay where I was. To make sure that I did what I was told the policeman stayed with me.

When the civilian emerged again he beckoned me to join him. 'Have you been inside the villa?' he asked, pointing at the now open doorway behind him.

'No.'

'Do you know what has happened inside?'

Again I answered no.

'Do you know the people who live here?'

'I know Patrick Mallow.'

'Then come with me,' he said. But as I started to follow him he had second thoughts. 'What is your name?' he asked.

'Julia Dylan. And yours?'

He looked surprised and simply answered 'Teixeira'. So this was the man from the Portuguese MI5 that Thomas had mentioned to me. What was he doing here? I had assumed that I was talking to a local policeman. I wondered why Thomas hadn't told me who he was when we'd seen him here the day before, then I remembered that Thomas and I weren't talking about anything at the time.

'There are two more bodies inside,' Teixeira announced. 'I need to identify them urgently, if you are willing come with me. Do not touch anything at all.'

It didn't take long. He led me upstairs. Patrick Mallow was lying on his bed. He looked almost peaceful; he had clearly been shot while still asleep. The blood and the silence added to the gloom of the shuttered room.

The maid looked as if she had been getting out of bed when she died, like Tiago Abreu. Her body was sprawled on the floor, one arm protruding through the open door of her tiny room. Rigor mortis seemed to be dissipating already. If that was the case she had probably died before Thomas and I arrived the previous day.

Teixeira took me gently by the arm and I let him guide me back downstairs. He was not to know that these three were not the first violent deaths I had seen. He carefully seated me in the back of the police car and then disappeared.

I tried to work out roughly when the three victims had died. The killers had obviously left before we arrived the day before. If they had only just left then the man who shot at us in Porto Moniz could not have been involved. If, on the other hand, Mallow had been killed during the night, the gun-happy Colombian in the wrecked Peugeot could easily have been the killer. Judging by where the victims were found, how they were dressed and signs that rigor mortis was starting to dissipate, I would guess that the Colombian couldn't be ruled out. It also struck me that the murders had probably taken place not long after Conor Byrne landed at Funchal airport.

Another police car arrived and then an ambulance. Teixeira reappeared. 'There is no more to do here,' he told me. 'The commissioner and the forensic team from Funchal will not be here for half an hour or more. Let us talk.'

He walked away and I followed. 'Mrs Dylan,' he started. 'Do you know who I am?'

'No. Why would I?'

'I thought perhaps Mr Dylan had told you.'

I said nothing.

'I have to make a decision,' he continued. 'Is this a police matter or is this a matter of state security? I met Mr Dylan recently, he is an officer of what I believe is called the Secret Intelligence Service. He was on Madeira representing that service. But I have never heard of a security official bringing his wife along on an overseas mission, so I must assume that you too are a representative of the SIS. I wonder how many more agents named Dylan Mr Dreyton has forgotten to tell me he has on the island.'

He looked at me quizzically. 'Of course you may tell me I am wrong. Whatever has happened in Quinta Moran is nothing to do with state security, you may say, you are not an agent of the SIS and you were here yesterday and today for some other entirely innocent purpose. In that case it would be best if you stay here and wait for the police commissioner from Funchal to arrive and you can explain your presence to him. You can tell him for example why the door to Mr Abreu's quarters was firmly locked when I was here yesterday but was wide open when I arrived today. On the other hand, if this is a matter for state security then I suggest that you and I leave before the commissioner arrives. We can then have a civilised discussion in which you tell me exactly what you and your supposed husband are doing here.'

He looked at me but again I thought it best not to answer directly. 'Perhaps I should talk to the British Consul before I speak to anyone else,' I suggested.

Teixeira nodded to himself. 'Not the Consul, I think, Mrs Dylan. Someone else has just arrived here in Madeira. An old friend of mine. Mr Ronald Silver. Perhaps you know him. He is from the British Embassy in Lisbon. I propose that we talk to him before we decide what to do next.' Thomas had mentioned Silver's name; he was the Head of Station in Lisbon.

'That sounds like a sensible idea,' I said. 'Shall we go to him now? I would be happy to follow you.'

Teixeira looked at me for a moment and then he smiled. It was a polite smile rather than a warm smile but a smile nevertheless. 'As you no doubt observed a police driver brought me here. I shall accompany you; that, I think, would be appropriate.' He beckoned one of the policemen over and spoke to him in rapid Portuguese. Then he marched off to the police car and spoke on the radio for nearly ten minutes. When he returned he led the way to the Mercedes. I started the car nervously, absurdly conscious of the gun in the glove box. We drove in silence for a while before Teixeira spoke again.

'How long have you been a member of British Intelligence?' he asked in what he hoped was a conversational tone.

'I'm not. One spy in the family is enough.' I glanced at him, hoping he would smile, but clearly he had used up his ration of smiles for the day.

'What were you really doing at Quinta Moran on your own?' he asked. 'I am told the man calling himself Mr Dylan left Madeira last night.'

'Let's wait until we meet Mr Silver,' I suggested, and Teixeira relapsed into an uncomfortable silence again.

As I drove it struck me that if I was to find out exactly what had happened to Roger Montacute I needed people like Teixeira on my side.

I could explain to him that I was in Madeira investigating the disappearance of Dr Montacute. Thomas had already told the police that when he visited the police station in Funchal on our first day. There was nothing to lose by going over it again with Teixeira. The problems would arise if he asked why Montacute was in Madeira. Could I tell him

Montacute was looking for Mourad Zineb? Knowing what we now knew about Zineb and the boat Thomas had seen delivering the needle missile, would Thomas be happy for me to lead the conversation in that direction?

I suspected that he wouldn't. That made me ask myself another, more fundamental, question: did it matter that Thomas might not be happy?

Thomas had changed since joining MI6.

In his first appraisal after transferring across from the Defence Intelligence Staff he had been described as self-effacing. That, he was told, could be a useful quality for a spy whose life might depend on not being noticed. Some women might also consider self-effacement a positive virtue for a husband. I wouldn't. I hadn't married someone who merged into the background. In my experience the only ones who do that were those who simply do as they're told. Thomas has always questioned authority; perhaps that's what had attracted me to him. But I wasn't sure that was true any more. MI6 consciously, and quite rightly, instilled a pride in its staff and that pride developed into an unquestioning loyalty. I had felt the same thing happening to me at the RAF Officers College. But an instinctive loyalty was one thing, unquestioning obedience was another.

I had told Thomas to go back to London, obey Dreyton's instruction, but I had to admit a tinge of disappointment when that's what he did.

As I had said before, I was in Madeira to discover what had happened to Roger Montacute. Loyalty to my country would of course take precedence over any obligation to Exodis and Lady Constance but that needn't mean rushing to protect whatever MI6 was up to on the island.

I had to say more to the man sitting beside me if I wanted the Portuguese authorities to stir themselves over Montacute's disappearance. The best place to start was with the truth. Teixeira needed to understand why I was on the island.

'Thomas and I really are married,' I told him without preamble. 'You know what he does, but I'm not here because of anything to do with his job. I'm here to discover what happened to Dr Montacute.'

It was clear Teixeira did not believe me. What was more surprising is that it soon became obvious that Teixeira had never heard of Roger Montacute. The labyrinthine local bureaucracy had ensured that nobody had briefed him. Thomas later told me that the police he had spoken to in Funchal when we arrived belonged to a different force to the men who had accompanied Teixeira to Quinta Moran. It occurred to me to wonder what Teixeira's own interest in Mallow and Quinta Moran might be if he was not investigating the disappearance of a British academic.

I explained that I had been hired by Roger Montacute's mother who was also Patrick Mallow's aunt. Her son had visited the island but had never returned, despite having booked a flight home and seemingly taken a taxi to the airport. Teixeira listened without comment, except to demand the name of the police commissioner in Funchal who was investigating Montacute's disappearance.

When I had finished he asked the obvious question: 'But why was Dr Montacute here in Madeira?'

I started to explain that Montacute thought he was on the trail of gold stolen in the Spanish Civil War. Teixeira's incredulity was almost palpable but I ploughed on. Montacute believed the gold had been stolen by a man named Mourad Zineb who now lived in Madeira. Montacute's cousin, Patrick Mallow, had offered to help but someone had given him a fake certificate showing that Zineb was dead. Montacute, we think, was suspicious about the certificate, and hired a taxi driven by Tiago Abreu's brother to take him to the registry office. Nobody has seen him since.

'And you really came here to investigate that?' Teixeira asked.

'Yes. We went to Zineb's old house in Porto Moniz and found Zineb fit and well. But before we could talk to him we were chased off by a Colombian named Moreno. He had a gun. So we came here to see Mallow again, as you know. That's it.'

Teixeira looked at me for a moment. 'No Mrs Dylan. That's not it. There are no mysterious Colombians in Madeira. And in any case how did you know his name?'

'That's what Zineb called him.'

'Zineb called him Moreno? No first name?'

'Carlos.'

'How did you know he was Colombian?'

'My husband recognised his accent.'

'And where is he now?'

'He left Madeira this morning,' I replied. 'With another man. I discovered they were staying at my hotel but they checked out first thing this morning. They took a taxi to the airport.'

He shook his head as if to say, 'Is that all?'

Of course that was not all. I wanted Teixeira to arrest Mourad Zineb and try to discover what had happened to Roger Montacute. But I was trying to be circumspect. I told him that Carlos Moreno had a gun but I didn't actually talk about the shooting in Porto Moniz. I didn't want the local police looking too closely at Moreno's car crash and asking themselves who was shooting at whom. After all Moreno and Zineb were the ones who had ended up off the road and I had ended up with a semi-automatic pistol in my car. Nor had I mentioned Mourad Zineb's boat the *Atiradora*. That would have to wait until Ronald Silver was present. If Teixeira interrogated Zineb and learned about Zineb's link with Haystack that wouldn't be my fault.

'That's all,' I replied.

We were approaching Funchal but Teixeira gave me directions away from the city. It soon became obvious that we were heading for the airport.

'So Ronald Silver is not actually here yet,' I commented.

'He arrived last night,' Teixeira responded. 'It is someone else I hope to see at the airport. I have told Mr Silver to ensure that the man you tell me is your husband returns to the island immediately.'

XXVII

Julia had been arrested, Brasenose said. What was he talking about? It wasn't possible. He'd mentioned triple murder. What triple murder? Who was dead? How? Julia could not be involved.

I needed to be there. I had to get back to Funchal immediately.

There was a brief delay at the airport. The smiling woman behind the check-in counter went away to consult someone and returned with a piece of paper bearing the airline logo and a handwritten telephone number that I was to call urgently. When I did so I was put straight through to Dreyton.

He sounded less bombastic than he had an hour or so earlier. 'Mr Brasenose is perfectly correct,' he started, 'Dr Montacute's disappearance must be resolved. Any assistance you can provide to the Portuguese authorities in their enquiries you must provide.' I waited for the but... 'However, there are details of Operation Haystack that must remain top secret. They clearly have no bearing on Dr Montacute's disappearance. Mr Teixeira knows as much about the operation as he needs to. I fully briefed him before he and his men met us at Sao Roque. In particular you are not to mention anything at all about the previous evening. How the contraband reached that warehouse is not a matter for the Portuguese. Do you understand?'

'Yes I do, of course, but I don't think he wants to ask about ships that may have passed in the night. Apparently three people have been killed.'

'I am well aware of that. Neil White has briefed me. But I don't think you need be concerned.'

'Why not? My wife has been arrested. Who the hell was killed?'

'You don't know?'

'Of course I don't know. How would I?'

'I see. Well I can tell you.' But instead of telling me what I wanted to know Dreyton launched into a monologue centred on himself.

'When I learned of this new development I immediately phoned Senhor Teixeira myself. It seems that the arrangements made for the arrival of Conor Byrne at Funchal airport were not as I expected. Rather than a taxi collecting him the Portuguese police have established that Byrne left the airport in Patrick Mallow's car. Senhor Teixeira naturally wanted to interview Mallow and attempted to do that this morning. But when he arrived at Mallow's villa he found Mallow and two of his employees inside, dead, and your wife outside—'

'Is Julia injured?' I interrupted.

'No, I believe not. And I trust she can explain what she was doing there. Clearly Montacute and Mallow have been fishing in some very dangerous waters. If the murders occurred after Byrne left Madeira then he must have had accomplices on the island. Or perhaps he was not alone when he landed and the surveillance at the airport failed to pick that up. I must say the quality of the surveillance does not appear to meet the standards we ourselves expect.'

With that Dreyton rang off but not before repeating that Operation Haystack had to be protected and informing me that Ronald Silver, our Head of Station in Lisbon, would be accompanying me at all times.

So Mallow was dead. If the other two were his employees, the chances were they were his driver, Tiago Abreu, and the maid. The implications were chilling. There hadn't seemed to be anything of enormous value in the house, so robbery was an unlikely motive. Either the three had been killed to shut them up or as a warning to somebody else. In either event it had been particularly ruthless, more like gangland retribution than a considered Intelligence operation.

I hoped that was good news. Teixeira would be aware that, whatever may be portrayed on the big screen, British Intelligence does not go around butchering civilians.

***

The Service had managed to book me on a direct tourist flight so I avoided changing planes in Lisbon. I still had plenty of time to think on the plane.

It occurred to me that in all the discussions with Dreyton neither of us had ever mentioned the *Atiradora*. I hadn't actually seen the name clearly on the night it delivered the missile and neither Dreyton nor his two men had mentioned the boat by name. Dreyton had referred to it as a trawler, which it certainly wasn't.

At the Foreign Office meeting I described seeing Zineb on the *Atiradora* in Porto Moniz. Even then Dreyton had said nothing to suggest that he was familiar with the name of either the boat or Zineb. But that didn't make sense. If he knew about Vilafermosa how could he not have known about Zineb?

I tried looking at it from the other end of the telescope. What did Dreyton know? He knew that the IRA were buying a missile, according to him from the Israelis. He knew it was being brought to Madeira by one of Vilafermosa's ships. He knew exactly where it was being landed and when. He knew about the plans the IRA had made for Conor Byrne to inspect the missile. And he knew that Patrick Mallow was the key player in arranging for the missile to reach Ireland and how he intended to do it. The only thing he didn't know is who would physically smuggle the missile onto the island. What was unbelievable is that all this information had apparently come from one man, Michael Sheehan, an at best dubious source who had never before been trusted with anything significant by anyone.

When I arrived in Funchal our man in Lisbon, Ronald Silver, was waiting for me.

'I've spoken to your wife,' he greeted me. 'Strong woman. She seems to have impressed Teixeira although she hasn't been entirely open with him.'

'Then why's she been arrested?'

Silver looked puzzled. 'Something lost in translation there, old chap. I think the expression is she's helping police with their enquiries. Although that's a bit of an exaggeration. All she's said is that she went to see Quinta Moran to look for Roger Montacute and found the driver's house with the door wide open. Nobody is accusing her of murdering anyone, they were dead long before she got there. But three people shot in their beds isn't the sort of thing that happens here so there's a bit of a kerfuffle. And, of course, the local police never like the Security Services getting involved. Teixeira is waiting here at the airport to see you.'

Silver's tone was reassuring. Our Heads of Station in Istanbul and Lisbon could not have been more different. Vernon Forbes in the Turkish capital had been young, ambitious and keen to establish our relative positions in the social hierarchy, both within the service and in the wider world. Ronald Silver, by contrast, was a man at ease with himself, with his role and above all with his approaching retirement.

'Can't understand why anyone would want to retire to the Algarve,' he told me as he led the way through the airport building. 'We have a place on the Douro.' The idea of retiring back to England clearly wasn't even worth thinking about. He was, he informed me, 'an old Portugal hand.' He had found his niche and felt no need to explore the world outside. It turned out that this was his first visit to Madeira. 'Everything in this country happens in Lisbon,' he said before explaining that his wife had been mortified that he was having to miss their regular Thursday bridge night.

Silver led the way to a small meeting room behind immigration, flashing an official pass he had somehow acquired. A stern-looking woman appeared and spoke to Silver. 'Teixeira is on his way, he's bringing your wife,' he translated. 'She should be here soon.' He was clearly in the habit of translating everything for visitors from London.

Most of the airport terminal was underground. Silver had been provided with a room for his own use. It was a windowless office with frosted glass panels on the wall separating it from a long and echoing corridor. He had been reading the *Expresso* broadsheet while the monthly *Madeira*

Island Bulletin and the Lisbon daily *Correio da Manhã* were lying crumpled on the chair next to him. According to the headlines, tensions between the United States and Panama were boiling over.

'Rum do this,' Silver told me, and he wasn't referring to the events in Panama. 'Gun running, Irish terrorists and now these three poor sods shot in their beds. That sort of thing doesn't happen in Lisbon and like I said before it certainly doesn't happen down here. It's not the Wild West. Portugal has one of the lowest crime rates in Europe. Always has. Perfectly safe place.'

'Unless you're Humberto Delgado,' I quipped. I wanted to show Silver that I knew Portugal well myself. Delgado, the exiled Portuguese opposition leader, had been murdered by the PIDE secret police back in the days of the Salazar dictatorship. If Silver noticed my familiarity with his territory he didn't acknowledge it.

'Don't make that sort of remark to Teixeira,' Silver warned. 'No sense of humour. He is a good man, one of the few survivors from the old days, but he can be a bit of a stickler. The Portuguese are our oldest allies, you know, and to them it's an alliance of equals. What you need to remember is that Teixeira is a proud man. Not sure our friend Dreyton really understands that. You don't want to try to be clever with him. No sense of humour.' Silver had an old man's habit of repeating himself. 'There's only one thing he wants and it's not flattery: it's respect.'

Before Teixeira arrived I had to know whether Julia had told anyone about our being shot at in Porto Moniz. If she had then she must have mentioned Mourad Zineb and that name would lead Teixeira to the boat, the *Atiradora*, which

251

was exactly what Dreyton didn't want the Portuguese to know about.

'Does Teixeira know about the gunman in Porto Moniz?' I asked Silver. 'Have you told him? Do you think Julia will mention it on the way here?'

'Yes, she told him. The first thing he did when he got here was rush off to see if the two Colombians are still on the island. I'm not sure she told him everything, mind you. She assured me she had said nothing about Haystack. I told her she shouldn't have known anything about Haystack.' He paused and cast me a look of mild displeasure. I wondered if Mr and Mrs Silver ever discussed his real role at the Embassy. 'Your wife assured me she knew nothing about the operation here and that Teixeira had been the first to mention Haystack. Quite a breach of security on his part if that's true. I advised your wife to be open about everything. After all, the attack on you had nothing to do with Haystack. The sooner we can get you two off the island again the better.'

Julia arrived a few minutes later with Teixeira. I was inordinately relieved to see her but being British showed it only by giving her an embarrassed peck on the cheek.

'Are you alright?'

'Of course.'

Teixeira invited everyone to sit down; he was not the sort for emotional reunions.

When I had met Teixeira before, most of the talking had been done by the Marine officer with him. I remembered the Portuguese Intelligence man as someone content to listen. He was short, although he had not seemed so when standing next to Clive Dreyton, but he stood erect. A trim figure with a neatly trimmed moustache and wire-framed glasses. He wore an expensive single-breasted suit, dark tie and highly polished shoes. He placed a leather document case, almost certainly handmade and bearing the monogram JCTC, on the table in front of him and removed a legal notepad. Beside it he placed an Otto Hutt silver fountain pen.

'It is time to talk, I think.' He smiled weakly in my direction.

I had expected a police interrogation, but this was very different. Teixeira clearly intended to conduct the meeting on his own; he was going to play good cop. I wondered if he had dispensed entirely with the bad cop; he had certainly put Dreyton in his place. There was no tape recording. Most surprisingly, Julia and I were being interviewed together so that Teixeira had robbed himself of the opportunity of testing our stories against each other.

It was obvious that Teixeira and Silver knew each other well. Silver's role was 'declared', which meant that the Portuguese Security Services had been notified of his appointment as our Lisbon Head of Station. This was very different to the usual posting, such as my old role in Moscow, and added an extra dimension to the proceedings. In normal circumstances the Service's continuing good relations with our Portuguese hosts would be far more important to Silver than the well-being of a British citizen caught up in a murder investigation. Hopefully, Operation Haystack made the circumstances anything but normal.

Teixeira looked across the table at me.

'I have been instructed to cooperate fully with your investigation,' I said.

'Then let us start with a simple question, Mr Dylan. Why are you here? This lady tells me she is your wife and that she works not for Mr Dreyton but for a private investigation company, although she insists she is not a private detective herself. You, I suspect, are going to tell me you are an officer of your country's Secret Intelligence Service but you are not here as a spy. Like Mrs Dylan you are simply looking for one of your fellow countrymen, Dr Montacute. And yet, where do I see you first? In Sao Roque do Faial where Mr Dreyton introduces you as one of his team for what he chooses to call Operation Haystack. Now what am I going to make of that Mr Dylan?'

'You have it exactly right,' I replied. 'I was here to help my wife find Roger Montacute, naturally Clive Dreyton was aware that I was on the island and decided an extra hand would be useful for a night's surveillance.'

I was telling the truth but even to my ears it sounded hollow. It was also beside the point. Teixeira didn't need to know why I was here, he needed to know whether the deaths at Quinta Moran were connected with Roger Montacute's disappearance or with Operation Haystack, or both. I had the same question but I thought I had the answer. Montacute had disappeared trying to find Mourad Zineb. Mourad Zineb was the link between Haystack and Montacute and Mallow. He was the man Montacute had come to Madeira to find, the man Mallow had insisted was dead, and he was surely the man I had seen unloading a needle missile from the *Atiradora*. But should I tell Teixeira? Dreyton had prohibited any mention of our having seen the needle arriving at the warehouse. Well, I wouldn't mention it but if Teixeira put two and two together that was Dreyton's problem. I was determined that the attack on Julia and I would be investigated by the Portuguese authorities and for that to happen I needed to be as open as possible. I didn't know then that Julia had already gone through the same thoughts in her own mind and reached the same conclusions. It suddenly struck me that I was more concerned with achieving justice for Lady Montacute than clearing up the loose ends from a failed IRA arms smuggling plot.

'Let's be frank with each other,' I suggested, before giving Teixeira the full story, although of course suitably curtailed, redacted and abridged.

I didn't realise that although Julia had mentioned the gunman in Porto Moniz to Teixeira she had thought it wiser not to talk about the car chase and our forcing the Peugeot off the road. When I reached that part I could sense Teixeira's surprise, although whether at the thought of someone shooting at us or at the female driver coming off the better I wasn't sure.

When I had finished Teixeira said nothing. Then he suddenly stood up. 'Stay here,' he ordered and disappeared.

He was away nearly half an hour. When he returned he sat down again before speaking.

'Two Colombians, one named Carlos Moreno, the name you gave me, left Funchal this morning for London. I have spoken to Mr Brasenose and, as usual, he has been most cooperative. I asked him to arrest the two men for the attempted murder of two of his agents. I have also spoken to Aloisio Abreu, he is with the police investigating his brother's murder. He confirms that he drove Dr Montacute to the Câmara Municipal in Santa Cruz, as you said. So we now have two possible motives for the three murders at Quinta Moran. Were those deaths connected to Irish terrorists or Spanish gold? Or perhaps both?'

'Not both,' Ronald Silver cut in. 'Dr Montacute's disappearance has nothing at all to do with our Operation Haystack. There's no connection between the two.'

'I disagree. Too many people are involved with both.'

'Only Mallow,' persisted Silver. 'He's the only connection and that's probably just coincidence.'

Teixeira smiled, the first genuine smile I had seen from him. 'Come now Ronald. There is certainly more than one connection. You forget we also have Mr and Mrs Dylan here. Mrs Dylan is searching for Dr Montacute while Mr Dylan is a colleague of yours. Another coincidence apparently. And then there is Aloisio Abreu.

'Today you tell me he was the last person to see Dr Montacute. But only yesterday I interviewed him about the death of his brother and he told me a rather odd story. He claims his brother asked him to pick up an Irishman at the airport and take him to a disused quayside on the north coast. He was to wait for the Irishman there and then drive him to a hotel near the airport. However, at the last minute his brother Tiago phoned him and cancelled the plans. Tiago told him that he was going to the airport instead but that Mallow would compensate him for the lost fare.

'All coincidences perhaps, or perhaps not, but certainly connections.'

There was a knock at the door and when Teixeira answered someone passed him a note. After glancing at it he announced 'A message from Mr Brasenose. The two Colombians had already left London on a plane for Bogotá. I suspect we will find it impossible to arrest them there. But some good news: Mr Dreyton is on his way back to the island.'

I expected a lot more questions but Teixeira again stood up abruptly. 'I need to talk to the Police Commissioner in Funchal. I will return to meet Mr Dreyton when he arrives. Perhaps then I will learn the whole truth.' He looked at Ronald Silver. 'I am not sure, my friend, that your colleagues understand the magnitude of what has happened. Three Portuguese citizens have been killed in their beds. This is a national scandal. If it becomes known that your Service is involved in any way that is very dangerous for all of us. I hope Mr Dreyton understands that.'

He led the way outside. The black Nissan I had seen before was waiting for him. 'I'll have that airport pass back now, Ronald,' he said. 'I intend to see Mr Dreyton alone when he disembarks. No doubt you will be in Arrivals when we are finished.'

When Teixeira had been driven away Silver turned to me. 'Teixeira's not happy. I've not seen him like that before. Let's hope that when Dreyton gets here he's at his emollient best. We might as well go and find somewhere to eat.'

'No thanks. We're going back to our hotel.'

'You're not waiting for Dreyton?'

'No. I know what he wants to do. He did tell you about our X-suffix asset?'

'Oh yes. Basil Rosen. We're visiting him tomorrow first thing.'

'Well you'd better pick me up at the hotel first. Nine o'clock?'

Silver looked puzzled. 'I didn't realise you were coming along.'

'Of course I am. I'm Rosen's designated handler. In any case, Dreyton doesn't have Rosen's address. I didn't want him charging in there on his own. Rosen's a complicated man.'

'I gave him the address,' Silver answered.

'How the hell did you get that?'

'Your desk officer Neil White gave it to me. Weeks ago. I was asked to send a postcard to an address in Funchal announcing that Tom would be visiting. I reported the address to Dreyton when he phoned this morning.'

I smiled. I had forgotten how we had responded to the first cryptic message from Rosen. For some odd reason I was looking forward to seeing Rosen again. He was a complicated man but in his own way, I thought, a trustworthy one. Perhaps the only trustworthy one. I certainly couldn't trust anyone on my own side. Except Julia of course. What I really wanted was for us both to get away and talk. I thought of the physical shock I felt when Brasenose told me she had been arrested. I took her hand.

'Come on. Let's find this wonderful car of yours.'

She kissed me, and Silver marched away.

But in the car I couldn't help thinking about the next day's meeting. Basil Rosen and Clive Dreyton could not be more different, except that they were both a mass of contradictions. Dreyton, who clung to his Englishness like a security blanket and craved status and power but had chosen a secret world where none but a select few would ever appreciate what he had achieved. A political animal always keen to wave the flag while waiving the values it stood for. Rosen, the Russian who had thrown off all things Russian to become as self-contained as it was possible to be. Rosen, I was convinced, would kill to stop anyone puncturing the protective bubble he had built around himself. And yet, despite discarding his past, Rosen took time out once a year to toast his brother,

258

not to celebrate his birthday but to commemorate his death with quiet dignity. There was nothing quiet about Dreyton's dignity and when it was punctured, as it had been by Brasenose at the Foreign Office meeting, I had seen Dreyton pirouetting away like a deflating balloon. Rosen's reaction to danger would be what it had been while he was stealing his country's secrets: cold blooded calculation. Dreyton facing danger would be torn between turning tail and hopeless heroics.

Rosen and Dreyton could be an explosive combination – I didn't realise how explosive until the bullets started to fly, again.

XXVIII

Julia was subdued next morning. Perhaps seeing the three bodies at Quinta Moran had been more disturbing than she wanted to admit. I hadn't seen them but I felt something similar. Being shot at by Carlos Moreno and Mourad Zineb in Porto Moniz had been alarming but also exciting. The adrenaline had been flowing. We had triumphed and were then ready for the next battle. The cold-blooded killing of Mallow and the other two was different. We were both left numbed, struggling with just one simple question: why?

The murders felt like revenge, but for what? What had Mallow done? And why shoot Mallow's driver and maid? Had they seen something? Was someone afraid of what they might tell? Was Mallow killed not because of something he had done but because of something he was about to do?

Silver phoned early the next morning. 'Dreyton says you can be there if you want, 9.15 at Rosen's house. Don't be late.' He seemed to have picked up Dreyton's imperious tone and I guessed he was repeating Dreyton's message word for word.

'I'll be there.'

Julia had decided she was coming with me.

'Dreyton won't like that,' I said.

'I'll wait outside. Then perhaps another visit to Mourad Zineb in Porto Moniz. See if he will say anything without his bodyguard.'

'He'll surely be in police custody by now.'

'You would think so,' said Julia. 'But nothing here seems to work as we would expect. I still can't believe Teixeira didn't know anything about Montacute's disappearance when he went to Quinta Moran.'

I insisted on setting off for Rosen's house in plenty of time. Nine fifteen Silver had said, but I wouldn't put it past Dreyton to start early. We drove along Rua do Lazareto just after nine and spotted Dreyton and Silver at the side gate to Rosen's house. I jumped out of the car and ran up the hill to join them. Dreyton didn't look happy to see me but he said nothing. Silver half smiled a greeting.

Dreyton opened the gate and walked past the parked Renault that had been there before.

As we approached the house there came the sound of music from inside, not the Tchaikovsky or Wagner I might have expected but Leonard Cohen singing something about Joseph looking for a manger. Rosen really was a strange man. As Dreyton was reaching for the doorbell the music suddenly stopped. Dreyton halted but, as there was no sound of movement inside, pressed fiercely on the bell. There was no response. He tried again and the sound of the bell seemed to echo in the silence.

'Is there another way in?' Dreyton asked.

'Only when you're invited,' I replied. 'Let me try.'

There was no letterbox so I rapped on the door with my knuckles. 'It's me, Tom,' I shouted.

A voice emerged from a small grating in the wall beside the door. 'What do you want?'

'We have a photograph to show you.'

'And you need three people to show me a photograph?'

'This is very important. My colleagues have come from London just to see you.'

'They are more senior than you?'

'Much more.'

'Wait one minute.'

There was silence and then the door slowly opened. Rosen stood just inside, one hand on the door and the other behind his back.

'You may bring one person inside. The other must wait outside. It is a small house.'

I pushed past Rosen and Dreyton followed suit. 'Wait here,' Dreyton told Silver.

Rosen pushed the door closed behind us. As he turned round I realised he had a gun under his shirt, stuffed into his belt. He hadn't thought that necessary before.

'Where is the photograph?' he asked.

'I have it here,' replied Dreyton. 'As Thomas said I have come all the way from London just to show it to you.'

'Not just for that. You want to see for yourself if I am the sort of man who can be trusted, but the truth is you have no choice. What is in the photo?'

'A man. I want to know if you recognise him.'

Dreyton took two photographs from his inside pocket. The top one was a head and shoulder shot, black and white. I recognised George Ffortiscue. It might have been his passport photo. The other I couldn't see. Dreyton moved across the room before passing them to Rosen, in doing so making sure I couldn't see the bottom one clearly. It seemed to be another black and white head and shoulder shot.

Rosen looked at the top one and replied immediately. 'It is George Ffortiscue, the man I saw at Reid's hotel.'

'And the other?'

Rosen examined the second photo. 'This man I don't know.'

Dreyton was watching him closely. 'I believe you,' was his only comment.

'You can go now,' said Rosen. 'Do not come back.'

Dreyton was about to say something when there was a knock at the door. Without pausing to think he spun round, and pulled the door open. 'What is it, Silver?' I heard him ask sharply before he was cut off.

Ronald Silver catapulted into the room, helped on his way by a double-barrelled shotgun smashing into the back of his head. Dreyton was flung back by the swinging door. A burly man in a red checked shirt pushed into the room, shotgun now in the crook of his arm. He was followed by two other men. The first, much taller and better dressed, with a semi-automatic pistol in his hand. Another stockier, bearded figure slammed the door shut and took up position with his back to it. The tall man was evidently in charge. He hesitated and at first I thought he clearly hadn't expected to find three of us inside the house. He waved his gun towards us as if he was deciding what to do next and then stopped.

A Walther P38 had somehow appeared in Basil Rosen's hand.

I hadn't seen any of these men before, but there was a spark of recognition on Rosen's face. Rosen started to lift his gun and I realised he was going to shoot.

For a split second it seemed that nobody moved. Then the truly unexpected happened. Dreyton launched himself at the man with the shotgun. It was like an overweight monkey jumping on a giraffe. The man swung round to shake Dreyton off but Dreyton refused to let go. He must have clawed at the shotgun because suddenly it exploded. The gun was pointing towards the floor but the tall stranger let out a yell as pellets struck his foot and leg. His leg seemed to give way and he lost his balance, dropping his own gun as he did so. He screamed at his two companions in a language I did not recognise. I could guess what he was saying: 'Kill them all.' I dived for his gun.

Redshirt had cast Dreyton aside and was levelling his shotgun at him. The bearded man by the door advanced into the room, reaching under his jacket for the handgun stuffed into his belt. As he did so the door behind him swung open again and almost simultaneously shots rocked the room.

Rosen had fired three times. The man with the shotgun collapsed, his red shirt perforated by bullet holes in the sort of tight grouping that wins pistol-shooting medals. There had been a fourth shot and the bearded man who had been guarding the door fell forward towards me. I looked up to see Julia in the doorway, the Smith & Wesson in her hand.

'Close the door,' shouted Rosen bizarrely, as if his biggest concern was disturbing the neighbours.

The tall man started to get up, blood clearly visible on the leg of his trousers. I couldn't make out if his face was twisted in pain or rage. He grabbed at his gun on the floor and I did the same. Before I could say anything Rosen stepped past me, put his gun against the man's nose and pulled the trigger. The man was dead the instant his brain stem exploded.

Despite what had gone before, Rosen's action stunned us all. Dreyton, Julia and I looked at him in utter disbelief.

'Why did you do that?' screamed Dreyton. 'We don't even know who he was.'

'He was the man I saw with the Russians at Reid's,' responded Rosen coldly. 'You must go.'

Rosen appeared to be in total control of himself. He was talking as if nothing unusual had happened. It was unreal. There were two dead men on the floor, perhaps three, but Rosen was calmly telling us to leave.

Ronald Silver struggled to get to his feet as Dreyton wiped blood from his face. I wasn't sure where that came from. Julia and I both stood with guns in our hands and no idea where to point them.

'You must go,' Rosen repeated. 'I will clear up here. You must give me twenty-four hours.'

'What are you talking about?' I demanded. 'We can't just walk away.'

'We must call the police,' added Julia.

'You can't do that,' said Rosen. 'This is my sanctuary, my manger, you promised me protection and you failed. You owe me now.'

'It doesn't work like that,' I responded. 'After what's happened we must let the Portuguese authorities take over. We will find you somewhere else.'

Rosen still had a gun in his hand and for a moment I thought he was going to use it.

'That is impossible,' he insisted.

'Of course it's not,' responded Julia. 'We need an ambulance.'

Rosen just shook his head. 'I told you I will find my own way. Go now. This is my house.'

It struck me that Rosen might be on the edge of the sort of nervous breakdown he had experienced when his brother had died in the Hungarian uprising. What did he mean by finding his own way?

Dreyton, who a few moments ago had been screaming at Basil Rosen, suddenly turned and spoke quietly, almost matter-of-factly, as if someone had flipped a switch. 'Who were those men?'

Rosen leaned over the man he had just shot and rifled through his pockets.

'Check his watch,' said Julia. I looked at the man's wrist and saw merely a round watch with a black face and leather strap. Julia saw a Patek Philippe Calatrava in 18-carat white gold, probably worth more than I earned. 'That's Roger Montacute's watch,' she said.

I looked again. The crown used to wind the watch was on the left-hand side. Montacute had worn his watch on the right wrist.

Rosen found a Moroccan passport and tossed it across to Dreyton.

'Hachim Zineb,' Dreyton read out. 'Who's he?'

'Mourad Zineb's son,' I told him. 'The man who threatened Roger Montacute in Morocco.'

Nobody responded. Now was not the time to worry about what had just happened or what had led us here. It was time to decide what to do right now.

Ronald Silver pulled himself up and walked shakily towards the phone. 'I'm going to call Teixeira.'

'No you're not,' said Dreyton. 'This is my operation. Mr Rosen is right. It's time to return to London. Everyone except for you Ronald.'

'That's ridiculous,' insisted Silver. 'This is the biggest balls-up we've had in this country since the Second World War. We can't run away from it.'

'We are not running away from anything but the Service

can't be involved in this. I will call you at nine o'clock tomorrow morning Mr Rosen. We will decide what to do then. Ronald, take a taxi to the nearest hospital and get yourself looked at. Tell them you fell over. Then return to your hotel and be back here with Mr Rosen when I call at nine.'

'That's impossible,' Silver persisted. 'I've got to work with Teixeira. I can't say nothing to him until tomorrow. What am I supposed to say then? Sorry I forgot to tell you three men jumped me and they all ended up shot?'

'You tell him you had concussion. You can blame me if you want. Tell him you thought that I would contact him. In any case, I spoke to him this morning and he won't be here, he's going to Ponta Delgado. I've made my decision. Tomorrow nine o'clock.' Dreyton turned to Rosen. 'If you can convince me when I call that you have found a way to keep the local authorities away from your door, then I will guarantee not to mention your name to them. I believe you saved my life; we owe you the right to continue undisturbed with your life here.'

I was watching Dreyton carefully as he spoke but I couldn't work out what he was thinking. How could Rosen possibly continue with his life here 'undisturbed'? Perhaps Dreyton really did think he owed Rosen the chance to preserve the life he had made for himself in Madeira. Or maybe he just wanted time to get off the island himself so that when this all blew up he would be back in London spinning the story his own way. Or then again perhaps he was just frightened of Rosen with a gun in his hand and planned to call Teixeira as soon as he got out of the house. One thing was sure, I was seeing a different side of Clive Dreyton.

'You look after Ronald,' Dreyton said to Julia. 'Get him

267

to his hotel and make sure he calls a doctor. Thomas will drive me to the airport.'

In normal circumstances Julia would have objected, pointing out that she didn't work for the Service and being a woman didn't make her the automatic candidate for nursemaid, but she said nothing. Nor did Silver; perhaps he was used to being spoken about as if he wasn't present. Julia stepped past me to Hachim Zineb's lifeless body and removed the watch on his wrist. 'This is for Lady Constance.'

Dreyton picked up the phone. 'Can I make an international call from here?' he asked Rosen.

'Of course.'

Within minutes he was through to someone in London. Rosen stood beside him, gun still in hand. Dreyton ignored him.

'I need to return to London. Now,' Dreyton barked into the phone.

The person at the other end must have started asking questions but Dreyton cut them off. 'I don't care what route, what airline, what class or how long it takes. I'm going to Funchal airport now and I want a ticket waiting for me when I get there.' He slammed down the phone.

He turned towards Rosen. 'This wasn't our fault,' he said. 'None of this was our fault.'

'Yes it was,' said Rosen. 'You led those men here. It doesn't matter who they were or why they wanted to kill us. My sanctuary has gone.'

Dreyton nodded an acknowledgement. We all knew Rosen was right. 'Come on,' he said to me, and then before leaving turned and uttered a farewell to Rosen: '*Dasvidaniya.*' It was the same mangled Russian I had heard in Turkey and in the back of my mind a bell started ringing. There was something wrong with that expression, but I didn't have time to worry about it right then.

Julia and Silver were following Dreyton out of the door when Rosen handed me the two photographs he had inspected earlier. The top one, as he'd identified, was a black and white passport shot of George Ffortiscue, the bottom one was someone else entirely. The photograph Rosen said he didn't recognise was of Justin Brasenose.

I was stunned. What could that mean? Dreyton couldn't imagine that Brasenose had somehow been involved in buying missiles.

As we left the house I noticed that Dreyton's hands were shaking.

'Did you mean it?' I asked. 'We do nothing until nine tomorrow?'

Dreyton gave me a look I couldn't understand. 'Of course I meant it. We could have been killed but for Rosen.'

I still wasn't sure whether I believed him. 'Why did you show Rosen a photo of Brasenose?' I asked as we approached Silver's car.

Dreyton didn't answer my question, so I repeated it. 'Why show Rosen Brasenose's photo?'

This time Dreyton responded, angrily. 'Because Haystack's a total disaster and somebody's responsible. Brasenose or Ffortiscue or both. I'm going to get to the bottom of it. Somebody phoned Quinta Moran from London on the evening Byrne flew in to inspect the missile. Teixeira told me. Somebody who knew enough to block the number they were calling from. They must have warned Mallow that we were waiting for Byrne. It had to be Ffortiscue or Brasenose.

It couldn't have been you. You were with me watching the warehouse.'

'Me! Why would I have wanted to warn Mallow?'

'Who knows? You asked Mallow about Ffortiscue when you first went to Mallow's villa with your wife. Why did you do that? That's when the operation started to unwind. You spooked Mallow and he frightened off Conor Byrne. You could have got us all killed. Why have you poked your nose in?'

'I'm not poking my nose in. I'm just doing my job. It's a pity others aren't doing the same instead of playing their own private games.'

'How dare you,' shouted Dreyton. 'I'm doing what's best for the country. It would have been a disaster if that missile had ended up in Ireland. I stopped that.'

A taxi appeared heading into town and Dreyton stepped out into the road and flagged it down. He was about to get into the cab when he remembered that his overnight bag was in Silver's car. After retrieving the bag, he jumped into the taxi without another word and disappeared.

Silver was standing beside his car. 'Let's go,' I said to him. 'You need a doctor.'

'No I don't, I need a drink. I'm getting too old for this business.'

He was booked into the Windsor, the hotel the Service had decided was suitable for me on my first visit. You had to have Dreyton's seniority to justify Reid's Hotel. 'I'll drive you there, I know where it is. Julia can go back to our hotel and pack.'

'The shit will hit the fan tomorrow,' proclaimed Silver, as we set off. 'You mark my words. Bodies all over the place and Dreyton just runs away. Teixeira can't keep us out of this. The local police are already furious with him for interfering with the investigation at Quinta Moran. You've no idea how bitter these bureaucratic battles can become.' He was silent for a moment before the real horror of the situation struck him. 'I could get kicked out of the country.'

I left him at the Hotel Windsor to nurse his sorrows and a sore head and grabbed a taxi back to the Casino Park Hotel.

Dreyton's whole body had been shaking at Rosen's house and I now realised I was doing something very similar. I could feel my heart still racing. I consciously slowed my breathing, switching my mind from near paralysis to analysis. Something Dreyton had said alarmed me. He blamed me for mentioning Ffortiscue to Mallow. How did Dreyton know what I had said to Mallow? I hadn't told anyone in London. It had been a mistake to ask Mallow about Ffortiscue and I didn't broadcast my mistakes. Mallow must have told someone, Sheehan or Ffortiscue probably, and one of them had told Dreyton.

When I arrived at the hotel I discovered I wasn't the only one still in a state of shock. 'You're all mad,' were the words Julia greeted me with. 'Three dead bodies at Quinta Moran. Two, probably three, at Rosen's house. Moreno trying to shoot us from a moving car in broad daylight. What the hell's happening? Dreyton seems to think he's directing a *Dirty Harry* film, the rogue cop gets away with killing all the bad guys. But he's no Clint Eastwood, and neither are you. We have to talk to Teixeira. Just think what would happen if Portuguese agents acted like this in London.'

'But the Portuguese wouldn't send agents to London.'

'Oh don't be so stupid Thomas. You know what I mean. If the CIA got involved in a shoot-out in London with dead bodies everywhere, what would we think? Imagine if Bill Merryweather killed someone and then just left the country, there would be hell to pay, special relationship or no special relationship. We can't just march in here as if we own the place.'

I understood what Julia meant but Dreyton was right. There was nothing more we could do here. And the sooner we were both off the island the better, especially Julia. My diplomatic passport didn't protect her. I was amazed the police had not interviewed her already. We must have Teixeira to thank for that; the Security Services clearly had more authority here than at home.

'If we stay here Dreyton will dump us in it. Whatever's gone wrong will be our fault. We have to go.'

I expected Julia to argue but despite her earlier outburst she had already realised that, with Dreyton gone, we had no choice but to follow suit.

'I know,' she admitted. 'I've checked the flights. There's only one direct flight today, to Gatwick, and we've missed it. I doubt if Dreyton managed to catch it.'

'Then we take an indirect flight.'

Julia managed a weak smile. 'That's what I've done. We fly via Lisbon and Amsterdam. It's the only way to get back today. We need to leave now.'

Returning to the airport was a risk but we had no alternative. There was no sign of Dreyton; it seemed he had somehow caught the earlier flight. I half expected to see Teixeira but we checked in with no problem.

'I wonder where Teixeira disappeared to,' I commented.

272

'Perhaps he's found a witness of some sort. Dreyton mentioned Ponta Delgado. I've no idea where that is.'

'It's the civilian airport in the Azores,' Julia replied. 'It must be something important for Teixeira to fly all that way with everything going on here.'

I nodded. We were both thinking the same thing: in our world the only thing of note in the Azores is Lajes Field, the US Air Force base.

XXXIX

For once Dreyton was on time. He sat behind his enormous desk chewing the end of a cheap biro. At nine o'clock his secretary put through the call to Funchal, except that it wasn't really a call, just a Portuguese ringtone. Nobody answered.

His secretary stood just inside the office and Dreyton gave her a questioning look.

'Are you sure you got the number right?'

'Quite sure,' she replied but moved quickly back to her own desk and we heard her phoning again. The result was the same.

'Where the hell is Rosen?' Dreyton demanded, looking at me as if I was somehow responsible for Rosen's non-appearance.

'No idea.'

'And if he's not there why doesn't Silver answer?'

Again I just shook my head.

'I'll get Comms to check the line,' Dreyton's secretary announced. We waited in silence. Dreyton busied himself initialling a stack of papers in a tray marked 'urgent'. The only other tray on his desk, empty when I walked in, was labelled 'actioned'.

I wondered how Julia was getting on. I suspected I was having the easier time. Julia had insisted that she be the one to break the news to Lady Constance that her son would not be returning. We hadn't found his body, it was no doubt weighted down at the bottom of the Atlantic, but the watch on Hachim Zineb's wrist was all the evidence that was needed. It was inscribed on the back with Roger Montacute's initials and the date of his twenty-first birthday.

After ten minutes Dreyton's secretary returned with the news that there was nothing wrong with the line.

'Then try again,' Dreyton instructed.

After a further five minutes the contents of the urgent tray had all been initialled and passed to the actioned tray. It was clear Rosen was not going to answer. 'You can go,' Dreyton told me, but as I stood up the phone rang. 'It's Mr Silver,' I heard the secretary say.

Dreyton grabbed the receiver. 'Ronald, what's going on? Where have you been? Where's Rosen?'

He had forgotten that the phone was on speaker and his voice echoed around the room. His secretary closed the office door.

'I can't get into the house,' reported Silver. 'The door's locked. I'm phoning you from a bar near the fort.'

'Is his car still there?' I asked.

'Yes. Everything's as it was yesterday.'

Dreyton thought about that for a minute before deciding what to do next. 'You'll have to go back and break in.'

Silver was obviously not pleased with that. 'That's going to make me very visible. And what are we trying to get inside for? If Rosen's inside he must be dead. If he's not inside we can't talk to him.' Silver's voice was muffled; he was obviously anxious not to be overheard.

'Just get into that house,' Dreyton snapped. 'I want to know why he's not answered my call.'

'Try the window on the side away from the road,' I suggested. 'It's not overlooked.'

Silver didn't argue and the phone clicked off.

Ten minutes later Silver phoned again. 'I'm inside. No sign of Rosen. Nothing's changed, nothing. Two very dead bodies and the man Mrs Dylan shot isn't moving. Everything is just as we left it.'

'Shit,' said Dreyton. 'You'd better get out, get back to Lisbon.'

'That's the worst thing we can do,' I interjected. 'The bodies will be discovered eventually and our fingerprints are all over the place. Ronald must search the house.' I moved closer to the phone. 'Try to work out whether Rosen has taken a runner. Is his toothbrush missing, or razor? Does it look like he's taken some of his clothes? Or a suitcase? If you find his British passport make sure you keep it, it's one of ours. Then get hold of Teixeira. Tell him we found Rosen's address in Montacute's papers in Cambridge, you went to his house this morning and found the window broken. Then you found the bodies.'

'What about our fingerprints?' Dreyton queried. 'The police are bound to find them.'

'There's nothing we can do about that. Ronald's can be explained away and he can try to clean up now but he's bound to miss something. At some stage you will have to talk to Teixeira but this at least buys you time to invent a convincing story. Haystack's your operation.'

I could see Dreyton thinking that through. His instinct was to take charge, to give orders, but he didn't know what orders to give. It had been the same at Rosen's house the previous day. I almost felt sorry for him. He suddenly sat upright. 'Ronald. Do just as Thomas says. But don't phone Teixeira until you get back to Lisbon. And if you find anything in the house let me know right away.' Then he ended the call.

He got up and looked out of the window. It was raining. 'Haystack's been a success,' he said, softly, as if speaking to himself. 'It stopped the terrorists getting their hands on that missile. Let's get that fact established before we start the damage limitation.'

He looked at me quietly. 'What are you going to tell Brasenose?'

'I don't report to Brasenose.'

I needed to say more than that. Dreyton was fragile, introspective in a way I hadn't seen him before. Perhaps he would open up. He had very nearly been killed the previous day. It must have affected him. His judgement was all over the place. I had a vivid picture of him in my mind, jumping onto the man with the shotgun. It was a totally mad thing to do but in the end it may have saved our lives. We could all have been killed. Perhaps this was the moment to try to convince him that we were all on the same side.

'You seem to think I'm Brasenose's pawn. It's not true. My wife is working for Roger Montacute's mother. You know that. But Lady Montacute didn't just pick out Julia's name in the phone book. Brasenose sent her. He's known the Montacute family for years. He must have known Lady Montacute's connection to Patrick Mallow. Mallow's her nephew. Brasenose wanted us poking around in Madeira long before I'd ever heard of Operation Haystack. He's been pulling my strings and I want to know why.'

Dreyton considered that for a moment. When he spoke

there was something faraway in his voice. 'Brasenose would have ordered the Navy to intercept Mallow's consignment. Did you know that?'

'I don't understand.'

'Operation Haystack wasn't supposed to end in Madeira. Conor Byrne was supposed to check the missile, confirm it was the real thing, tell New York and go back to Ireland. Then one of my men would have gone into the warehouse, disarmed the needle and let Mallow ship it to Cork. The Irish authorities would have picked up whoever collected it. Successful Anglo-Irish cooperation, terrorist plot thwarted, ringleaders including Byrne arrested. Everybody's happy.'

'So why did you bring Teixeira and the Portuguese marines along with you to the quayside? They were obviously expecting to grab Byrne.'

'Why do you think?'

'I don't know.'

'Because of Justin bloody Brasenose of course. He couldn't bear the thought of anyone else running a really successful operation in the field. He was always sniffing around. The Israelis couldn't risk getting caught supplying arms to the IRA, so they subcontracted the delivery of the needle to a reputable Spanish company, Vilafermosa. Somehow Brasenose got involved. Your wife started poking around, Brasenose planted a Parliamentary Question. He sent you down to Madeira. Then he turned up in Gibraltar. He was arranging for the ship carrying Mallow's cargo to Ireland to be diverted to The Rock. The missile would then be discovered by his people. The credit that belonged to this Service would go somewhere else.'

'What evidence do you have for any of that?'

'Evidence? Just look at the map. Any ship from Madeira to Cork has to pass Gibraltar. Brasenose claimed he was in Gibraltar investigating confidential information being leaked to some television programme, but he could have done that from here. The leak was ages ago. I wouldn't put anything past him.'

Dreyton looked at me as if pleading for my support. I said nothing. Saying just look at the map wasn't evidence, any more than it had been when Dreyton had insisted the missiles were bound for Polisario guerillas in Morocco. Mallow's shipment would cross the Bay of Biscay miles away from Gibraltar.

'The only way for us to control the outcome was to let the Portuguese seize Byrne and the missile,' Dreyton continued. 'Perhaps I should have let them grab Vilafermosa's trawler when it delivered the bloody thing. I was protecting my asset.'

'You mean Sheehan.'

'Of course, Sheehan. He was the lynchpin. He'd brought together the New York Jews who were selling the needle and the New York Irish who were buying it. He knew Mallow from his student days. He arranged for the Israelis to deliver the missile to Vilafermosa and Vilafermosa to land it in Madeira. But he was back in New York when it got there. It was up to Mallow and Byrne to sort out the arrangements for getting it to Ireland. If anything happened to the missile before Mallow had collected it from that warehouse the IRA would blame Sheehan. But if we let the Irish authorities discover the needle when it arrived in Ireland Sheehan would be in the clear, he knew nothing about the Irish end of things. Brasenose ruined the whole plan. We had to cobble together a plan B, let the Portuguese find the missile and persuade the IRA it was just bad luck, a Portuguese anti-smuggling operation. We had to make them believe that the Portuguese Navy had spotted something the night before, but of course we couldn't let the Portuguese actually spot anything. Protecting Sheehan meant also protecting the Jews bringing the missile in on that Spanish trawler.'

Dreyton's earlier nervousness had gone now; he was speaking with utter conviction. But he was living in a fantasy world. He had no evidence that Brasenose being in Gibraltar was anything to do with Operation Haystack. New York Jews and New York Irish conspiring to murder the Queen was the stuff of cheap fiction. Michael Sheehan as some sort of IRA mastermind was impossible to imagine. Equally unimaginable was the picture Dreyton was painting of Patrick Mallow, sitting in Quinta Moran calmly organising an arms shipment to Ireland

I got up and stood looking out the window as Dreyton had earlier.

There was something wrong in all of this. Something was missing, a half-remembered piece that refused to slot into place. We were both silent as if each of us were following chains of thought that were too fantastic to put into words.

When Julia discovered that, despite my Modern Languages degree, her conversational French was better than mine, she had presented me with a book, *Je me souviens*. It consisted of four or five hundred uncomplicated sentences each beginning 'I remember...' Somehow, in a collection of random memories Georges Perec had conjured up not only the story of his own life but a picture of France that was instantly recognisable.

Something similar was happening now. Dreyton's words

had triggered connections that had been niggling at the back of my mind. Fragments of memories suddenly came together. Something about Israelis, and something about that Russian word I kept hearing.

Back at Rosen's house Dreyton had shouted '*dasvidaniya*'. It was a farewell I had heard before, in Turkey. I remembered that PM's body had been in the boot of his car, waiting to be driven away, when a great bull of a man appeared and, like Dreyton, shouted a mispronounced Russian farewell. He had casually waved goodbye to the men PM had travelled from Beirut to meet.

It was the wave that triggered the memory now. That's how memory works. Not a gently flowing river but individual splashes on the surface of a lake that ripple away and only occasionally merge into something larger.

Now that wave, that Russian word, Dreyton's anti-Semitic fantasies were the random fragments that conjured up the truth.

I had only seen the man in Ağva momentarily, but even on a rainy night his silhouette and that wave had been unmistakeable. And I had seen that wave again, recently.

Just a couple of days ago at the Foreign Office. A relaxed wave goodbye from a great bull of a man but this time accompanied with a Texan-accented 'so long' rather than a Texan-accented '*dasvidaniya*.'

'The Israelis never had those missiles,' I said, as much to myself as to Dreyton. 'They're not involved in this at all. New York Jews peddling missiles is nonsense. It never happened.'

Dreyton looked at me as if I were mad, but suddenly I knew.

When I first met Merryweather at the US Embassy

he had seemed very familiar. I remember thinking then that I knew his type, but it wasn't his type I knew, it was Merryweather himself. I'd seen him before.

The men who had shot out my tyres in such a theatrical way were not Israelis at all. They were Company men. It was the CIA who had followed PM from the airport and tried to stop me doing the same. The Israelis hadn't taken PM's place, the Americans had. And now one of the missiles they had arranged to buy in Turkey had ended up in Madeira, intended for use by Irish terrorists.

What game was Merryweather playing?

XXX

'You said it was the Israelis who shot at you,' insisted Dreyton. 'That was your theory. We all agreed with you. The Americans themselves said the Israelis had those needle missiles. The only one to doubt your theory was Brasenose. What are you and Brasenose cooking up now?'

'It's nothing to do with Brasenose. The man I saw in Ağva was Merryweather. I'm sure of it. The Americans had the needles themselves all this time. That's why they didn't carry on looking for them.'

'That can't be true,' insisted Dreyton. He was pleading with me to deny it. But even as he answered I realised that Merryweather wasn't the only ghost in the story. Another man linked the pieces together.

'Ffortiscue's the key.'

Dreyton looked startled. 'Why are you all talking about Ffortiscue? You, Brasenose, Merryweather, you're all obsessed with the man.'

'That's right, we are. You're the only one who thinks he's got nothing to do with any of this. Why are you so confident? Have you spoken to him?'

'He's not involved in this.'

'But you have seen him.'

'Of course, he's an old friend. It pays to stay in touch with old friends. We had dinner one evening when he was in London. We discussed my new role. Nothing indiscreet you understand, no operational details. We talked mainly about his life in the US and how naive he found Americans. How they didn't understand the dangers posed by left-wing terrorists, in Central America, in Italy, in Ireland.' I could see Dreyton's brain ticking away, trying to remember exactly what was said. 'I may have mentioned Sheehan's mad story about trying to shoot down the Queen's plane. At the time nobody took that seriously. When Neil West was stationed in Belfast he always claimed that Sheehan was a fantasist. It was only later that Sheehan produced any evidence.'

'What evidence?' I asked.

This time Dreyton had a more convincing response. 'Photographs of a surface-to-air missile, a Soviet needle, and its launcher and case. And one of the photos showed someone wearing a balaclava holding the missile and a recent copy of *Time* magazine. Sheehan said the photos came from the men selling the needle. The photo with the magazine could have been faked of course, you can do that quite easily these days. But I had it checked, our experts are 95 per cent certain the photo hadn't been played around with. Sheehan had a photo of a needle missile and that photo had been taken within the previous couple of days. He told me the missile would be delivered by a Spanish trawler to Patrick Mallow in Madeira. After that it was up to us. Mallow ships wine to Cork, so that was obviously how the needle would reach Ireland. Mallow is sending a consignment in ten days' time.'

'Not any more,' I commented. 'He's not sending anything anywhere.'

'Byrne must have realised he was being set up,' Dreyton replied. 'Perhaps the IRA found out about Brasenose's plan to intercept the missiles in Gibraltar and they sent what they call an active service unit down to Madeira to take out Mallow.'

'Why would they do that?' I asked. 'What threat was Mallow to them?'

Dreyton shrugged. 'Well, what do you suggest? If Byrne didn't kill Mallow who did?'

'The men who tried to kill us at Rosen's house. Hachim Zineb.'

It seemed obvious to me, but Dreyton latched on to the idea like a drowning man clings to a raft. 'Of course. Moroccans. Montacute was threatened in Morocco. Mallow must have been killed because he knew something about Montacute's disappearance. He was involved in some way. Nothing to do with Haystack.'

I realised Dreyton still had just half the picture.

Only a couple of minutes ago he had talked about the need to protect the Spanish trawler that had brought the missile to Madeira. Perhaps a Spanish trawler had been involved somewhere but the missile had been brought ashore on the *Atiradora*, by Mourad Zineb. I knew Vilafermosa and Zineb had been working together, a connection that went right back to the Spanish Civil War, a connection Montacute was digging into when he disappeared. That was what linked Haystack and Montacute's disappearance. Dreyton understood none of that.

'You saw the boat that delivered the missile that night,' I said. 'It wasn't a Spanish trawler. It was Mourad Zineb's boat from Porto Moniz. It was Mourad Zineb we saw unload the missile into the warehouse. And it was his son, Hachim Zineb, that Rosen saw at Reid's hotel with Vilafermosa and the Russians and Ffortiscue. You heard Rosen say that.'

Dreyton shook his head but he wasn't disagreeing. 'George swore to me he had never been to Madeira. I checked with Teixeira, there's no record of any George Ffortiscue arriving in Madeira.'

'Of course not. He didn't want you or the Americans to know he'd been anywhere near the place. He would have used a different passport. But he used his own name when he booked the dinner table because that was the name his guests all knew. He didn't think it mattered. Nobody would be checking table bookings.'

'But what was he doing there? Who's he working for?'

'He hasn't been working for you?' I asked.

'Of course not. Just the occasional advice.'

'Like what?'

'Innocuous stuff. Like when Sheehan told me that the needle would arrive on a Spanish trawler George suggested that was probably a Vilafermosa boat. The Vilafermosa company is close to the Spanish authorities, he said, and the Spanish Navy has been trying to get Vilafermosa registered as a NATO asset, something to do with their fishing dispute with Morocco. George suggested I support their efforts, try to ensure the Portuguese Navy leaves Vilfermosa alone, which of course I did.'

'And you didn't think to ask how George Ffortiscue over there in Miami or Panama or wherever would know that an obscure Spanish fishing business was trying to get NATO protected asset status?'

From his expression it was obvious Dreyton hadn't asked anything, he had just accepted, grateful for any help Ffortiscue could provide.

I was beginning to see what might have happened. In Turkey, Merryweather had reached some sort of deal with the Russians who had stolen the missiles from Khelvachauri. But the Americans wouldn't want to get too close to the actual missiles in case something went wrong and the Russian authorities accused them of being behind the original theft and the death of the two conscripts. So they turned to an intermediary: Ffortiscue. Ffortiscue was supposed to arrange the logistics with the Russians, just like he'd been doing for Merryweather in Central America.

Then Ffortiscue had a bright idea. Why didn't the Russians keep one missile back for a spot of private enterprise? A gang of Russian thieves who were naive enough to think that PM in Beirut was a major arms dealer, clearly lacked the right contacts but Ffortiscue had a potential buyer already. Dreyton had told him that the IRA had a fantasy to shoot down the Queen's plane and just lacked a missile. No doubt over a bottle or two, Ffortiscue and Dreyton had laughed over Michael Sheehan's wild ideas but where Dreyton saw a fantasist Ffortiscue saw a business opportunity.

As I explained all that to Dreyton I could see him coming round to the idea.

'So the Russians weren't selling missiles, when Rosen overheard them, they had already agreed that with the IRA. They were discussing delivery. The IRA wanted the missile delivering to Madeira because Mallow had a way of smuggling it into Ireland.'

'And,' I took over, 'Ffortiscue was staying with Mallow to make the arrangements. Mallow would have known Vilafermosa and Vilafermosa's agent on the island, Mourad Zineb. So Mallow arranged for Ffortiscue to meet them and when everything was finalised Ffortiscue reported back to Sheehan who promptly told you.'

'But Sheehan didn't tell me Ffortiscue had been involved. He claimed all the credit for himself, the little bastard. If I'd known George Ffortiscue was that deeply involved I would have smelled a rat.'

I doubted that. Dreyton only smelled what he wanted to smell.

'I've told Sheehan to come over here, now,' Dreyton continued. 'I'll sort him out once and for all.'

'And he's coming?'

'Of course. I want to know exactly what's been happening. Sheehan has no choice. If he doesn't cooperate he knows we could let the FBI know he's been buying Russian arms to ship to the IRA. At a minimum he wouldn't be able to stay in the US, and it would be dangerous for him back in Ireland. The IRA might blame him for what happened to their man Mallow.'

Dreyton was nodding vigorously now. 'So when it all went wrong Hachim Zineb, the son, the one who was killed yesterday, went to Mallow's home and shot him. He must have thought that Mallow had betrayed him.'

'Perhaps.' Killing three people in cold blood in Quinta Moran still seemed pretty drastic.

'And then Zineb tried to kill Rosen yesterday because our man could identify him.'

I shook my head at that but Dreyton ignored me. In his own mind he had resolved the deaths in Madeira and was back in the world he understood, Whitehall politics. He had already decided that one of his earlier theories must be true. It was amazing how quickly his mind could leap from one version of reality to another.

'We know the Provisional IRA have their eyes on The Rock, Gibraltar. It's not long since we managed to shoot three of the bastards there. They must have discovered that the Navy were mounting an operation to intercept the missile they had just bought. That's why Byrne aborted his mission. If Brasenose hadn't involved the Navy, Operation Haystack would have been a success.'

Dreyton had an almost Trumpian ability to persuade himself that what he wanted to have happened actually had. He wanted Haystack to have failed because Brasenose had been plotting against it, and therefore that's what happened, even though he clearly had no actual evidence that Brasenose had plotted anything of the sort.

He paused before looking directly at me. He seemed to have now decided that I was on his side. 'You must go and see Brasenose. Tell him what's happened. I'll tell him you're coming.' The buck was about to be passed.

He picked up the phone and told his secretary to get Brasenose on the line.

'Justin. How are you? Just thought I should let you know we've found out why the Provisionals aborted the business in Madeira. It seems they picked up some silly story in Gibraltar about the Navy preparing to intercept a weapons consignment being shipped to Ireland by Patrick Mallow. We don't know how they got hold of that yet but we'll get it investigated, just wanted you to know. On another note, there have been some alarming developments on the ground concerning the X-suffix asset we mentioned, not a current asset of course, left over from your days. Don't want to go into details on the phone but I'm sending your man Dylan over to brief you. We may need to talk to Teixeira about why you wanted Dylan and his wife down there.'

He put the phone down with something approaching a smile on his face. 'Let's see how he handles that. It's down to him now. He needs to get Teixeira onside. And Her Majesty's Government needs an agreed position in case the press starts smelling any connection between the Portuguese intercepting IRA gun runners and all these dead bodies. "Gang warfare on holiday isle" we can live with; any suggestion of British involvement is definitely off limits. Let me know what line Brasenose proposes to take.'

With that I was dismissed. Dreyton, I concluded, was cracking up. He was lurching from theory to theory, one minute completely lost and the next consumed by an overpowering certainty. It was less than twenty-four hours since he had been brought face to face with men determined to kill him. I could almost smell the gunpowder still on him, gunpowder and fear. And still he couldn't tell the truth.

Whatever crackpot theories he came up with, the fact remained that Hachim Zineb had discovered Basil Rosen's address and there was only one possible way that could have happened. Directly or indirectly, it must have come from Dreyton. My guess was that despite his denials Dreyton had been in touch with Ffortiscue and Ffortiscue had passed the information on to Hachim Zineb.

But Dreyton's suggestion that Zineb wanted to kill Rosen because Rosen had seen him at the dinner with the Russians didn't make sense. Rosen hadn't recognised Zineb. It was Ffortiscue whom Rosen had recognised.

290

XXXI

Back in my office I called Brasenose and was told he had time to see me at noon.

I then phoned Julia who was just setting off to see Lady Montacute. 'Why don't you come with me?' she suggested. We met at Sloane Square. Fortunately there was no time to window shop on King's Road or even pop into Peter Jones. We walked down towards what I've always called the Chelsea Hospital but which Julia pointed out is, more correctly, the Royal Hospital Chelsea.

'We still don't know why Roger Montacute was killed,' Julia commented when she was sure there was nobody in eavesdropping range.

'He must have learned something he shouldn't have, overheard a conversation not meant for him. We'll never know exactly what it was.'

Julia was silent for a moment. 'Perhaps it was me,' she murmured.

'What do you mean?'

'Well Montacute came to see me before he went to Madeira. Told me all about the gold, Vilafermosa and all that. Suppose he did the same in Madeira. He arrived unexpectedly. Sheehan and Ffortiscue were already there. What did they talk about over dinner? Certainly not Russian missiles and the IRA.'

'I suppose if he mentioned Vilafermosa then ears would really have pricked up.'

Julia nodded. 'He certainly mentioned Zineb because somehow Mallow got hold of a fake death certificate. But suppose he mentioned Exodis. We've been on the BBC. People in the business know us, that's how we survive. We feed off our contacts, which is just what Ffortiscue does. Montacute could have talked about using Exodis to investigate Vilafermosa. Ffortiscue would know that Exodis is plugged into the Security Services. And if Montacute had actually mentioned me by name, I'm sure Ffortiscue won't have forgotten what happened last time we met. He wouldn't have wanted me turning up in Madeira asking questions.'

'Possibly,' I agreed, although I didn't want Julia thinking along those lines. There was no way she was responsible for Montacute's death. 'I think it's far more likely that Montacute died because of his persistence in tracking down Mourad Zineb. He wouldn't let up once Mallow had produced the fake certificate. Somebody decided that having him prowling around was too big a risk.'

Julia was not satisfied with that but reluctantly agreed that we would never have the full story of Roger Montacute's death.

When we arrived at the Montacute townhouse in Swan Walk the front door was opened by an elderly maid, uncomfortably reminding us of the events at Quinta Moran. She led us upstairs to a drawing room looking out on to Chelsea Physic Garden. Lady Constance was seated by the window. She rose to greet us. She seemed shrunken, her face thinner, the silk scarf looser at her throat. The fragile handshakes completed, she quickly sat down again.

'You have bad news,' she said.

There was no point in beating about the bush. 'Yes, we have. The man who threatened your son in Morocco has been killed, he was wearing what we believe is your son's watch.'

Julia passed the watch over. Lady Constance looked at it for a moment before turning it over. 'I gave it to him, on his twenty-first birthday. His father gave him a new sports car, rather ephemeral I thought. The watch will remind you of me when I've gone, I told him.'

I thought a tear was going to escape but instead she reached for a small bell on the table beside and summoned her maid. 'I always have tea at this hour, you'll join me of course. A nice strong Darjeeling will revive us.'

When the maid had left the room Lady Constance turned away from us. 'What happened?'

The question was aimed at both of us. Julia looked in my direction, not sure how much we should reveal. As little as possible had to be the answer.

'We don't know exactly how your son died,' I said. 'A gang of Moroccans seems to have been targeting foreigners. Roger stopped in an area called Santa Cruz on his way to the airport, we don't know why. Perhaps to buy some last-minute souvenir. Our theory is that he probably hailed a taxi to continue to the airport but was robbed and killed. It appears that the gang found that he had been staying at Quinta Moran. As a result your nephew Patrick's house was burgled. Three people, including Mr Mallow, were murdered.'

'Yes, I know that,' Lady Constance interjected. 'Mr Sheehan told me.'

I let that go for now. 'Yesterday the same men attacked the house of another British resident but were interrupted and two of them were killed, including their leader. He was wearing your son's watch.'

Lady Constance looked out of the window. 'We must trust that Roger didn't suffer.' There was silence for a minute. Then she turned to Julia again. 'Roger was an innocent abroad. I thought perhaps he had been carried away with his stories of Spanish gold and done something silly, but it seems not. I suppose that should be a comfort. You must send me your bill my dear. You did as I asked.'

It was time to leave. It was best not to wait for the Darjeeling to arrive. As we stood, I asked casually, 'You've seen Michael Sheehan?'

'He phoned to find out if there was any news about Roger. He and Roger used to be very close friends. I hadn't realised they were still in touch, but they had both been staying with my nephew in Madeira. Michael assumed I had heard about the murders at Patrick's villa, he was clearly very shocked.'

'I'm surprised the news reached New York so quickly.'

'Oh Michael is in this country. He's in Marlow for some sort of meeting.'

Dreyton had certainly brought him to London quickly.

After the maid had shown us out Julia suggested we try to find Sheehan and question him. I shook my head; my priority was talking to Brasenose.

XXXII

'What the hell has been happening?' Brasenose asked when I was shown into his office. 'You and Julia seem to have left dead bodies all over the place. I've just been speaking to Teixeira. And before that I had Clive Dreyton on babbling about a ship being intercepted in Gibraltar.'

Brasenose was seated behind his enormous desk. Neither the desk nor his leather chair were standard civil service issue.

'Dreyton thinks you were planning to steal all the credit for Operation Haystack by intercepting his missile before it reached Cork,' I said.

Without being asked I sat down at a round meeting table, ignoring the two seats lined up in front of his desk.

'Dreyton's mad,' Brasenose responded. 'He stopped that missile reaching Ireland himself by letting the Portuguese seize it in Madeira. Tell me what happened down there.'

I did as he asked, leaving only one thing out. He said nothing until I had finished.

'You did right to come back. All hell is breaking loose in Portugal. To say that Texeira's upset would be an understatement. I don't think our friend Dreyton will be welcome at any EU security symposia from now on. What you've just told me ties in with what Teixeira said. Silver phoned him last night and when the police arrived at Rosen's house it was exactly as Silver had described. Two men dead, one badly wounded and unlikely to live and Rosen nowhere to be found. It seems Rosen's clothes were found on the beach near the fort in Funchal this morning. Teixeira is working on the assumption that Rosen just swam out to sea and decided not to swim back. Seems highly unlikely to me. I should think he's done a runner somewhere. He can't have gone far.'

'No,' I said. 'I think Teixeira is right. Rosen told me the very first time we met that that's exactly where his path would end.'

Brasenose wasn't convinced. 'Just swimming out to sea is funny way to kill yourself, especially when you say he had a gun. We'll see what Sheehan says about it all.'

'Dreyton's told him to come over to London,' I said.

'Did he? I didn't know Dreyton had done that. It explains why Sheehan's here. Merryweather told me he arrived this morning. Apparently the FBI have him on their watchlist and when he left New York Merryweather was alerted.'

'Does Merryweather get alerted every time someone on an FBI list leaves the country?' I asked.

'What do you mean? Sheehan was heading our way, so the Embassy here was alerted.'

'Alerting the Embassy I understand, but why Merryweather in particular? And why did he tell you? You see I haven't told you one part of the story yet. Something totally unexpected. I realised who had attacked me in Turkey: it wasn't the Israelis. They don't come into it at all.'

'I never thought they did. It's not their style at all.'

'It was our friends in Grosvenor Square,' I said. 'The Company. I recognised Merryweather. He was there, no doubt at all. He has that way of waving farewell with his hand over his head, that and the sheer size and shape of the man. I'm certain it was him. Like we thought, those two men in Ağva weren't shooting at me to hit me, they were just trying to delay me and showing off. They were Americans.'

Brasenose didn't reply at once; when he did his reaction wasn't what I expected.

'I thought it might be them. One minute they're frantic to find out what had happened to those stolen missiles and the next minute they lose all interest. And like you say, just about anybody else would've shot at you, not at your tyres. What the hell is Merryweather up to? I happened to know that the US Air Force flew him down to the Azores yesterday and Teixeira this morning mentioned that he too was there. I would guess that Teixeira had been summoned to a council of war.'

'There is a question we ought to ask but which doesn't seem to have occurred to Dreyton,' I suggested. 'What happened to the other missiles? If they stole thirty and sold one to the IRA, what happened to the other twenty-nine? If the Company had shipped them back to the US for inspection we would have heard about it. So the Company still has them somewhere. What are they doing with them? They surely can't still be shipping things like that to the Contras in Nicaragua, not after all the fuss Congress made last year. Just in the last week there's been another very public row over what the Company's been getting up to. And now with Bush sending his troops into Panama they won't want anything more blowing up in that part of the world. It just doesn't make sense.'

Brasenose didn't say anything. The whereabouts of the remaining missiles was a loose end Brasenose appeared happy to leave hanging in the air. But one thing I had learned working for Brasenose is that he never, ever left a loose end hanging. There was something unsettling in the way he was shepherding me through the conversation.

What the hell is Merryweather up to? he had asked. But it was a rhetorical question. He hadn't tried to supply an answer or wait for me to do so. He knew Merryweather had flown down to the Azores to talk to Teixeira but didn't try to suggest why. And now he was ignoring the possibility that a container load of Soviet missiles had gone missing.

'You knew,' I said. 'You knew it was the Americans in Turkey. You knew they bought the missiles and you know what they're doing with them.'

I thought Brasenose would deny it but he slowly smiled. 'I trained you well. I didn't know, I guessed. Someone on the Defence Intelligence Staff was at a briefing in Washington a while back that included pictures and a technical assessment of the latest Soviet SAM-18; he was told that a couple of missiles and their launcher had just been flown in from Incirlik, the US airbase in Turkey.'

I shook my head. 'The other thing you taught me is that half a lie is always better than a whole lie. That's not all of it. There were thirty missiles stolen and you didn't just guess the Americans had them, you knew. Once you suspected who had the missiles you would have wanted to know what they were doing with them. And you would have found out. You're nothing if not persistent. Although the Joint Intelligence Committee is a British Cabinet committee the CIA is always there; eventually someone would have taken you aside and let you in on the secret.

'Although you kept asking me what Merryweather was

up to, the truth is that you knew perfectly well,' I continued. 'Merryweather was doing what he had been posted to Europe to do, what he'd been doing in Central America. He was still trying to bring down the Sandinista government in Nicaragua. After everything that's come out about the Iran-Contra affair the Company has still been trying to channel weapons to the Contra rebels behind the back of the US Congress.'

'Well it isn't now,' Brasenose responded quickly. 'Things have changed. The Sandinista government agreed to free elections, so US strategy has moved from encouraging the Contra's terror campaign to supporting the anti-Sandinista parties at the polls. When that happened Merryweather's more politically savvy masters in Washington told him to abort what he'd kicked off in Turkey. And they told him to destroy any evidence that Congressional investigators or the media might stumble across.'

That made sense but it didn't explain how one of those missiles ended up in a decrepit warehouse on the north coast of Madeira.

'Did you arrange for one of Merryweather's missiles to be shipped to Madeira and then feed all that IRA story to Dreyton? Was Dreyton right after all? Were you arranging for Mallow to get hold of a missile and then ship it north, allowing you to divert the shipment to Gibraltar where you could discover the missile? That way the public could see British Intelligence foiling a terrorist plot and in Whitehall the credit would naturally go to you.'

'Don't be ridiculous Thomas. I've never been anywhere near Gibraltar.'

'But you headed up the internal enquiry into that

Gibraltar TV programme. That wasn't a secret.'

'Yes I did. But I didn't actually go there. The leak was here. You really are sounding as deranged as Dreyton. It's madness.'

It did sound mad but in there somewhere was the truth. Brasenose may not have known that one of the Russian missiles would end up in Madeira but I knew Brasenose. He could be devious and even though Dreyton was conjuring up a conspiracy that didn't exist, one thing I would bet on: Operation Haystack had been blown off course not by anything that happened in Madeira but by competing ambitions in London.

There was one more question I wanted to ask before he ushered me out of his office. 'What happened to the two Colombians who flew to London from Funchal? Carlos Moreno who shot at Julia and me in Porto Moniz, and his friend.'

'They're back in Colombia now,' replied Brasenose. 'Our man in Bogotá knew quite a lot about both of them. Just as we expected when anyone mentions Colombia the first thing that comes to mind is drugs. Carlos Moreno is an enforcer for one of the big Colombian drug cartels.'

I remembered that when I mentioned Moreno's name at the Foreign Office meeting it was obvious that Merryweather recognised him, but he didn't say anything. I still wondered why not.

'What about the other man?'

'In some ways that was even more interesting. It seems that he is a member of the family that controls one of the drug cartels in Cali. His name is Geronimo Estriquez.'

Another piece of the jigsaw fell into place.

Right at the very beginning Roger Montacute had mentioned three names to Julia: Vilafermosa who had commanded the troop that had allegedly stolen the gold; Mourad Zineb, his second in command; and Emiliano Estriquez, his superior. It was Estriquez who had altered the records to hide the fact that the Tiradores de Ifni had ever been anywhere near San Blas de la Ciduela. Roger Montacute had not interviewed him because after the war was over Estriquez had emigrated; we now knew where he had gone.

The three men who had no doubt divided up the stolen gold had clearly stayed in touch with each other. And fifty years later their sons, Mateo Vilafermosa, Hachim Zineb and Geronimo Estriquez, had come together in Madeira: why?

XXXIII

Finding Sheehan's hotel had been easier than Julia expected. In Marlow the first place anyone would look is the Compleat Angler.

After the meeting with Brasenose I took the Tube from Westminster and Julia picked me up outside Earl's Court.

I filled her in on the meeting but nothing I said seemed to surprise her until I mentioned Geronimo Estriquez.

'So Roger Montacute starts raking over the story of the missing Spanish gold and the younger generation decide to act to protect the reputations of their fathers,' Julia commented. But even as she said it, we both realised how implausible that sounded. We were still missing something.

I had already recounted my conversation with Dreyton on our way to see Lady Constance that morning. Julia had obviously been mulling it over.

'Dreyton was in shock yesterday,' she said. 'He couldn't handle what he was seeing. The dead bodies, and Rosen shooting that man the way he did. Dreyton flipped. You could see that when we were there: he just didn't know what to do and his first reaction was to get away, anywhere, just away. Everything was going wrong. He wanted to lash out at someone. Find someone to blame. He's inventing things and then convincing himself they must be true. That story about Brasenose ordering the Navy to intercept a ship on the high seas just to disrupt Dreyton's operation is obviously nonsense. If Brasenose had done that the Service would have demanded an enquiry and his career would be over.'

I agreed. Brasenose was far more subtle than that.

'Brasenose wasn't planning to steal Dreyton's glory, but he didn't want Dreyton getting any glory either,' I said. 'Somebody sabotaged Operation Haystack, something spooked Conor Byrne. I thought it was my asking Mallow about George Ffortiscue, but if that was the case Byrne would never have travelled to Madeira. Whatever caused him to turn round and go back happened after he arrived. Dreyton is right, it was the phone call from this country. The call that the Portuguese haven't been able to identify. I bet that was Brasenose, just as Dreyton said.'

Julia shook her head. 'No Thomas, I don't think that's right. Brasenose can't have phoned Mallow. At that stage we hadn't mentioned Mallow's name to anyone in London and we certainly didn't suspect that Mallow was involved with the IRA. We didn't add that piece to the puzzle until later.'

Julia was right but as we turned off the M4 she answered her own objection.

'We've been conned,' she said suddenly. 'Brasenose has been ahead of us all the time. Just think: Roger Montacute disappears and what does Brasenose do?'

'He sends Lady Constance to you.'

'But that can't be what he did first. Brasenose is not like that. He would have investigated the disappearance himself. We know he confirmed that Montacute had booked a flight but hadn't taken it. He must have done more than that. Lady Constance, he told us, is an old friend of the family. If he knows Lady Constance so well he must have known that her sister moved to Madeira and had a son who still lived there. In any case Lady Constance would have told him where Roger was staying. Brasenose would have surely phoned Mallow as soon as Montacute disappeared, and Mallow would have waffled on about Montacute's stay. He must have mentioned the dinner they had with his friends Michael and George.'

Julia was right. Mallow had greeted us by asking after Lady Constance and commenting that he had been told that she was as formidable as ever, still acting the 'grande dame'. Who would have told him that? It wasn't the type of expression her son would have used about her, surely. But it was exactly the sort of phrase Brasenose might use, and indeed had used to us.

'And once Brasenose discovered that George Ffortiscue had been staying at Quinta Moran,' I pointed out, 'his antennae would really start quivering. What was he doing there and who was the Michael Sheehan who was staying there at the same time? It wouldn't take Brasenose long to discover exactly who Sheehan was and that Clive Dreyton had just taken over from Neil White as Sheehan's handler.'

I remembered Brasenose casually asking Neil White about Sheehan after the Foreign Office meeting. 'The name Sheehan rings a bell,' he had said. 'One of your ops, wasn't it?' By that time Brasenose would have known all about Michael Sheehan and his stories about plans to murder the royal family. He could have put all the pieces together: Merryweather telling Dreyton's old friend Ffortiscue to get rid of the Russian missiles he no longer needed; Ffortiscue and Sheehan meeting at Quinta Moran; Dreyton taking over as Sheehan's handler and then warning people off Vilafermosa's boats and chasing off to Madeira. It all pointed to Dreyton trying to mount some sort of operation in Madeira involving Sheehan, Ffortiscue and the missing missiles.

Brasenose had no more evidence for his theories about Dreyton than Dreyton had for his theories about Brasenose, but Brasenose was an operator, he knew how our secret world really worked. As he often said, he could smell something suspicious.

Brasenose had taught me to always follow my instincts, but I also wanted evidence. I had been wrong about the Israelis in Turkey and sent Dreyton chasing off down his own peculiar cul de sac. Hopefully, Michael Sheehan would soon provide solid evidence.

In the event I never spoke to Sheehan. As we approached Marlow we saw a black Chevrolet van coming in the opposite direction, over the Marlow Bridge. It turned into the Compleat Angler's car park. We followed it in and I noticed the van had diplomatic plates with the prefix 271. Julia had noticed the same thing. 'What's an American diplomatic vehicle doing here?' she asked. The answer was soon apparent as Bill Merryweather jumped out leaving his driver to park the van. He didn't look back and marched into the hotel.

We had decided that Julia should be the one to approach Sheehan. She would tell him that we were working for Lady Constance. There was no need for him to realise that I was connected with the Security Services. But Merryweather's appearance changed things.

'He must be here to see Sheehan,' I said, 'in which case we should try to join them. Let me do the talking. I won't introduce you. They can assume you are my assistant, no need to tell them you have no official status.'

Julia agreed with a theatrical grimace, but inside the

hotel our plans had to change again. Merryweather had gone through to the terrace at the back where despite the cold winter weather two men were standing by the river. They turned round as Merryweather approached. He obviously wasn't expected.

Julia and I were hanging back trying to decide what to do, when Merryweather appeared to push one of the men away. 'Michael Sheehan,' I told Julia, who hadn't seen the photo that Neil White had shown me. Sheehan seemed to be waiting for the third man to make a move.

As the man turned Julia gave a startled gasp. 'That's George Ffortiscue.' She was right. The last time we had seen him in the flesh was years ago when a mission he was running in Sicily went disastrously wrong and a member of Julia's family had been killed.

There was no time to wonder what he might be doing here.

It was clear that Merryweather wasn't here to see Sheehan. It might be that Merryweather's team had tracked Sheehan from Heathrow but it was when they reported that Sheehan was meeting Ffortiscue that the American decided to intervene.

Ffortiscue said something to the Irishman and Sheehan turned away and came towards us.

'I'll talk to Merryweather and Ffortiscue,' I said.

Behind me Sheehan was entering the hotel reception and I could hear Julia ask him if she could have a moment of his time.

I walked towards the river where the two men seemed to be arguing fiercely. They didn't notice me approaching.

'Fancy seeing you two here,' I interrupted. They both

spun round. I don't think Ffortiscue recognised me but Merryweather certainly did.

'What the hell are you doing here?' he demanded.

'I was just going to ask you that.'

'Just piss off,' snarled Merryweather. 'This is Agency business.'

'And this is England,' I responded. 'You don't give instructions here. We're not in Ağva now and your sidekicks aren't pointing guns at me. What the hell is going on?'

Merryweather looked at me for a moment. 'You're out of your depth, just like you were in Turkey. Go talk to Brasenose.'

Ffortiscue had recognised me and broke the silence. 'Dylan,' he said, 'Thomas Dylan. What's happening? What are you doing here?'

'Trying to work out why so many people have been killed just to stop our friend Bill here discovering that you were in Madeira. He didn't expect you to go there, did he, when he entrusted those missiles to you? You weren't supposed to take them all to Madeira.'

I was making it up as I went along but it was the only explanation that made sense. I kept going before they could interrupt.

I turned to Merryweather. 'You had to think on your feet in Ağva, didn't you? You weren't sure what you would find when you followed Poghos Mkrtchyan to that house. But you certainly thought quickly. Why should some Lebanese amateur get hold of SAM-18s? God knows what he would do with them. Far better to buy them yourself, get them off the market, or even better find something positive to do with them. But the Agency couldn't be involved directly. Not with the US Congress investigating the CIA's private enterprise arms smuggling. And you certainly didn't want to risk the Russians linking the United States to the murder of two Russian soldiers in Georgia and the hijacking of their brand new missiles. So what are you to do? You turn to Mr Fixit, Mr Ffortiscue, well known as a useful, deniable middleman in Central America. What did you say to George? We've got these missiles in Turkey. Put a couple on a truck and get them driven right across the country to Adana and our airbase at Incirlik without anybody noticing. And find a way to get the rest delivered to our friends in Central America, again without anybody noticing. If you can do that there will be a nice little commission for you. But George had other ideas. He doesn't want a nice little commission. He realised he could sell one of the missiles on the side. You probably wouldn't notice and even if you did what could you do about it?'

Ffortiscue looked as if he was going to protest but I kept going. I wanted to keep the initiative for a bit longer. 'So George set up this crazy Irish project and sucked my Service in. And it nearly worked. Dreyton was really convinced that the IRA were planning an attack on the Queen's flight and were in the market for surface-to-air missiles. But the IRA didn't know anything about it, did they? It was all a fantasy that only existed in Michael Sheehan's head. Only when you told Sheehan that you could really produce a missile did it become serious. And then Sheehan told you about Patrick Mallow. An old university friend with wildly romantic ideas about his Irish ancestry. And, more importantly, who regularly shipped wine from Madeira to Ireland. That's when even the IRA became interested and agreed to send Conor Byrne down to take a look—'

'That's enough,' interrupted Merryweather, grabbing my arm. 'I'm not interested in what a bunch of crazy Irishmen are doing. Like I said, go sort that out with Brasenose, Dreyton and all those stuffed shirts in London. George and I have real business to deal with.'

'That's right,' I said. 'The other missiles. That's what you want to know about. What happened to them? Where were they supposed to go? Where did they go? Because George had plans for them as well, didn't he? That's why you've been looking for him. You didn't know he was in Madeira. When that came up at our meeting in the Foreign Office you were really shocked. You hoped he'd done what you asked him to do. Dump them in the Atlantic perhaps and then hole up in Latin America somewhere like Butch Cassidy and the Sundance Kid.'

'Like I said,' Merryweather responded, grabbing my lapel. 'This is company business. Nothing to do with you, nothing to do with Dreyton, nothing to do with MI6. So fuck off, or else.'

'Or else what?' It was Ffortiscue who asked the question. 'Or else what, Bill? Are you going to broadcast the fact that you wanted to send a pallet load of Russian missiles to the Contras just at the very time Congress is beating the Agency up about doing exactly that? Do you want that on the evening news?'

'Don't try to threaten me, George,' Merryweather responded. 'We told you everything had changed, we told you not to take the missiles anywhere near Lanzarote. Just dump the fricking things in the ocean. But you didn't, did you? You thought you could make money by sticking to the original plan with a few little changes. You arranged to ship the missiles on a Bulgarian freighter heading for Angola but instead of unloading them into Vilafermosa's trawler off Lanzarote, like we'd originally planned, you drop them off in Madeira. And instead of sending them on to Nicaragua, you and that lunatic Estriquez were going to sell them to Noriega. Here we are planning to invade his two-bit country and you want to sell Russian missiles to some half-assed dictator so he can use them to shoot down American aircraft. You're insane, totally insane.'

'Not totally insane,' I said, as it dawned on me the full scale of what Ffortiscue had been planning. 'With your help he had already arranged that there would be no surveillance by the Portuguese Navy so he could unload the missiles onto one of Vilafermosa's trawlers wherever he wanted. Then the trawler brought them in shore where one would be put onto Zineb's boat, the *Atiradora*, for Mallow and Sheehan. The rest were brought into Porto Moniz and put in that boat shed.'

I turned to Ffortiscue. 'What were you going to do with them then? If Bill's right and you were going to sell them to Noriega, how were you getting them to Panama, in one of Vilafermosa's reefer ships?'

Ffortiscue just stared at me but Merryweather couldn't resist the opportunity to show that he knew far more than anyone else. The chance to boast outweighed his frustration at my arrival.

'I'll tell you what he did. He put them on a truck and took them across the island to the port in Caniçal. But you see, George, that's where everything went wrong for you. Because as soon as I heard you'd been in Madeira I took a little look at the map. It was obvious what you'd done. Like I said, rather than taking the missiles to Lanzarote, or dumping them in the ocean, you were offloading them in Madeira. So I talked to my good friend Teixeira and discovered that a certain Panamanian registered ship owned by Vilafermosa SRL that was supposed to call in at Arrecife, Lanzarote instead called in at Caniçal, Madeira. What's unfortunate for you is we calculate it will take another five days for that ship to reach Panama. You must have seen today's news. President Bush has finally given the go ahead to getting rid of that arsehole Noriega. Operation Just Cause. Twenty thousand US troops in there already. And if ever Uncle Sam needed a reason for invading Panama we now have a shipload of reasons – brand new Russian missiles just about to be handed over to the man who is now America's public enemy number one.'

Ffortiscue looked deflated, but he wasn't the sort to be deflated for long. 'Well, you win some, you lose some,' he said.

'But when you lose,' said Merryweather, 'you lose big-time, George. You and your friends have been playing for big stakes, mucho dollars. Your friends in Colombia will want their share.'

'Well they won't get anything, just like me. Noriega hasn't paid for the bloody things yet. And I don't suppose he will now.'

'Oh, but he did pay George. You see when we intercept that ship we'll need a reason. How did we know there were missiles onboard? Because we followed the funds, we'll say. It turns out that Noriega paid a hell of a lot of money to a European intermediary who bought the missiles from the Russians and arranged to get them on that ship.'

'That's not true,' Ffortiscue protested.

'You'll find it difficult to convince people of that,'

responded Merryweather. 'When Noriega's gone everyone will be asking what happened to all his money. And you think they'll believe some of it didn't go on those missiles? Are you going to tell Estriquez that Noriega didn't pay you in advance when the US Government is brandishing receipts with your name on? Emiliano Estriquez is an important man. Nobody makes a fool of him, or of his son Jeronimo. They're not going to be happy when the missiles they promised their friend Noriega disappear.'

'Estriquez won't worry about Noriega now,' insisted Ffortiscue. 'He'll move on. You don't know the man.'

'But you do,' I said. 'Both of you. I bet the CIA have been using Estriquez for years. A mutual backscratch. The Agency turns a blind idea to all those flights from secret airstrips in Honduras or Guatemala to the Florida Keys, the drug routes your colleagues in DEA are now trying to close, and in return Estriquez helps you use the same airstrips to smuggle weapons to the Contras in Nicaragua.'

'Did you help operate those routes, George?' I asked. 'I bet your name's all over them. Your friend Bill here organised a meeting in London between my Service and a woman from the DEA, the war on drugs' people. At the end of the meeting Bill made some strange remarks about you. He asked Dreyton to call you back to London. Implied you were still working for the Service. Dreyton didn't know what Bill was talking about. But that's no surprise, Bill wasn't talking to Dreyton, he was talking to the woman from the DEA, putting up a big sign saying George Ffortiscue is nothing to do with me.'

Ffortiscue shrugged. 'The Agency won't want any of this coming out. There's been too much dirty linen washed in public.' Like so many people, Ffortiscue seemed to speak primarily in cliches when flustered.

'After Noriega goes that will all be history,' declared Merryweather. 'My Agency has always been able to bury its history.'

'I think you've missed the point,' I replied. 'It's not Estriquez and his history that George needs to worry about, it's Estriquez and his plans for the future. The links between the Estriquez, Vilafermosa and Zineb families go back a long way. Back to the Spanish Civil War and the event that set them all on their way: the hijacking of a government gold shipment. The families have stayed in touch since then. Right up to now when the pressure on the drug routes into the US is increasing every day. Estriquez decided to diversify geographically. And to do that he called on his old family friends.'

I was guessing now but the expression on Ffortiscue's face showed that I was on the right track.

'Morocco's always been free and easy when it comes to drugs,' I continued. 'Tangiers was a magnet to the beat generation after the war. Europe is just across the Straits of Gibraltar. Drugs have been smuggled across the Straits for years but with Franco gone it's a lot easier now. Somebody saw an opportunity. A route through Morocco to Europe to parallel the routes through Central America to the US. Estriquez starts sending his merchandise to the Canaries. That would be easy, nearly everything in the Canaries is imported, just put the cocaine in with sacks of coffee or tins of pineapple. Then Vilafermosa moves it to Morocco and the Zineb family move it up north and into Europe. When the fishing disputes between Spain and Morocco make the route too risky they shift operations from Lanzarote up to Madeira.

'And then Bill Merryweather presents you with a container of missiles and a month or so later tells you to dump them in the sea. It must have seemed that fortune was smiling on you. There's a dictator in Panama facing a probable invasion willing to pay whatever it takes to get anti-aircraft missiles. And your friends Vilafermosa and Estriquez have a ready-made way of getting them there. As long as nobody finds out until the missiles are delivered and paid for, you're fine. One big, enormous final deal and you're off to retire somewhere the Americans can't extradite you.

'But then Dreyton tells you that your name has come up in connection with the sale of needle missiles in Madeira. That's a potential disaster. Dreyton has to believe that the IRA are behind everything, with Sheehan masterminding the sale. If he suspects you've put everything together he may get cold feet, or more dangerously he may mention your name – and if Bill Merryweather hears he won't take long to work out what's happened to his missiles. So Dreyton must be persuaded that it's a lie, you've never been to Madeira. That's easy because Dreyton wants to believe you. But then Julia and I start poking around and suddenly I'm on to Mallow who's not the committed IRA man Dreyton imagines but a lonely romantic who might say anything. So he has to go, along with the staff who met you. And then Dreyton tells you about Rosen, the witness who saw you in Madeira with Vilafermosa and Hachim Zineb. So he will have to go, too.'

If I expected Ffortiscue to break down and confess all I was disappointed. 'Fairy tales. All of it. Pure fairy tale.' Ffortiscue had been around Whitehall long enough to have learned the very first rule of politics: never admit you've made a mistake. 'You've absolutely no evidence for any of it.'

It was Merryweather who responded. 'You may be right, George. Mr Dylan here can't act without proof. Neither can we. But Jeronimo Estriquez can. If Dylan is right, Estriquez father and son had a nice little set-up in Madeira when suddenly the shooting starts and Jeronimo has to run away in a hurry. He could have been charged with murder. Jeronimo's not going to be a happy man. Remember Patrick Mallow found out exactly what happens when Jeronimo Estriquez is unhappy. You'll spend the rest of your life looking over your shoulder. It could be a very short life.'

With that Merryweather turned to go. He clapped me on the shoulder. 'So long pal.' He waved his hand over his head in farewell and marched towards the hotel. Ffortiscue turned to do the same as Julia emerged.

Ffortiscue hadn't recognised me but he recognised Julia. 'Mrs Dylan. We meet in unfortunate circumstances again.'

'Unfortunate circumstances? I saw the three butchered bodies in Quinta Moran. I wouldn't call that an unfortunate circumstance.'

'Oh dear, still the sensitive one, are we? The events at Quinta Moran represent what the Americans in Vietnam learned to call "collateral damage". I call it an unfortunate circumstance.'

'Deliberate, cold-blooded murder is never merely "unfortunate" Mr Ffortiscue. I trust you will discover that for yourself one day.'

Ffortiscue turned away and instead of continuing into the hotel strode off towards the river.

'Come on,' said Julia. 'Let's go home. I need a drink.

Sheehan had nothing to add.'

Outside, Merryweather was standing next to the Chevrolet. He was speaking to a short man in a long black coat and dark fedora, who had been inside the hotel earlier. Merryweather turned and clambered into the Chevrolet, which immediately drove off. The man in the fedora walked slowly off in the direction taken by Ffortiscue, towards the river.

'He looks familiar,' I said. 'Reminds me of the guy who shot at us in Porto Moniz.'

'If only that were so,' said Julia, who had a far better look at the man earlier. She swung the car door open, smiling to herself. 'Come on. If I put my foot down we'll be in time to surprise Eveline at school.'

XXXIV

Postscript December 2014

Nowadays everything is digital. The Service spends far more on computers than human beings. The old tradecraft skills of dead letter box, invisible ink and microfilm have disappeared. Not entirely disappeared, of course, there are relics of the old days scattered around. One of them is an innocent looking Camden postal address which is still kept alive in case some long forgotten operation creaks back to life.

In the Internet age of electronic communication nobody really expected that address to be needed again. Only lawyers and a few dusty parts of the civil service still use what the young men and women joining the Service today disparagingly refer to as snail-mail.

The letter with the Canadian postmark that arrived at the Camden address just a couple of weeks ago was from a lawyer. It says something about the way the Service's old procedures are being maintained that it took longer for the letter to travel from Camden to the Service's new headquarters at Vauxhall Cross than it had taken to wing its way across the Atlantic.

I was in my study contemplating yet another missive from the Service's legal department requesting that I delete, or as they put it, 'redact' certain passages from the memoir I was trying to write. When the phone rang, it was a voice I hadn't heard since my retirement. At first I didn't recognise it.

'Thomas,' said the voice. 'It's Camilla.'

I racked my brains trying to remember Camilla before realising that it was a young girl who had joined the Soviet Operations Desk just before it was disbanded. Except now of course she wasn't a young girl anymore and in any case we were no longer allowed to use the term 'girl' to describe anyone in the Service.

'I'll come straight to the point,' the voice continued. 'We have a bit of a mystery here. A letter's arrived in Camden addressed to you.'

'Who from?' I asked. 'What does it say?'

I had no illusions. Any letter arriving at that address would have been opened and carefully studied before anyone would think of contacting me.

'I think we've worked out what it means,' Camilla responded, without directly answering my question. 'But we thought it might be worth sending it over to you. Perhaps you could take a look at it.'

'Certainly. Fax it over,' I said, conscious that fax was now itself a very old-fashioned technology. 'Or just attach it to an email,' I corrected myself.

'I'd rather courier it over,' Camilla replied. 'In case you spot anything we missed on the original. The courier can wait there, save you the bother of having to get it back to us.'

And making sure that I don't photograph it myself, I thought. Nothing changes. Suspicion becomes second nature.

When the courier arrived, I was waiting for him.

'Do you want a coffee?' I asked. 'You can help yourself in the kitchen.'

'That's fine thank you. I'm already swimming in coffee.'

He followed me into the study and I opened the package he had brought. There were three items inside: an envelope, a letter and a certificate.

The address on the front of the envelope had been typed and on the reverse was printed the name and address of a firm of lawyers in Nanaimo, British Columbia.

The lawyer's letter was addressed to me. It could not have been more succinct. The firm was acting as executor for the late Mr David Lucas of Galiano Island, British Columbia. Regretfully Mr Lucas had disappeared at sea on the fourth of October. His body was found four days later and had been interred in the St Margaret cemetery. Mr Lucas left his estate in its entirety to the Pender Island Public Library. The only other instruction in his will was that a copy of his death certificate be sent to me. That was the third item in the package.

Not all Canadian death certificates show place of birth. British Columbia's do. The birthplace of David Lucas was given as Funchal, Madeira, Portugal.

I smiled to myself. He had been prepared.

At our first meeting he had told me that none of us follow the path we would have chosen. 'We can only choose where that path will end.' I had decided that Rosen had chosen to end his path in the Atlantic off Madeira. But at our last meeting he had been quoting from Leonard Cohen's 'Stranger Song': we were taking away his sanctuary, his manger, he said. But there was another image in that song, of an unending highway always curling up like smoke above the stranger's shoulder.

It was only now that the last wish of Vasily Kornelyuk

alias Oleg Buriakov alias Hans Schmidt alias Basil Rosen and now alias David Lucas had been fulfilled: he had contrived to choose where his path would end. In a watery death. Like George Ffortiscue, whose body had been found all those years ago, in the River Thames at Marlow.

ABOUT THE AUTHOR

After giving up on an academic career, and deciding not to join the government spy agency GCHQ, Brian Landers helped a former Director General of Defence Intelligence and a motley collection of ex-spooks set up a political intelligence unit in the City of London. Out of that experience sprang the character of Thomas Dylan, a novice who over the years progresses through the labyrinthine world of British Intelligence.

Brian Landers has lived in various parts of North and South America and Europe. He has worked in every corner of the globe from Beirut to Bali, Cape Town to Warsaw and points in between, and in industries as varied as insurance, family planning, retailing, manufacturing and management consultancy. He saw the inside of more prisons than most during three years as a director of HM Prison Service. He has a Politics Degree from the University of Exeter and an MBA from London Business School. In his spare time he helped set up the Financial Ombudsman Service, served on the boards of Amnesty UK and the Royal Armouries, and was Chairman of Companies House.

Landers subsidised his university bar bills by writing a column for the local paper and since then has written articles for various journals, newspapers and websites. As a director of Waterstones and later Penguin his passion for writing was rekindled. His first book, *Empires Apart*, published in the UK, US and India, was a history of the Russian and American Empires. His next book was going to be *Trump, Putin and the Lessons of History* but the subject was so depressing that he turned to fiction.

In 2018 Brian Landers was awarded an OBE in the Queen's Birthday Honours.

brianlanders.co.uk

THE DYLAN SERIES

Exodus
of
Spies

Brian
Landers

THE DYLAN SERIES

Awakening
of Spies

Brian
Landers

THE DYLAN SERIES

Families
of Spies

Brian
Landers

THE DYLAN SERIES

Brian
Landers

Coincidence
of Spies

THE DYLAN SERIES

Peter Oborne: an unmissable series of novels.

Awakening of Spies. In 1974 newcomer Thomas Dylan has a safe desk job in the Ministry of Defence. But British Intelligence needs someone who will just do as he's told. They have the wrong man. Thomas is sent to Zandvoort, Chicago and then the dangerous streets of Rio de Janeiro. The woman sent with him clearly knows more than he does. But can she be trusted?

Families of Spies. Thomas and Julia are on honeymoon in Rome when Julia's aunt and her Iranian husband are murdered in Sicily. There is a Russian spy at a US airbase on the island, but could that be a red herring? Are the murders linked to the past - to a coup in Iran perhaps or to an infamous mafia massacre?

Coincidence of Spies. The Cold War is about to end. The CIA thinks it can hurry on its way and when Thomas joins MI6 he is sent to Warsaw to help. But the American operation goes disastrously wrong. Thomas is left dangerously exposed. Only one person can help. Back in London newly pregnant Julia discovers that everything Thomas was told in Warsaw is a lie.

Exodus of Spies. The founder of Julia's security consultancy is murdered in the Caribbean. At first that seems nothing to do with Cubans and South Africans fighting a bitter war in Angola. But when an Angolan minister is assassinated in

London things change. Apartheid arouses strong emotions in the Intelligence world on both sides of the Atlantic. The action moves from Angola to New York and Antigua before the surprising conclusion in Lisbon.

AVAILABLE FROM ALL GOOD BOOKSHOPS